The Beiderbecke Connection

also by Alan Plater

The Beiderbecke Affair
The Beiderbecke Tapes

ALAN PLATER

The Beiderbecke Connection

Methuen

For
Peter, John and Paul

First published in Great Britain in 1992
by Methuen London
Michelin House, 81 Fulham Road, London SW3 6RB

A CIP catalogue record for this book
is available from the British Library
ISBN 0 413 61230 9

Typeset by Goodfellow & Egan Ltd, Cambridge
Printed in Great Britain
by Clays Ltd, St Ives plc

I

Oh Look!

Prams, Trevor Chaplin decided, were not what they used to be. When he was a lad in the North-East, prams were vehicles of substance, designed by the spiritual descendants of Brunel and Stephenson, and built by time-served craftsmen, wise old welders, blacksmiths and sheet-metal workers with grey-flecked hair. A pram was high, wide and handsome. It would scrape the paintwork on both sides of the hall simultaneously. On the road it would carry, with ease, the designated baby, plus a week's groceries, a couple of footballs, supplementary kids hitching a lift, fish and chips for the family and still have room left over for a bag of coal.

By comparison, the thing Trevor was pushing was a puny affair: a small, irregular plastic bubble, shaped like a glass-blower's failed audition piece. All you could do with it was push it. Though he was a woodwork teacher, Trevor gave occasional thought to the meaning of words, under the powerful influence of Jill Swinburne, who taught English and was the mother of his child. The word pram was derived from perambulator, and that was what you did with a proper old-fashioned pram. You perambulated: you marked the boundaries of your domain, defined the borders of your bailiwick, stated the terms of your very existence. You couldn't do that with a shampoo sachet mounted on eezy-glide ball-bearings.

All that being so, Trevor Chaplin didn't perambulate. He walked. If you walked, you kept yourself to yourself. If you perambulated, you spoke to people and patted dogs; but Trevor was walking, with headphones on his ears. At the moment he entered the park he was listening to the Duke Ellington Band's 'Cotton Tail' recorded on 4 May 1940 in Hollywood, with the famous solo by Ben Webster. This information may have been irrelevant to most of the people in the park but it was as essential to Trevor's daily round as his red corpuscles and the halftime scores. Against the furry, laid-back sound of Webster's tenor sax, he heard the voice from the bowling green.

'Oh look. It's average-sized Trevor Chaplin.'

The voice belonged to Big Al, long-time acquaintance of Trevor and Jill. Once upon a time, they had been instrumental in lifting up a few stones in the neighbourhood and uncovering enough creepy-crawlies to send a senior police officer and several local councillors to prison. Trevor still didn't quite understand why. He was better at listening to music than he was at unravelling sinister plots. He decided he would listen to the end of 'Cotton Tail' before attending to Al.

On the bowling green, a little local dispute had developed between Big Al and his opponent, Little Norm. They claimed to be brothers, though on the available evidence it was an unlikely proposition. Al gave the impression that he had been quarried from a Pennine. He moved with the slow inevitability of a glacier. People in the moonstruck outer limits of Leeds who found themselves with problems, from the temporal to the spiritual, generally cut out the middlemen. Why waste your time with bank manager or priest when you could go straight to Big Al?

Little Norm was smaller than Al; hence the prefix. He looked as if he had been assembled in a hurry on a day when the factory was running short of components. The faster his legs moved, the more slowly he travelled, and Al always arrived first. Maybe for that reason, they argued a great deal.

'You're always doing that,' said Norm.

'Doing what?' said Al, calmly. Their arguments generated indignation in the smaller man, tranquillity in the larger. It was all part of the fraternal fabric.

'Talking, just as I'm taking my shot. You put me off.'

Norm pointed to his bowl, as it dropped into the gutter at the far side of the green.

'It's only a game, Norm. And what is a mere game, compared with becoming reunited with an old and valued friend?'

'What old and valued friend?'

'Average-sized Trevor Chaplin.'

Al moved with slow and graceful precision across the bowling green in the direction of the path where Trevor lingered, waiting for a neat juxtaposition between Al's arrival and the end of the Ellington piece. It worked.

'Now then, Trev!' said Al, as Trevor removed the headphones. 'You remember me? Big Al? And my brother, Little Norm?'

'Yes, I remember. You used to have a warehouse full of jazz records.'

The sinister plot involving the councillors and the senior police officer had begun with Trevor's purchase, at unrepeatable prices, of some Bix Beiderbecke records. After that it had got complicated.

'The warehouse was part of my early period, Trev,' said Al, peering at the push-chair, his mind already two stops along a branch line.

'I see your union has been blessed with issue.'

'The NUT?' said Trevor, who was still back in the land of cheap Beiderbecke LPs.

'Unto you a child is born.'

Al touched the peak of his cap in homage, like an Old Testament prophet on a day trip to the twentieth century. It was very much part of the Big Al street style.

'Well, yes, sort of, only . . .' Trevor hesitated.

'That baby's cornflakes,' said Little Norm, who was small enough and eager enough to do a thorough check of the vehicle.

'That remark doesn't make a lot of sense, Norm. Babies, as a rule, are not cornflakes.'

'It's true. You've only to look.'

Al looked closely at the push-chair. Norm was right. It was packed tightly with groceries and a large box of cornflakes lay snug against the pillow.

'My apologies, Norm. Your remark makes complete sense. That baby is a box of cornflakes.'

'There isn't room for the baby and the shopping in this thing,' said Trevor. 'Prams aren't what they were when I was a lad.'

'Nothing is,' said Norm. 'The way I look at it, everything in life is rottener today than it was yesterday. Definitely rottener.'

Al was less concerned with Norm's cosmic reflections than with Trevor's shopping problems.

'Haven't you still got your little yellow van, Trev? Ideal for carrying groceries I would have thought. And a child too, if deemed appropriate.'

'This way I get the exercise,' explained Trevor. 'It's all to do with fibre and metabolism.'

'Fibre and what?' asked Norm.

'Metabolism.'

'Oh.'

The fibre and metabolism, in their turn, were to do with Trevor's now long-standing relationship with Jill. She had gently but firmly weaned him away from takeaway junk food in the general direction of good health and a concern for the environment.

Little Norm had managed without metabolism all his life and had no intention of tangling with it now. It was just something else to get rottener with each succeeding day. But Big Al was intrigued by the metabolism talk.

'If you're committed to fibre and metabolism, does that mean, perchance, that average-sized Mrs Swinburne is still part of your life? Indeed, does she have some profound connection with your absentee baby?'

'Yes. She is the . . . mother of my child,' said Trevor.

'Very nice. Don't you reckon, Norm? Very nice?'

'Yes, very nice.' Little Norm nodded, agreeing about the niceness of the arrangement, especially in a world growing rottener. He peered into the pram. 'There, there. Cheeky face,' he said.

'You are cooing at a packet of cornflakes, Norm,' said Big Al.

'I know. It's a joke.'

'Don't attempt jokes, Norm. It doesn't become you.'

Trevor looked at his watch.

'I'll have to be getting a shift on. You'll be wanting to get on with your game of bowls, and I said I'd be back by . . .'

Al hadn't finished yet.

'Is Mrs Swinburne still busy cleansing Society of the many evils therein? Despite the onset of motherhood?'

'Oh yes. She's been getting stuck into the ozone layer and the tropical rain forests.'

'Excellent,' said Al. Clearly it was the answer he had been hoping for.

'Tell Mrs Swinburne from me . . . We Shall Not Be Moved.' He said it with capital letters.

'Right,' said Trevor.

'We're in the middle of a game,' said Al, looking back towards the bowling green. 'We'll have to be moving.'

'You just said you wouldn't be moved,' said Little Norm.

Jill Swinburne and Trevor Chaplin lived in Hotspur Street, artisan terraces built in the shadow of World War One by a speculative developer with a lurking admiration for the earthier elements in Shakespeare's plays. Quickly Crescent and Timon Terrace were just around the corner, leading into Bottom Row where, twice a year, the residents got up a petition to have its name changed, then couldn't think of anyone to send it to.

Jill sat in the through lounge of Number 17, Hotspur Street, pondering the changes that had swept across the room in the last few weeks. Her posters proclaiming continued allegiance to the Planet Earth and Trevor's record shelves, neatly stacked with the Planet's All-Time-Jazz-Greats – these were now overlaid with a new presence called Baby. Talcum powder hung upon the air. Trevor had said that morning: 'The whole house smells of pink.' He didn't seem to mind.

In addition to the pinkness, soft and cuddly toys squatted and slouched on every available surface: a green elephant, a blue rabbit, a yellow bear that looked drunk, and multi-coloured species yet to be discovered, identified, classified and filmed by Bellamy or Attenborough. Most of these had been gifts from kids at San Quentin High. Jill suspected a third year project. The results projected all over the room.

She was also living with the immediate challenge of becoming a working mother. It seemed very simple when you read about it in the *Guardian*: all those keen-eyed women with three kids, a film company, a publishing house, a country retreat in Oxfordshire, a *pied-à-terre* in uptown Camden, a couple of Hockneys above the retrieved and restored Victorian fireplace, a live-in lover from the media and lapsed membership of the SDP. What Jill had was a sticky boy-child, a live-in jazz-crazed woodwork teacher, a planet to save and a new school term starting three days from now. She wondered whether those *Guardian* women were ever confronted by a girl like Emma.

It had, to be fair, been an amiable and democratic agreement. Trevor would do the shopping while Jill interviewed the prospective child-minders. A card in the betting-shop window had produced a cluster of applications from unemployed school-leavers. San Quentin High specialised in producing these; indeed, it produced very little else. And sure as God made Granny Smiths, it had produced Emma.

Emma was lumpen without being proletarian. Her father was a newsagent with a sideline in dirty videos and, according to the caste system around San Quentin, any family with its own shop was right up there among the crowned heads of Europe. All the same, Emma was unquestionably and irredeemably lumpen. It was said that when approaching an unfamiliar door she would read the word aloud – 'Push' or 'Pull' as the case may be – before attempting to open it. If the door carried no instructions, she would wait for help from a friendly passer-by.

Jill tried, for the eighth time, to explain the nature of the job on offer.

'I suppose what we're looking for is a sort of . . . au pair.'

She knew immediately it was a mistake.

'Oh what?' said Emma.

'Pair.'

Emma stared, face blank as two coats of cream emulsion paint. Jill persevered, with patience honed by years spent in classrooms confronting such faces, thirty-five at a time.

'Do you know what I'm talking about?'

'I know what pear means.'

Emma glanced towards a bowl of fruit on a nearby table, wedged between a panda and a Postman Pat.

'Not pear as in fruit bowl. Pair. As in . . . au pair.'

Jill felt as if she were trapped in an old Abbott and Costello routine. It was not where she wanted to be. But Emma's face brightened, and a glimmer of understanding crept warily into her eyes.

'Pair. It means two, doesn't it. Pair.'

'Yes, dear, pair means two.'

The glimmer of understanding departed, as fleetingly as it had arrived.

'You're looking for an oh two?'

Jill pondered on a reply then decided to quit while she was still losing.

It was the final, decisive moment in the bowls match between Big Al and Little Norm.

'Very timely, seeing Trev again,' said Al, as Norm took his shot.

'You're doing it again.'

'What am I doing, Norm?'

'Talking when I'm taking my shot. Putting me off.'

'The salient point,' said Al, ignoring Norm's passionate

complaints and gazing into the middle distance like a Chekhovian heroine, 'is that average-sized Trevor Chaplin is alive, well and in possession of his faculties and his little yellow van.'

'What of it?'

'A little yellow van signifies movement and transport, Norm. It will take things from A to B. Or from B to A. Not to mention C and D.'

'I know that,' said Norm, keen to avoid a meditative ramble through the entire alphabet. 'Everybody knows what a van's for. What's it got to do with us?'

Al prepared to take his final shot.

'I'll deal with affairs of state in the fullness of time. First, let me finish my game of bowls.'

The wood travelled with poetic precision, its natural left-hand bias gently compensating for the right-hand bias created by the crown of the green, and came to rest against the jack, tenderly, like a parent reunited with a long-lost child.

'Game shot, I believe, Norm.'

There was nothing lumpen about Yvonne. Across the broad acres around San Quentin High, she had street credibility in streets where even tomcats patrolled in twos. Mr Carter, the staffroom's self-appointed cynic, had once accused her of being an existentialist.

'You, child, are an existentialist.'

'Is that good, sir?'

'You consider that reality as existence can only be lived, but can never become the object of thought.'

'Sorry, sir. I never think about it.'

Her school career had been punctuated by explosions of varying nature and dimension. When the dust settled, Yvonne was generally to be found close at hand, bearing a cheerful smile and the charred remains of the blue touch-paper.

The smile, Jill noted, was as cheerful and guileless as ever, but an inevitable question hung in the space between them in the living room: what mother in her right mind would entrust her child to the care of a streetwise existentialist?

Jill played for time.

'Yvonne . . . formerly of 5C, and before that, 3B.'

These classes had found their place in history alongside Goths, Picts, Vandals, Vikings and Vlad the Impaler's first team squad.

'You're not going to hold that against me, are you, miss?' said Yvonne, who could spot an innuendo at a thousand paces. Jill, despite the milk of liberal-mindedness that flowed through her soul, was a little inclined to hold it against Yvonne. She threw a morsel of evidence into the debate.

'You were deported from Holland halfway through the school trip.'

'Not just me, miss. All of us. It was just youthful high spirits. And a deprived childhood.'

'You? Deprived?'

Yvonne shrugged. 'A bit.'

Jill realised she knew nothing of Yvonne's childhood or family circumstances. Though the good book said you should take a keen interest in such matters, as an aid to effective education, the staff at San Quentin tended to avoid social probing into the lives of the kids. The teachers spent enough time picking their own scabs and squeezing their own boils, without starting on other people's.

Jill filed Yvonne's alleged childhood deprivation in a box marked 'For Future Reference on a Quiet Day', and moved on.

'What have you done since you left school?'

'Been on two schemes and had one job, miss.'

'A job?'

'Sort of, miss.'

'How did you manage that? Did you win the raffle?'

It was a joke, much loved in the parish, that whenever the Job Centre came by anything resembling proper employment, the staff sold tickets and organised a draw by some local celebrity – a Rugby League player for preference – with an official presentation and a brass band. A kid like Yvonne getting a decent job would have been an occasion for *Son et*

Lumière in the grounds of Fountains Abbey, with the Hallé Orchestra and a guest appearance by Stevie Wonder.

Yvonne explained. 'It wasn't a proper job. I had to sell cavity wall insulation on the telephone. No wages. Just commission.'

'That doesn't sound easy.'

'Half the punters hadn't even got walls. I chucked it after three days. Is yours a proper job?'

'Yes. But you have to answer a simple question.'

'Ready, miss.' Yvonne sat forward in her seat, eager and unafraid. Jill remembered the pose from 3B and 5C days, when Yvonne's answers were legendary for being prompt, inventive and wrong.

'Do you know what an au pair is?'

Yvonne smiled.

'Yes, that's dead easy, miss. You look after a baby and you learn a foreign language.'

'You wouldn't have to learn a foreign language.'

'I could learn to talk proper like you, miss.'

With her spare antennae, Jill had noticed Trevor walking up the path with his precious cargo of cornflakes. He walked into the living room while the idea of learning to talk proper still hung upon the atmosphere.

'You could learn to talk proper like Mr Chaplin.'

'He doesn't talk as proper as you, miss.'

'Don't understand,' said Trevor, unconcerned. He took it for granted that 98.4 per cent of the world around him would never make any sense, and it didn't worry him. As long as he could play a little blues at midnight, he and his universe stayed cool. He even stayed cool when he recognised their visitor.

'Yvonne, isn't it?'

'Yes sir.'

'You used to be in 5C . . . and before that 3B . . .'

'Yes sir.'

Jill interceded.

'It's all right, Trevor. We've talked it through.'

'That's all right then,' said Trevor, adding a footnote for

Yvonne's benefit. 'We do a lot of that here. Talking through. Also we like to keep in touch with our feelings.'

'Knock it off,' said Jill.

Trevor wandered into the kitchen with the groceries, to file them in their allotted compartments, cupboards and crannies. Jill found herself responsible for two simultaneous conversations, like a Wimbledon umpire negotiating a line dispute at one end of the court and new balls at the other.

'You'll never guess who I saw in the park,' said Trevor.

'The famous five having filthy fun in the shrubbery?'

'Big Al and Little Norm.'

'I was close,' said Jill, turning to Yvonne to ask: 'So would you like to be an au pair? Providing you don't have to learn any languages?'

'Yes please, miss. It'll be dead magic.'

'He's grown a beard,' said Trevor.

'Which one?'

'The one on his chin.'

There were moments in their gentle relationship when Trevor's laconic humour drove Jill to the edge of the perimeter of the precipice of irritation.

'I mean which one has grown a beard. Big Al or Little Norm?'

'Big Al.'

Somehow Trevor made Jill seem silly for asking. Radical changes in a man's life-style, like growing a beard, were obviously Big Al's *métier*, rather than his lesser-known brother's. Jill became aware of Yvonne's keen interest in the conversation. Her face implied: I am not used to living with day-to-day surrealism.

'Are you sure you want this job?' asked Jill.

There was no need to worry.

'Yes, miss, course I do. Am I allowed to ask questions?'

'It's a free and democratic household,' said Jill, preparing herself for in-depth probing on the subject of wages, overtime, holiday pay, incentive schemes and worker participation.

'Where's the baby?'

'Ah,' said Jill, who had momentarily forgotten about the baby.

Trevor walked, on tiptoe, into the living room, fingers to lips. All three listened intently. From upstairs came the sound of a child crying.

'I'll go,' he said.

Trevor disappeared upstairs.

'He's a very good father,' said Jill.

It was true. Jill loved their child, but Trevor was totally and terminally besotted. If she suggested buying a small but gaily painted Thomas the Tank Engine, he would put in a counter-claim for a comprehensive and fully integrated transport system. He had discovered, very quickly, that being a father was a season ticket to a second childhood and he wasn't going to waste it, especially as second time round you had some sort of control over the budget.

'If it's a democratic household, does that mean I can ask another question, miss?' said Yvonne.

'Ask as many as you like.'

'Have you and Mr Chaplin got married?'

'Certainly not.'

'Good.'

'Now that sounds like you're making a moral judgement and we don't encourage moral judgements.'

As she said it Jill thought: am I making a moral judgement by saying this in the first place? She needn't have worried.

'It's not a problem, miss, on account of I've got no idea what you're talking about.'

Trevor walked into the middle of their becalmed moral dialectic. He held in his arms a six-month-old boy child of surpassing innocence and beauty.

'Meet First-Born,' said Jill.

'You're supposed to say "Ah",' said Trevor.

Yvonne said: 'Ah.'

On the first day of the new term at the institution known to the world as San Quentin High, the students and staff rolled along the drive with all the evangelical fervour of sludge flowing up a steep hill.

'I'm worried,' said Trevor, as he parked the yellow van that was as much a part of his life-style as his resolute cool in the face of the world's 98.4 per cent absurdity quotient.

'What are you worried about?' said Jill.

'First-Born. Is he going to be all right with Yvonne?'

'Of course he'll be all right.'

'She's sure to let the milk boil over, and I've just got my kitchen looking nice, and she'll ruin all my surfaces and . . .'

'Oh look,' said Jill.

Trevor stopped worrying about his kitchen surfaces and looked. A large banner draped between two upper-storey classroom windows bore the message: 'WELCOME BACK MISS!'

Jill was touched, moved and puzzled.

'I can never get used to the idea of being popular.'

'Why not?' said Trevor. 'I like you. I know it took a year or two but I persevered and . . .'

'Trevor!'

He shrugged. It was his normal response to a reprimand. The trouble was Jill couldn't tell when he was joking. Nor, for that matter, could he. It was a small problem, no bigger than a person's hand, and he very rarely worried about it. Nor did he worry when he saw Mr Wheeler, the headmaster, bearing down on them, academic gown blowing in the wind, with a searing cry.

'Mrs Swinburne!'

'Good morning, Mr Wheeler,' said Jill.

'Good morning, Mr Wheeler,' said Trevor.

They had long ago refined their anti-Wheeler tactics. They countered his blinkered zealotry with a precise blend of non-sequiturs and a totally unrelenting niceness. At times the niceness was so nice it became aggressive.

'Are you responsible for that?' said Mr Wheeler, flinging an arm towards the banner like Klemperer cueing in a crescendo.

Jill smiled with honey sweetness.

'No, I think my class is responsible for that.'

'They think she's very beautiful, very gracious, very talented and they do love her madly,' said Trevor, quoting Duke Ellington by way of objective evidence.

'And what do you observe about it, Mrs Swinburne?'

Jill assessed the banner with the flattering device.

'The lettering's neat. The spelling's perfect. Admittedly, any word with more than two syllables gives them trouble. But generally, I'd say it's pretty good.'

'I think we had better discuss this in my study.'

'Discuss what?' asked Jill, still fumbling for the agenda.

'In private!'

Mr Wheeler turned on his heel, gown flaring and headed towards the main door of the school, like a bat returning to Hell.

'I'll see you later,' said Trevor.

'Both of you!' said Mr Wheeler, who had ears in the back of his head.

'Both of us,' said Trevor.

Both of them wandered towards the entrance through the crowd of kids hanging around the doorway, comparing notes about holidays, parents, scholarship and the starting prices at Catterick.

'Well done, miss, we're proud of you,' said Glenda, a vapid third-former who had stuffed First-Born's drunken yellow bear.

'Thank you, my dear,' said Jill.

'Well done, sir. That'll stop the rumours,' said Spike, a streetwise fourth-former who believed in enterprise culture and ran protection in the bike sheds.

'I'll have you, sunbeam,' said Trevor.

Trevor Chaplin and Jill Swinburne stood in front of Mr Wheeler's desk. The atmosphere was exactly as Jill remembered it, heavy with fading dreams and ambition turning sour in the bottle. Mr Wheeler's problem was very simple. He wanted to be Dr Arnold of Rugby, educating the sons of self-elected gentlefolk to play up and play the game and, in their spare moments, run the British Empire. It probably wasn't all that easy for Dr Arnold. For Mr Wheeler, in a decaying, under-funded state school situated on a housing estate in the moonstruck outer limits of Leeds, it was, quite clearly, impossible. That the headmaster continued to sustain his fantasy, in the face of such overwhelming odds, could be construed as a kind of manic heroism. But most people just thought he was stupid.

He explained his current agony to Jill and Trevor.

'The crucial word on the banner that so offended me this morning is . . . Miss.'

'But all the kids call her miss,' said Trevor.

'The children, Mr Chaplin, the children.'

Mr Wheeler cherished the notion that the students could be properly classified as children, despite the fact that the word implied a degree of innocence, and the prospects of finding innocence in and around the school was on a par with finding diamonds beneath the cracked tarmac of the playground.

Trevor persisted with his thesis.

'They call the women teachers miss and the men teachers sir. If we're lucky.'

'Apart from Mr Bickerstaffe,' said Jill.

'Mr Bickerstaffe is a separate issue!' snapped Mr Wheeler.

'So I've heard,' said Trevor.

The Bickerstaffe saga was a no-go area in the headmaster's study, which is why Jill had mentioned it. Mr Wheeler had appointed the young man because he had attended a minor public school and was therefore, according to the Wheeler doctrine, potential officer class. It was a star-crossed hypothesis, which Mr Carter, staffroom cynic, had gleefully spotted within seconds of Mr Bickerstaffe's arrival at San Quentin.

'He is a mere boy. A sensitive flower. He has no hope of survival in this atmosphere. We need men about us who are rhubarb, who will flourish on filth. My nostrils are already quivering with the scent of imminent catastrophe.'

Mr Bickerstaffe had indeed hobbled from crisis to crisis.

The crises had embraced his sexuality, his identity and what passed for his relationships with other members of the human race, both fully-paid-up and lapsed. His most recent problem was mere manifestation. He hadn't been seen for weeks. Nobody took over his classes because nobody could remember what he had been appointed to teach.

'He is now a non-person,' Mr Carter had concluded, the day Mr Bickerstaffe's name disappeared from the timetable, adding: 'Non-being sounds very attractive. I shall send away for a kit.'

All this was the sub-text to Mr Wheeler's snappiness. It was an Achilles heel of his own making, and he hated to be caught out in the act of limping. He resumed his case for the prosecution of Jill Swinburne.

'You have returned from maternity leave, Mrs Swinburne. Yet, if we are to believe the word written on that banner, you are, in the eyes of the children, miss. And in the eyes of the law, you are miss.'

'It isn't as simple as that, Mr Wheeler. I am still called Swinburne, in the eyes of everybody, even though I inherited the name from my ex-husband, and I threw him out years ago. Most of my letters are addressed to *Mrs* Swinburne. Fellow-conservationists and peace-lovers address me as *Ms* Swinburne, or comrade, or sister. It's very complicated, this whole question of forms of address, don't you agree?'

'It isn't at all complicated. You have returned to school, as the mother of a young child, but you are not married to its father.'

'I think we already know that,' said Jill, with a glance at Trevor who added:

'Yes, I know that.'

'Is that the kind of example we should be setting to the children?'

'Oh, I see, it's a moral question,' said Jill.

She knew the battle was over; neither won nor lost, but definitely over. On questions of personal morality, she and Mr Wheeler lived out a surly truce. She believed you should do as you like, providing you didn't hurt any living creature. He believed you should be bound and gagged by his personal version of the Commandments which numbered a hundred and nineteen at the last count. Trevor believed you should stay cool and listen to the music, which wasn't much use as a mediating stance.

Mr Wheeler eased into the closing rites.

'As you know, I am not one to preach about personal morality . . .' he began.

But he was. He knew it and they knew it.

'Please continue, Mr Wheeler,' said Jill.

'Did you want to preach about personal morality?' said Trevor.

'I simply ask you to think very carefully about what I have said.'

Within minutes Jill and Trevor were in the corridor, on their way to their classes.

'I've thought very carefully about what Mr Wheeler had to say,' said Trevor.

'And?'

'I'm ignoring him.'

Jill felt at home again. She and the headmaster had argued themselves into a moral cul-de-sac and now she was sitting in the San Quentin dining hall contemplating her lunch, with Trevor to one side, and Mr Carter to the other. All round her were the familiar sounds of school meals: the clatter of cutlery as it struck the food, the keen-edged debates as to the nature of the substances lying on the plate, the subdued hum of bacilli entering digestive tracts and the defiant laughter of intestines, large and small, as they hauled themselves into a defensive posture.

But the greatest of these sounds was the voice of Mr Carter, adding his characteristic editorial comments on the surrounding fabric of their shared existence.

'I have to tell you, Mrs Swinburne, that yours has been the longest pregnancy in the history of conception.'

'I'd have agreed with you, until today.'

'Without you to inflame my erotic fantasies, my life, and especially my lunchtime oasis, nay, my entire world, has been an aching void of infinite nothingness.'

'Obviously,' said Trevor. 'If it was a somethingness it wouldn't be a void.'

When Trevor strayed into metaphysics, people generally left him alone. He was usually out again quite quickly. Mr Carter's declarations about his erotic fantasies were a daily happening, Monday-to-Friday in term time. They had always remained strictly fantastical and, as far as Jill knew, had never frightened the horses. It was all familiar as an old song.

'Sitting here,' she said, 'I feel as if I've never been away. Everything's exactly the same. The food. Your erotic fantasies. We even started the day with a moralising sermon from Mr Wheeler.'

'Ignore it. The man is clinically insane, even by the standards of the teaching profession.'

'And I then discover I have to teach thirty-eight kids in 5A the inner truth about *Tess of the D'Urbervilles* with only two copies of the book.'

'Send them out to steal some more,' said Trevor.

'They suggested that. They said it would make a good project.'

Mr Carter nodded, approvingly. 'They're a bright lot, 5A, by our admittedly sub-human standards. I would expect them to be exceedingly competent shop-lifters.'

Jill found the courage to lift the merest whisper of food from her plate halfway to her lips, and then examined it for signs of movement.

'Correction. Some things have changed. The food is even worse.'

Mr Carter nodded.

'Well spotted, Mrs Swinburne. The food has been privatised. Franchised out. I wrote a letter to the education committee, complaining about the taste of the artificial flavouring. I had a reply from Milton Keynes.'

'Is he the chairman of the education committee?' asked Trevor.

'Trevor,' explained Jill, 'Milton Keynes is the name of a place in the South of England where large corporations have their headquarters and plan the continued exploitation of the planet . . .'

Then she realised, too late, that Trevor had known all along about Milton Keynes. His remark was a joke. Trevor always signalled his jokes by concealing all signs of mirth, real or potential. Though they shared a house, a bed, a child and a life, Jill rarely spotted his jokes at the moment they took place. Compared with Trevor, Buster Keaton was a compulsive giggler.

'Don't you want to hear about the reply I received from Milton Keynes,' said Mr Carter, plaintively.

'Not very much,' said Trevor.

'Of course we do,' said Jill.

'I wrote complaining about the taste of the artificial flavouring. I had a reply, written on a computer in Milton Keynes.'

'With an apology?' suggested Jill.

'And a replacement pudding?' suggested Trevor.

'No. I received six glossy brochures about their special offer cavity wall insulation.'

The sun was setting on Hotspur Street. It was behind the clouds at the time, and the effect was to increase the density of greyness draped over the rooftops.

'And the lights go on at seven at the start of another English summer,' said Jill, paraphrasing Larkin, as Trevor came into the room.

'What?'

'It's an oblique literary reference.'

'That's cool.'

He sat down in his armchair and searched the *Guardian* for the sports pages. Jill sat at the table marking the new term's first consignment of exercise books: thirty-eight essays on the subject, 'What I would have liked to do in the school holidays if I'd had any money to do it.'

'Is he sleeping?' said Jill.

'Yes. Like a baby.'

It was a joke. She spotted it.

'You must have told him a story.'

'Yes. I told him a story.'

'Goldilocks and The Three Bears?'

'No. Woody Herman and The Four Brothers.'

'What?'

'It's an oblique jazz reference.'

'That's cool.'

Trevor had become the specialist teller of bedtime stories. Jill tucked First-Born snugly in his cot and kissed him good night. Then she left the room before Trevor started his story. Bedtime stories were a sacred act of communion between parent and child. They were nobody else's business.

She had no idea what the stories were about but she sensed that floppy-eared rabbits and naughty pixies were thin on the ground in Trevor's narrative landscape. Saxophone players and low-down blues were the stuff his dreams were made on. Maybe one night she would persuade him to tell *her* a bedtime story under the duvet. She had ways of making him talk.

Trevor put down his newspaper.

'I've just realised something,' he said.

'What have you just realised?'

'It's like being a family, isn't it? Mother. Father. Child. House. Family.'

'Yes, Trevor. Very like being a family. Almost indistinguishable to the naked eye, I should think.'

'I could get a pipe and some slippers. Wash the van on Sunday morning. Do a bit of gardening. Lag some pipes. Have we got any pipes?'

The doorbell rang.

'You could answer the door,' said Jill.

'I think I'll answer the door.'

Trevor went into the hallway. Jill heard half-familiar voices and was on her feet as Trevor returned with Big Al and Little Norm. Big Al's presence had the effect of making the room seem half its previous size.

'We come bearing gifts for the first-born,' he announced.

'Thank you,' said Jill.

'Norm. Where's the gift?'

'It's here.'

From behind his back, Little Norm produced a plastic carrier bag, bearing the logo of a famous supermarket chain with a head office in Milton Keynes. He handed it to Big Al.

Al hauled out an old-fashioned shoe-box, many times recycled, tied around with a piece of pre-war string. He handed the box to Jill.

'Unfortunately we're right out of gold, frankincense and myrrh down at the warehouse,' he said.

'Been a bit of a run, you see,' explained Little Norm, with a near-miss at a smile.

'In addition to which,' Al continued, 'we've only got two wise men, if you include Norm, that is. We have a lot of debates about that on the bowling green.'

Jill looked warily at the box. Its shape, size, texture and demeanour suggested it might harbour a living creature. You saw tense people in vets' waiting rooms, nursing boxes like these. They contained ferrets or lemmings, nervously rustling in straw as they waited for their tetanus shots.

'Shall I open it?' she said, half hoping, despite all her principles, that Trevor would flex his muscles and say, 'This is man's work – leave it to me, my dear.'

But all he said was, 'Yes. Open it. It's a guaranteed way of finding out what's inside.'

She disentangled the string and removed the lid from the box. Inside was a tightly packed bundle of thin, plastic-covered wire.

'Oh look. Wire.'

'I was only saying the other day, we're getting a bit short of wire,' said Trevor.

'Allow me,' said Big Al, taking the box from Jill, dragging out the bundle of wire and revealing, within its meshes, two small boxes. He held them up, one in each hand.

'In my left hand, Component A. In my right hand, Component B. Component A is a combined microphone and loudspeaker. So is Component B. They are linked by wire of a sufficiency to girdle the earth.'

'It's an intercom,' said Norm, always the first to flag in the face of Al's soliloquies. But the big man was building up a head of steam.

'You place Component A in First-Born's bedroom, close to his manger. You place Component B here in the living room. First-Born cries. Mummy and/or Daddy hears him, presses the button marked BUTTON, and says, "There there, Mummy and/or Daddy is on his or her way with a dry nappy and a cheerful nursery rhyme."'

Al handed the bundle to Norm.

'Fix it, Norm,' he said, before turning to Jill and Trevor with yet another of the footnotes vital to his condition.

'It's a fraternal partnership. I deal with cosmic reflections, street wisdom and political dialectic. Norm deals with the installations.'

Norm planted Component B on one of Trevor's stereo speakers then asked: 'Can one of you direct me to the manger?'

'I'll show you,' said Trevor.

He and Little Norm went up the stairs, trailing wire behind them. Jill, as ever and always, was delighted, intrigued and baffled by Big Al. He was an enigma, double-wrapped in mystery, spiced with earthy gallantry and a disconcerting passion for truth.

'This is very thoughtful of you,' she said.

Al touched the peak of his cloth cap, with respect but no hint of deference.

'There's not many of us left, Mrs Swinburne. We have to stand together against the forces of darkness.'

'Do you still have your warehouse?'

It was Big Al's warehouse and his creation of a comprehensive black economy in the county – an economy he claimed, with justice, to be cleaner, cheaper and nicer than the so-called real thing – which had first drawn Trevor and Jill into his mighty orbit.

'I still have access to the warehouse, Mrs Swinburne, should you require any consumer durables at competitive prices. But I no longer run it. I am concentrating on affairs of the planet. My brother is in charge of the warehouse.'

'Little Norm?'

'No. My brother.'

Jill had never worked out the number, variety or geographical spread of Al's brothers and sisters. His extended family extended further than the eye could see, or the authorities investigate. Mostly they didn't bother. She was tempted to ask about the warehouse brother, if only to fill in another name on the infinite crossword puzzle of Big Al's empire, but she was interrupted by the voice of Little Norm, distorted by the microphone of Component A and the loudspeaker of Component B.

'Are you receiving me? Over.'

Al pressed the button marked BUTTON and replied: 'Big Al receiving Little Norm loud and clear. Over and out.'

There were a number of clicks from upstairs, followed by the eager sound of Trevor's voice: 'Hey, this is fantastic! BD to Z Victor One. We are on the brink of a new era if only . . .'

'Trevor! This is not a toy! Come downstairs at once! You'll wake First-Born!'

Jill had always been quick to learn about buttons marked BUTTON.

'Sorry. I'll come downstairs,' said Trevor.

'A very pleasing test run,' said Big Al, as the new technology of Component B fell silent.

'Thank you again,' said Jill.

'Good bit of installation, that, I reckon,' said Little Norm, stumbling over a trailing end of superfluous wire as he and

Trevor returned to the living room. They were very pleased with themselves.

'British craftsmanship,' said Trevor, 'is still alive and well and . . .'

'And living in penury,' said Big Al, powerfully. Nobody argued. They all knew that long ago Al had worked in the building trade. Then came redundancy. They had heard the speech.

'The system said to me: Al, you are redundant. Your skills are no longer required. Ever since, I have been saying bollocks to the system. It's the only sensible thing you can say to systems. Bollocks.'

People sometimes thought Big Al was a joke. He was not a joke. He concealed the mighty rage of a rejected craftsman. He had been known to tilt the West Riding on its axis. If he could do that, the planet would present few problems. Any Yorkshireman would confirm that truth.

Before leaving, he said to Jill, 'May I confirm, Mrs Swinburne, that you are still dedicated to cleansing Society of all evil?'

'Well, bearing in mind I have a full-time job and a child, yes, I am. Why do you ask?'

'No reason, Mrs Swinburne. Idle curiosity.'

'Al. Your curiosity is never idle.'

The big man smiled, acknowledging a palpable hit.

'Well spotted, Mrs Swinburne,' he said, then turned to his fraternal partner with a brisk, 'Come on, Norm. We mustn't waste good crusading time.'

After they had gone, Jill resumed marking her essays. Trevor moved his chair alongside Component B and settled down to read the paper.

'It was nice, seeing Big Al again,' said Jill.

'He's a bit unpredictable.'

'No, he isn't. He's *totally* unpredictable.'

Trevor stretched arms and legs and enjoyed a good yawn.

'My problem is when Al's around, things happen. I'd rather nothing happened. I'm beginning to enjoy predictable. The slippers. The pipe. The garden. Lagging pipes. I'm serious about all that.'

'Trevor. You are turning into a cabbage.'

'I like cabbage.'

They sat quietly and went about their business. Jill thought about the future of the planet. Trevor thought about cabbage.

2

A Formidable Police Presence

The police car cruised gently along an unwanted inner-city ring road. Its blue light flashed and its siren blared, giving a sense of urgency to its otherwise placid progress.

Joe, the driver, complained to his CID colleague.

'Would you mind switching all that stuff off? We're dazzling too many pedestrians and that noise hurts my ears. It's altogether too piercing, man.'

'Sorry,' said Ben, doing as his partner requested. Peace was restored to the car and its immediate environment.

'My psychiatrist would call that attention-seeking behaviour.'

'I hit the wrong button, that's all. I was looking for Radio Three.'

'I lost concentration with all that noise. Where are we supposed to be going?'

Ben checked in his notebook.

'Archer Street shopping precinct.'

'Why couldn't the thieves strike in some other place? It's murder, trying to park down there.'

The car approached a roundabout bearing two road signs, each reading: ARCHER STREET SHOPPING PRECINCT. Joe ignored both in favour of a gloomy ginnel, signposted: TO MUNICIPAL ABATTOIR.

It was characteristic of the team's circuitous approach to the maintenance of law and order. Joe and Ben were outstanding members of the local CID squad. They dressed much better than the average detective, and were dedicated professionals. The dedication took a slightly unusual form. Their constant quest was to produce the maximum of apparent results with an absolute minimum of actual effort. Expressed another way, they were bone idle; yet the indolence was concealed behind veneers of simulated efficiency, highly-polished jargon and calculated servile charm to superior officers.

They parked the car in the centre of the pedestrian precinct. With great precision they simultaneously blocked all access to the kiddies' playground, and the only decent view of the sculptural water feature.

A crumbling, well-loved Victorian market-hall had been demolished, overnight and illegally, to make way for the Archer Street development. A journalist on the local paper had discovered the precinct was jointly owned by a man in Dallas, Texas and another in Osaka. Neither of them knew anything about it. They re-directed all searching questions to a branch office in Milton Keynes. The journalist was given a sideways career move and now covered religious affairs and greyhound-racing.

Mrs Pringle was one of the few survivors from the old market-hall, where she had run a second-hand bookstall on a trestle table, catering to those elements in the population forced to juggle poverty and literacy without the aid of a net.

She assumed it was either an executive oversight or a computer error that had resulted in her appointment as manager of MEGABOOKS INC. She hated the name, but saw it as a small victory against the advertising consultants who wanted the shop to be called LIT 'N GLITZ. She dutifully supervised the weekly campaign whereby today's best-sellers were unveiled at the main entrance every Saturday, and sold off at half-price the following Friday by the rear door marked STAFF ONLY. From the old days she retained her trestle table, in a corner beside the fire extinguisher, most of her former customers, total recall of every worthwhile book published in the last hundred years and a violent hatred of a dangling participle or a misplaced apostrophe. She it was who had called the police and now found herself confronted by Joe and Ben. She deserved better, but was too well-read to expect absolute justice on the good earth.

'So what did the thieves take?' asked Joe.

'Books.'

Ben made a note of this, while Joe scanned the broad acres of shelving all around them.

'Books,' he said. 'Yes. That would make sense. Clearly they knew exactly what they were looking for and where to find it.'

'Can you give us a description?' asked Ben, keen to make more notes. He was an obsessive note-taker.

'Of what? The thieves or the books?'

The two detectives looked at each other. Mrs Pringle's clarity of thought was an unexpected development. But speed of response was part of their detective training.

'Er . . .'

'Maybe . . .'

'Both?'

'One at a time, in order,' said Ben, finding solid ground.

'Starting with the . . .'

'Books.'

Mrs Pringle waited, to be sure they had finished, then announced, with great precision. 'He, she or they took two books. The title of the first book is *An Alphabetical Guide to Sexual Behaviour, Volume One*.'

'*Volume One*?' said Ben, who was writing it all down.

'*A to K*.'

'A very good place to start, in my experience,' said Joe.

'And the other book?'

'*Tess of the D'Urbervilles* by Thomas Hardy.'

As they returned to the car, the two detectives shared thoughts on the theme of Sexual Behaviour beginning with A.

'Apologetic.'

'Amphibious.'

'Ambulatory.'

'Apprehensive.'

'All systems go.'

'Oh look.'

'That begins with O,' said Ben.

Joe pointed at the car. A small, brown-paper package was wedged beneath one of the windscreen wipers.

It was Ben's turn to drive. He fancied a trip to the park. Joe unwrapped the parcel. It contained a video-cassette.

'One experienced glance tells me this is a video,' he said.

'Even money says it's the now legendary pilot episode of *Hill Street Blues*.'

'It seems to be a homemade video.'

'Often the best sort.'

'With a message attached.'

'A message?'

'Written on a mass-produced word processor of the kind that is ruining everyone's eyesight and making calligraphy a lost art, it reads, and I quote . . . "I THINK THE FORCES OF LAW AND ORDER SHOULD KNOW WHAT IS GOING ON IN A ONCE RESPECTABLE AREA" . . . all in capital letters. Heigh ho. What happened to the green ink we used to know and love?' sighed Joe.

'Any signature?' said Ben.

'No name. No signature.'

'Which makes it anonymous in my book.'

'Do you think we should leap into action?'

'Action sometimes gives me a migraine.'

They drove on in silence. Joe wiped his fingerprints from the cassette. Ben pondered the correlation between migraines and action.

'Solved it,' said Joe. 'We'll hand it in at the nearest police station.'

In room 19B on the first floor of San Quentin High, Jill was taking her English class.

'I'm delighted to say we now have *three* copies of *Tess of the D'Urbervilles* . . . well done, Sharon.'

Sharon smiled. She looked like the younger, lesser-known sister of a Botticelli angel, but wasn't.

'It was the last one in the shop, miss, but I think they're getting some more in.'

'Good. And with a bit of luck, you will all have a chance to read the book some time during the academic year, perhaps even in time for your examination. As and when you do read it, you will discover that *Tess of the D'Urbervilles* is a story about the ruthless exploitation of women by . . . by whom? I wonder if you can guess? All together now!'

'Men, miss!' yelled thirty-eight voices in chorus. They liked their teacher and knew how to make her happy.

'Excellent,' said Jill. 'Now we're getting somewhere.'

She glanced out of the window and saw Big Al and Little Norm. They were cycling across the playing field, being careful to avoid the more sensitive areas of the football pitch.

In the Woodwork Room on the ground floor of San Quentin High Trevor was sharing a problem with forty kids. He calculated that in this case a problem shared was a problem increased by a factor of forty, but he shared it anyway.

'I gather from Mr Wheeler that it will be at least a month before we get any fresh supplies of wood. Which is a bit of a problem, since what I'm supposed to teach you is woodwork.'

Gary put his hand up. He looked like the younger, lesser-known brother of a Hell's Angel, and he was.

'Sir, is it to do with all that crap about tropical rain forests, sir?'

'Hardly at all. It's to do with the school not having any money. That's the bad news. Now for the good news. Mr Wheeler has suggested that we spend the next few lessons studying the theory of wood. Now. I wonder if anybody can tell me what this is?'

Trevor unrolled a picture of a tree. The leaves were coloured green, the trunk was coloured brown and there were dotted lines to indicate the roots. As an additional clue to the uncertain, the word TREE was written underneath it, in red and underlined.

There were no suggestions forthcoming from the class.

'Oh, come on,' said Trevor, ' even I know what this is. I'll give you a clue. This thing is made out of wood. Apples grow on some of them.'

In his time Trevor had survived everything from flying chisels to sawdust in his sandwiches, but he had never been ignored. He turned to see the class staring out of the window and Gary with his hand up.

'Please sir, Big Al's outside, sir.'

Al was at the window, his nose pressed flat against the glass, beckoning to Trevor. It was a more interesting sight than a drawing of a tree.

Trevor walked across the room to the window. Al held up a large, hand-written sign, reading:

ARE YOU IN TONIGHT?

Trevor nodded. Al turned the sign around. On the back it read:

GOOD!

Big Al and Little Norm touched their caps, climbed on their bicycles and rode away.

'Do you know Big Al?' said Trevor to Gary.

'He's my uncle, sir.'

'I see.'

Trevor returned to the drawing of the tree.

'Are you any nearer deciding what this might be?'

'Sir!'

Gary's hand shot up, proud and confident.

'Yes?'

'We could get you some wood, sir.'

From various parts of the room, eager voices added their support to Gary's suggestion.

'My Dad knows a feller . . . anybody can get wood . . . dead easy, piece of piss . . . what sort do you want?'

Beneath the hubbub of the young voices, Trevor fancied he heard a deeper rumbling, as the surviving tropical rain forests ran for cover.

Joe and Ben sat in the CID room of Sherlock Road Police Station, playing back the videotape. They had considered delegating the task downwards or sideways, but Ben was concerned to fill a few more pages in his notebook, and they were both concerned with passing the remaining hours of the shift as painlessly as possible.

'Besides,' Ben had pointed out, 'the tape might contain a vital clue leading to an early arrest and an award for gallantry, but with no element of danger involved.'

'A consummation devoutly to be wished,' said Joe.

They had been mistaken. The tape showed a series of blurred, semi-abstract images of no discernible criminal import. There were shapes that resembled houses, a street, people walking in the street, a motor car, a dog and two men on bicycles.

'Tedious and pointless,' said Joe. 'Very nearly the most boring thing I've ever seen. Certainly on a par with synchronised swimming.'

They spent fifteen contented minutes listing the most boring things they had ever seen.

'The Boat Race.'

'Recorded highlights of the *Horse of the Year Show*.'

'Anything whatsoever on ice.'

A county cricket match between Sussex and Sussex.'

'The Home Counties South slow foxtrot formation team pulling out all the stops in the second semi-final of *Come Dancing*.'

'Oh look.'

The tape had run its course. The images had given way to a speckly configuration of dots and scratches, though it was hard to tell the difference.

'Clearly we have to refer this to *somebody*,' said Joe.

'But not downwards or sideways, both of whom will tell us to sod off.'

'Forensic?'

'Ballistics?'

'Upwards!' they cried in unison, as they remembered Inspector Hobson, their brand-new, hardly-used receptacle for unwanted dilemmas.

Hobson had first arrived at Sherlock Road four years

earlier, with a first-class degree and the rank of sergeant. He had fallen head first into an investigation involving Trevor Chaplin, Jill Swinburne, Big Al and Little Norm, and emerged triumphantly. It was his own little Watergate. He then departed, in pursuit of more letters, and had duly returned with a PhD, the rank of inspector and a knapsack containing a chief constable's baton, a change of underwear and a hundred floppy discs.

Inspector Hobson was the Prince of Information Storage and Retrieval. A modern Descartes, he lived by the principle: it is in the Computer, therefore it is. Applying this principle, he had won a Distinction for his PhD thesis, written on aspects of criminology so obscure they would have had great novelty value at Dartmoor and the Scrubs. At the Police Academy he had become famous for finishing his examination papers in half the allotted time, and whiling away the remaining hours writing learned critiques of the questions, pointing out where they were wrong.

His weakness was communication with other representatives of the human race. His head was terminally clogged with information, and his soul with ambition. He was the true child of a joyless decade, and he was no match for the streetwise coppers of the outer limits; least of all for Joe and Ben. The door to his office carried his name: INSPECTOR HOBSON. Ben had added 'PhD' with a felt-nibbed pen. Hobson didn't know whether to leave it or order its removal. It symbolised his uneasy relationship with the police force, the county of Yorkshire and Life.

Now, facing Joe and Ben across the broad sheen of his desk, the unease was once more upon him. He did not understand these people.

Ben placed the video-cassette on the desk.

'To be brutally honest, Inspector Hobson, we do not feel up to this task.'

'We are strictly old-fashioned, bare-knuckled policemen,' said Joe.

'Street fighters.'

'But life has moved on since Sir Robert Peel.'

'We acknowledge that freely and frankly.'

'We are dinosaurs.'

'I am reasonably clear about everybody's place in history,' said Hobson. 'But I am not at all clear what you are asking me to do.'

'Relieve us of our burden,' said Joe.

Ben pointed at the video-cassette.

'Inspector Hobson. This cassette is of your world, not ours. You have a mind that belongs to the 1990s. Video technology requires your sort of mind. You are, in our joint and humble opinion, ideally equipped to penetrate the heart of its mystery and reveal its innermost significance.'

'You have the mind. You have the technology.'

They looked across at the institution known to all at Sherlock Road Police Station as Hobson's Wall. The inspector had designed and built it, from self-assembly units. A complex stacking system housed two computers, a printer, a photocopier, a radio transmitter and receiver, two audio-tape decks, a video recorder and television set, a FAX machine and a number of related items so far unidentified. Originally christened the Starship Enterprise, a passing superintendent had commented:

'Yon bloody wall. It's twice as tall as Hadrian's and six times as impenetrable.'

Possessing and understanding such a wall made Hobson an obvious candidate for tedious and unwanted videos; and he was, in any case, more comfortable with hi-tech than low comedy.

'Leave it on my desk,' he said.

Casually, and with the speed of light, the two detectives were at the door.

'We'll get back on the streets where we belong,' said Joe.

In the corridor, Ben challenged his partner.

'What was all that stuff about getting back on the streets where we belong?'

'Merely a form of words to impress our superior officer.'

'As long as you didn't mean it.'

'When did we ever mean anything?'

'Fair comment.'

They moved on, in search of meaningless activity and amusing vantage points, where they might stand and stare until the end of the shift.

Inspector Hobson played back the videotape helped by part of his wall, and a remote control switch with facilities for studying the images in fast or slow motion, forwards or backwards, and for freezing the frame at any chosen point. Whatever permutation he selected, his conclusion was the same.

'Gobbledegook.'

He caught a momentary glimpse of a small van that was distantly familiar, like an echo of a long-forgotten song; but the words, music and title eluded him. His problem, though he did not know it, was that the videotape was in monochrome. Yellow looks grey in monochrome.

Trevor Chaplin's yellow van pulled up outside Number 17, Hotspur Street at the end of another long day. Teaching woodwork without wood and English without books was hard work. Jill, for once, owned up to tiredness.

'No exercise books to mark. As soon as First-Born's in bed, I'm going to put my feet up and be a cabbage.'

'I think Big Al and Little Norm are coming round.'

'They are?'

Trevor explained: 'Al pressed a note to the Woodwork Room window saying, ARE YOU IN TONIGHT? And I nodded. So I expect that means he or they is or are coming round tonight.'

'You even end up talking like Big Al.'

Their return to the house was recorded on video.

It is a fact of life in the English suburbs that any display of radical politics provokes an equal and opposite reactionary. Jill's passionate devotion to great and good causes had never been a secret. Her front room window carried a permanent display of posters declaring allegiance to the Planet Earth, its animal and plant life, and the poor and dispossessed of its people. The posters, by definition, also declared non-violent war on the many and various institutionalised villains whose prosperity was based on kicking the hell out of animals, plants and people.

The man opposite disagreed. He had gnomes and a wishing well in his front garden, which, in itself, indicated a shortage of radical zeal. He had spread rumours about Jill and Trevor and written anonymous letters to Mr Wheeler, with a precise catalogue of the depravity he had witnessed across the street.

Jill and Trevor did not know the man's name. There seemed no compelling reason to seek an introduction. Instead, they had created a mythology about him. He was, they decided, an unfrocked bank manager. For the purposes of daily conversation, this they simplified to UBM. In idle and vindictive moments, they added cheerful chapters to the UBM saga. Observing that he lived alone, they invented a series of grotesque wives, each of whom the UBM had murdered, usually in the bath, and then buried in the wishing well. Whenever a new gnome appeared, that was a sure sign that another bride had taken her final journey down the well, by way of the en suite bathroom.

What Jill and Trevor did not know was that their neighbourhood UBM had bought a video-camera and was dutifully recording the more sinister aspects of the street life as seen from behind his lace curtains. His plan, already implemented in part, was to pass these tapes on to the proper authority. He was still mastering the theory and practice of focus, and somewhere on the machine there was supposed to be a switch marked SWITCH. As soon as he found it, the pictures would be in colour, the evidence would be obvious to all, the authorities would act and Society would be cleansed. He had allowed himself three weeks for the job. The UBM was round the bend but as Mr Carter had once pointed out, 'In the present climate, round the bend, the lunatic fringe and the middle of the road are one and the same place. I may have to consider moving to somewhere less crowded.'

Big Al and Little Norm arrived, on their bicycles, as the UBM started a brand-new cassette.

'We are all old friends and we trust each other. I'm sure that's correct.' Big Al stood centre-stage in the living room not so much speaking as opening his mouth and addressing a multitude. He was talking to Trevor and Jill, so it was the lower end of the multitude scale. Little Norm, as usual, was present with observer status only.

'Is that correct, Mrs Swinburne? My understanding about the nature of our friendship?'

'Yes. That's correct.'

'Trev?'

'Yes. That's correct.'

'That being so, I wonder what you thought the other night, when me and Norm arrived, bearing a modest gift for your child?'

'I think I thought . . . thank you Al, thank you Norm.'

Jill turned to Trevor for confirmation of what she had thought.

'Yes. I think that's what we thought. I think we said so. Thank you Al. Thank you Norm.'

'You did,' said Little Norm. 'I remember you saying it.'

'That being so,' said Al, 'I wonder whether you thought to yourselves: we'll end up paying for this. Here comes Big Al with a present. You watch. He'll be back within the week, asking us to do him a big favour. You didn't think that, did you?'

'No. I certainly didn't think that. Did you, Trevor?'

'No. I just thought it was a really useful toy.'

Al moved his head up and down, twice, indicating this was the desired response.

'Good. Excellent. First class. A gift for its own sake. Presented out of admiration and affection, purely and simply.'

'That's what we wanted you to think,' said Norm.

'Precisely.'

''Cos that's what it was.'

They both nodded, agreeing with each other, not quite in unison.

'Good,' said Jill.

'Good,' said Trevor. 'And thank you. Again.'

The room fell silent. Al, Jill decided, was in his Samuel Beckett mode. If Godot ever turned up, he would be a dead ringer for Big Al.

'However.'

The word landed in the silence like the gong at the beginning of an old J. Arthur Rank movie.

'However?' said Jill.

'This, Mrs Swinburne and Mr Chaplin, is a genuine example of a pure and remarkable coincidence.'

'Is it?' said Trevor.

'Big Al brought you a present and here he is, back within the week, asking you to do him a big favour.'

'You're asking us for a big favour?' said Jill.

'It is a pure coincidence but yes please. We need . . .' Al looked around the room, as if checking the walls for ears, before continuing, ' . . . a safe house.'

'We thought this looked like a safe house,' said Little Norm.

'Is it a safe house?'

Trevor gave an artisan shrug.

'There's a bit of a leak on the verandah roof. The flashing's come adrift. Otherwise . . .'

'I don't think that's what they mean, Trevor. They mean a safe house where somebody can stay. Is that what you mean?'

'That is what we mean, Mrs Swinburne. A house where someone can stay in safety.'

'Unobserved,' said Norman, by way of clarification.

'Who and when and for how long?' said Jill.

'For one night only,' said Al.

'This night,' said Norm.

'Like tonight.'

'You haven't said who it is,' said Trevor, growing a little

impatient. He quite enjoyed suspense providing it didn't go on too long.

'There is no harm in revealing that we are talking about a man. At this stage it would be wise not to elaborate further.'

'We'd find out he was a man anyway, if he stayed here.'

'If?' said Jill, quietly. Though she had not declared herself, she was already thinking in terms of when and, beyond that, whether there were any clean towels.

'What's this feller done?' said Trevor. 'He must have done something if he wants to be unobserved. Like who does he want to be unobserved *by*?'

'He's more or less a refugee,' said Big Al.

'Who from?' asked Jill.

'It's obvious,' said Trevor. 'He's a refugee from whoever it is he wants to be unobserved by.'

'I was asking Al.'

'Sorry.'

'Al? Can you offer us a modest morsel of information?'

The big man nodded.

'Certainly, Mrs Swinburne. If I withhold certain salient factors it is purely in your own interest, since you cannot reveal what you do not know. But I can tell you this. Our man is on the run because of his involvement with what you might term the international peace movement. Also because he has the wrong sort of passport.'

'The wrong sort of passport?'

'Like he hasn't got one,' said Little Norm.

'Which, technically speaking, is very much like having the wrong sort,' said Al, content that he had now clarified every dot, comma, semi-colon and parenthesis of the situation, including asterisks and footnotes.

Jill glanced at Trevor. He was sitting in his armchair, legs crossed, idly picking at the frayed toe-ends of his venerable and much-loved slippers. She knew the gesture. It meant: I want no part of this. He tended to pick at his slippers when she suggested having a dental check-up, watching an award-winning Polish film, or changing to skimmed milk. They generally ended up going to the dentist, seeing the film and buying the milk. She would buy him some new slippers for Christmas.

'Where is your refugee now?' she said.

'Hiding.'

'In the park,' said Norm.

'The way I see it, if you want to loiter somewhere, the park's quite a good place, because it's full of people loitering.'

'And lurking and prowling,' said Norm.

'Philosophically speaking, if everybody's loitering, nobody appears to be loitering. Therefore, you may safely loiter, unobserved. A veritable sanctuary, a municipal park, in that respect.'

'*If* we say yes,' said Jill, still aware of the toe-picking, 'what happens next?'

'We bring the refugee here. Under cover of darkness.'

'He stays the night?'

'Yes. Please.'

'And then?'

'A little light breakfast, if you'd be so kind.'

'And then?'

'We take him away again.'

'In the morning?'

'That's about it, Mrs Swinburne.'

'It'll be light in the morning,' said Trevor.

'It often is. I've noticed that,' said Norm.

'What's the point of bringing him here under cover of darkness if you're going to take him away in broad daylight?'

'Thank you, Trev, you have spotted a flaw in my logic. I'll have to conceive a subterfuge to counteract the illumination of broad daylight. Don't let me forget about that, Norm.'

'Subterfuge.'

'Remind me.'

'Right.'

Al adjusted his cap, as if anticipating an early encounter with the night air.

'Do I take it you've agreed? Mrs Swinburne? Trev?'

By way of reply, the voice of First-Born emerged from Component B, a plaintive cry that ran, in translation: don't worry, folks, it's nothing serious, the nappy's dry and nothing hurts, but it would be nice to see one of you for a few minutes' idle chat on matters of mutual concern.

'Excuse me,' said Trevor, who understood every syllable.

'Lovely bit of wiring that, Norm. You can hear that baby's voice, as clear as a bell.'

'Thank you, Al,' said Jill. 'I can spot moral pressure at a range of a thousand miles.'

'Pardon?'

'Shhh!' said Norm.

They fell silent. Trevor was talking to his child, and nobody wanted to miss the programme.

They heard:

'There there, son, the old man's here. Your mother's busy downstairs, talking things through. I've got a pretty good idea she's about to save the Planet Earth. Again. It happens two or three times a week. You'll get used to it. The best thing's just to bob and weave, sway back against the ropes, and keep well out of the way. That's what I always do. You'll find out. Doesn't hurt. Rule number one where your mother's concerned. Keep quiet and, above all . . . stay cool, baby.'

Trevor's soliloquy was followed by a brief tone poem of shushing, gooing and gurgling: non-verbal communication of a high and precious order.

Jill looked at Big Al.

'Looks like you got yourself a safe house.'

'Thank you, Mrs Swinburne.'

Inspector Hobson had opted for a final brief dalliance with his wall before committing himself to the journey home through what people assured him was the real world.

He was playing back the UBM tape and had frozen the frame in a last, obsessive search for recognisable shapes and forms. Hobson screwed up his eyes, concentrating on the trembling image. He thought: it could be a house. But it could just as easily be a horse. And was it admissible evidence? A videotape of something that might be a house or might be a horse? Defending counsel would drive a horse and cart through it. Or a house and cart. And what was he trying to prove in the first place?

'I am going potty,' he said, thereby, for the first time placing himself in total agreement with the men under his command.

He switched off the television set and the video machine, and switched on his miniature tape recorder, loyal recipient of his minute-by-minute activities and cosmic broodings.

'Inspector Hobson, 21.06. Have completed preliminary visual assessment of anonymous videotape, identification number 2726B. It appears to be totally devoid of all meaning and purpose.'

Inspector Hobson switched off his wall at the mains, counted his pencils, set his burglar alarm, triple-locked his door and went home.

Jill Swinburne and Trevor Chaplin never had rows; they had gentle simmers. You could make chicken stock on their disagreements.

'You're doing it again, aren't you?' said Trevor, voice upraised like a television commentator reporting on the early stages of a minor indoor bowls tournament.

'What am I doing again?'

Unmoved and undisturbed, Jill carried on reading her Toni Morrison.

'Getting us involved.'

'We are providing accommodation for a homeless refugee. I think that's quite a good thing to do.'

'You know what happened last time. We ended up getting chased by armed men halfway across Europe.'

That had been another of their disorderly adventures, beginning when Trevor heard some Bix Beiderbecke music in a neighbourhood tavern, continuing with oppressive attention from MI5 to MI37 inclusive and ending with Jill's pregnancy.

It was, by any standards, an unusual sequence of events, giving little comfort to the Cause-and-Effect school of human development.

'Trevor. History does not repeat itself. It's a well-known historical fact.'

'What do you know about history? You teach English. I'll ask Mr Carter. He knows some history.'

Jill was always touched by Trevor's faith in the idea that teachers knew what they were teaching. It earned him a whisper of reassurance. She put her book down, sat on the arm of his chair and kissed the top of his head.

'I'll tell you what will happen. Big Al and Little Norm will arrive soon, with a man. He will stay the night. He will eat a little light breakfast.'

'I hope he likes muesli.'

'And in the morning he will go again. There. All over. It didn't hurt, did it?'

'Promise?'

'Promise.'

'Besides.'

'Besides what?'

Jill got up and crossed to the window.

'They seem to be on their own.'

'What?'

They looked out to see two men approaching the house. One was small and Norm-shaped. The other was large and Al-shaped.

Jill opened the front door to them. It was as they entered the living room that the truth was made manifest. The Norm-shaped man was indeed Little Norm, but the Al-shaped man was not Big Al.

'Now I understand,' said Jill. 'You're not Big Al.'

'One searching glance, that's all it takes,' said Trevor.

'He's disguised as Big Al. It's our security cover.'

The stranger wore one of Al's extensive range of identical cloth caps and a donkey jacket by McAlpine. He was as tall as Al, but with a lean, austere face. If Al was a Pennine, this man was a slender, ice-capped Carpathian.

'Does he have a name? Are we going to be introduced?'

'Ah. Well. Yes. So. Right. His name's Ivan. But Al says I have to tell you he isn't all that terrible.'

'I'm sure he isn't.'

'Ivan. This is Mrs Swinburne. This is Mr Chaplin.'

Ivan shook hands with each of them in turn. He seemed to regard it as a very serious business, involving much concentration.

'Hello Ivan. It's a pleasure to meet you,' said Jill.

Ivan smiled.

'Hi,' said Trevor.

Ivan smiled again.

'He doesn't speak any English,' said Norm.

'None at all?'

'I think he does the odd please and thank you. That's about his lot. He's foreign, you see. That's the explanation.'

Introductions over, Norm was eager to leave. His conversation accelerated as he headed for the door.

'I'll have to dash. I want to catch the chippy before all the halibut's gone.'

Jill wanted to catch Little Norm before he was gone.

'What about the arrangements for collecting Ivan?'

'Yes.'

'Yes? With the greatest of respect, Norm, that hardly constitutes an answer to my question.'

'It means yes, there'll be some arrangements. Good night.'

With one bound he was gone.

Jill and Trevor found themselves marooned, like wedding guests stuck with a silent mariner. A little primitive mime helped Ivan through the process of removing Al's cap and jacket. Jill hung them up in the hall, then returned with the resolute brightness of vintage Shirley Temple.

'Cup of tea?' she said, aware that she was taking the coward's way out.

'Good idea,' said Trevor.

'Tea?' they chanted at Ivan, Jill wondering whether he might prefer it made in a samovar.

Ivan examined the concept long and hard. Einstein was probably much swifter working out what E was equal to, even without a pocket calculator; but the answer emerged, at its true and chosen speed.

'Tea. Good. Thank you.'

'I'll make it,' said Trevor.

'No, I'll make it,' said Jill.

They practically collided on the way to the kitchen, then had a tug-of-war with the kettle. This was no simmer. This was a disagreement coming quickly to the boil, albeit in hushed voices.

'You stay and talk to Ivan,' said Jill.

'What am I supposed to talk about? What am I supposed to talk *with*? What do I use for words?'

'Use your initiative.'

'I'm a cabbage. Cabbages don't have any initiative. Cabbages don't want any initiative. That's the point of being a cabbage.'

'Cabbages get eaten.'

Jill won the kettle and filled it.

'Go and talk to Ivan!'

'I'll go,' said Trevor, 'but I won't talk to him. I'll sit in a corner. Sulking.'

'Do as you like. But in the name of God, go!'

Trevor trudged back to the living room, raking out the recesses of memory for lively topics with a Soviet tinge. His best offer comprised a couple of goalkeepers – Tiger Khomitch and Lev Yashin, and a Lithuanian piano player called Vyacheslav Ganelin: a fragile base for a meaningful conversation.

To his astonishment, Ivan spoke first, and the word was light.

'Bix!'

Ivan stood by the record shelves, with a Beiderbecke LP in his hand.

Trevor replied slowly and precisely, suddenly aware of a promised land, only a blue note away.

'You . . . like . . . Bix . . . Beiderbecke?'

Ivan nodded.

'Bix. Cool.'

'Cool. You bet. You . . . like to hear?'

'Bix. Cool. Good.'

The words emerged at equal intervals, like careful footprints on a sandy shore. They were heading in a Chaplin-approved direction. Jill arrived from the kitchen, bearing tea and biscuits. The sound of Beiderbecke's plaintive cornet danced upon the air and Trevor was giving Ivan a conducted tour of his record shelves. He continued to talk like a phrasebook in translation.

'These are all Duke Ellington. You like Duke Ellington?'

'Yes. Duke. Ellington. Cool.'

More footprints.

'And Charlie Parker. And Art Tatum. And Louis Armstrong. And . . .'

'Trevor.'

'Yes?'

'Do I take it you've made an exciting new friend?'

'He's a jazz freak. I came in and he was looking through the Beiderbecke albums.'

'Bix. Cool,' said Ivan.

Jill poured the tea.

'I see. You made a Beiderbecke connection.'

'Yes.'

Though she knew that history did not repeat itself and had said so, vehemently, within the last hour, Jill was aware that all of their previous misadventures on the mean, uptown streets of the West Riding and the even meaner boulevards of downtown Europe had begun, weirdly and inexplicably, with the music of Leon Bismark Bix Beiderbecke, whose playing sounded like bullets shot from a bell.

'I ask myself,' said Jill, 'is this a good connection?'

'It's the best there is,' said Trevor.

3

Hello, Sir. Hello, Miss

Trevor winced as Jill's muesli crashed into the bowl.

'What time did you come to bed?' she asked him.

'Three. Four. Something like that. A low number.'

'What were you drinking?'

'Ivan had this bottle in his bag. Sliv-something. Sounded like a foreign politician.'

'Slivovitz?'

Trevor nodded, winced again, then slid into Ivan-Speak.

'It . . . is . . . made . . . in . . . Yug . . . o . . . slav . . .ia. Cool? Yes?'

'How many glasses of this libation did you drink?'

'A high number. I counted five. After that it was the red mist.'

Yvonne arrived. Her smiling eagerness lit up the room and hurt Trevor's eyes.

'Hello, sir! Hello, miss! All ready for another day's au-pairing. Where's First-Born?'

'Still asleep,' said Jill. 'And be very gentle with Mr Chaplin.'

'Got pissed again, sir?'

'Take a week's notice.'

Yvonne ignored him.

'There's something else you should know,' said Jill. 'There's a foreign refugee in the spare room. Probably sleeping off the same hangover as Mr Chaplin. His name's Ivan.'

'And he likes Bix Beiderbecke,' said Trevor, keen, despite his pain, to give a complete and rounded portrait of their visitor.

'Nobody's perfect, sir.'

'Take another week's notice.'

'Don't do anything of the kind, Yvonne.'

'Wasn't going to, miss. Not after what you said to me.'

'What did Mrs Swinburne say to you?'

'She said: if Mr Chaplin says anything stupid, just ignore him.'

'Yes, that's excellent advice.'

It was obvious that Trevor would be unable to distinguish basic shapes and primary colours much before noon, so Jill drove the van to school. Trevor slumped in his seat, his entire world an unrelenting frown, wrapped around his head like a towel.

'Will Yvonne be all right?' he said, seeking the comfort of small anxieties.

'Don't understand.'

'With Ivan?'

'Of course she will. If you told her the Brigade of Guards and the Boston Philharmonic were in the spare room she'd say: that's all right, miss, as long as they don't mind instant. Anyway, Big Al's taking Ivan away this morning.'

As they parked the van, Jill noticed Mr Carter looking down from the staffroom window. He was a reliable barometer, his demeanour normally a sound guide to the day's prospects. On that basis today's destiny was a prolonged wallow in the deep end of doom.

The reason for Mr Carter's expression was the lowering presence of the headmaster. Mr Wheeler was lurking in the doorway with the shifty assurance of a dedicated and accomplished lurker. He was trying to make a speech.

'If I might have your attention!' he cried.

The teachers were unwilling to spare him even one milligramme of attention. They were preoccupied with the final fix of tabloid, caffeine or nicotine before embarking on the trench warfare of scholarship. Mr Wheeler tried again.

'If I might have your attention!'

A shaven-headed figure in a track suit handed him a whistle, without losing concentration on the day's runners at Doncaster. Mr Wheeler took a deep breath and gave a piercing blast on the whistle. There were scattered cries of 'Offside Ref!' and 'Stop, thief, in the name of the Law!' followed by a gradual and truculent silence.

'Thank you. I'm sorry to disturb you at a time when you are all so busy preparing your lessons . . .'

It was a bizarre distortion of reality but since they all knew the headmaster was clinically insane, nobody saw the need to comment. In any case, a more amusing diversion walked into the room.

'Who's the silly sod blowing whistles? I've got a head like a bucket.'

Jill was close behind Trevor, and swift to the rescue.

'Mr Chaplin has a head like a bucket, but it's almost better now.'

'Yes. Fully recovered. Thank you.'

Trevor sat down on the nearest unbroken chair while Jill stroked the headmaster's psyche with a pre-emptive cringe.

'Do forgive us, Mr Wheeler. We didn't mean to interrupt your flow of wisdom.'

She indicated with a gracious gesture that the floor and, come to that, the entire universe, was his. He tried again.

'I am sorry to disturb you at a time when most of you, or at least some of you, are preparing your lessons, but it is to inform you of a special emergency meeting I am calling this evening. As you know, the school is desperately short of vital equipment . . . textbooks, exercise books, materials . . .'

'Pens, pencils, paper, water, oxygen,' murmured Mr Carter.

'And it seems to me that our proper response is not to whinge and whine but to stand on our own feet and be self-reliant. Therefore, I am asking you all to attend a special meeting in the school hall this evening, at seven-thirty prompt. I am also inviting all parents to attend. I will see you all tonight. Seven-thirty! Prompt! And don't forget . . . bring your ideas with you!'

With a mighty swirl of his academic gown, Mr Wheeler left the stage. Across the room there was a rustling of diaries like the flapping of sails at the start of a round-the-world yacht race.

'Ideas!' said Mr Carter, outraged. 'What does the man mean? Ideas! The only constructive idea anybody's ever had at this school was when 3B tried to burn it down.'

'He means jumble sales,' said Jill. 'Isn't it time you had a new suit, Mr Carter?'

'He's not having my suit. It's been in the family for several generations. This isn't a suit. This is the history of our great nation.'

'A thing of shreds and patches?' Jill suggested.

'*Quod erat demonstrandum*, Mrs Swinburne.'

'Well we can't go to any meeting,' said Trevor. 'We haven't got a baby-sitter.'

'I'll baby-sit for you,' said Mr Carter. 'Everybody in this room will baby-sit for you.'

Jill and Trevor were suddenly besieged by prospective baby-sitters, including some whose hatred of children verged on the psychotic. Anything was better than the headmaster addressing a meeting in his Agincourt mode. Jill was not to be moved.

'Go away everybody! We went to the trouble of breeding our excuse and we are sticking to him.'

One day, when she was seven years old, Yvonne had helped her mother take up an old carpet, to make way for a new carpet. Buried beneath the old carpet Yvonne had found layers of old comics: *Radio Fun*, *Film Fun*, *Dandy*, *Beano* and *Knockout*. She had disappeared to her room with the comics, leaving the carpets, ancient and modern, to her mother.

She remembered that one of the comics broke up the longer

words with hyphens, so the young reader arrived at the syllables one at a time. She was grateful for the memory. It was useful when dealing with passing refugees.

She wandered into the living room, where Ivan sat listening to cool music on Trevor's headphones. She indicated her need to talk. He emerged from his music.

'I am go-ing out,' said Yvonne. 'I am ta-king the ba-by. We are go-ing to the su-per-mar-ket and to my Mam's and per-haps to the bet-ting shop.'

'Good. Cool.'

'No prob-lem. I am ta-king my an-o-rak.'

Ivan stood up, polite and smiling.

'Goodbye, miss.'

'Good-bye, I-van.'

Across the street, the Unfrocked Bank Manager used his zoom lens with reforming zeal as Yvonne left the house, pushing First-Born in his wheeled capsule. He then caught a glimpse of a strange face at the window. The UBM frowned. Strange faces at windows were a sure sign of subversion. Admittedly, his own face was at the window, but that was his birthright, fought for and won by his kith and kin. All other faces should go back where they belonged: Moscow for preference.

The Unfrocked Bank Manager was under no illusions about *glasnost* and *perestroika*; Russian bears didn't change their spots and had he been in a position of high authority over High Authority, at that very instant, officers of the law would have been rounding up the usual suspects and hurling them into a portable cell, addressed to The Kremlin, cash on delivery.

Joe and Ben, the ace detective duo, were doing nothing of the sort. They were doodling around the inner ring road, well within the speed limit, though to be fair, they were also contemplating a little genteel investigation. Joe was on the radio to headquarters, confirming this intention.

'Francis Albert Seven to Control. Responding to your call. We are proceeding with all possible haste to the scene of the crime. Over.'

'Control to Francis Albert Seven. We are profoundly impressed by your fine example of duty and purpose. Over and out.'

'Are you serious about all possible haste?' said Ben.

'You're driving. I leave it entirely to your discretion.'

'More haste, less speed. I read that on a matchbox only last year. Tedious Old Proverbs and Wisdom, Number 48 in a series of 50.'

'So take your time, partner. We'll be there quicker.'

The scene of the reported crime was once more MEGA-BOOKS INC. in the Archer Street Shopping Precinct.

'This could be a copycat crime,' said Ben as he parked the car in a bay reserved for disabled drivers. Inside the shop he tested his theory with Mrs Pringle.

'Would we be right in supposing that more books have been stolen?'

'Yes.'

'And can you describe the books, assuming you had a clear sight of them?'

'Yes. Two books. *Tess of the D'Urbervilles* by Thomas Hardy and *An Alphabetical Guide to Sexual Behaviour, Volume Two*.'

'*Volume Two*?' said Joe, making a highly detailed record of the conversation in his notebook.

'*Volume Two. L to Z*.'

Joe checked back in his notes.

'According to your previous statement, Mrs Pringle, the last occasion this particular gang struck they stole *The Alphabetical Guide to Sexual Behaviour, Volume One. A to K*. Would that be correct?'

'Yes.'

'Which means, according to my deductive powers, that the thieves are in possession of the complete set, A to Z, sexual-behaviour-wise.'

'Yes. That's correct.'

'Perhaps they'll be satisfied now,' said Ben.

Returning to the car, it seemed normal and natural to discuss Sexual Behaviour beginning with L.

'Loud.'
'Lewd.'
'Limp.'
'Look.'
'You're not supposed to look,' said Ben. 'That's voyeurism. Which stunts your growth and begins with V.'
'Look at the windscreen.'
They looked at the windscreen. It was exactly the same as they had left it, half an hour earlier.
'May I remind you,' said Joe, 'that yesterday when we parked here, an anonymous person left a video-cassette wedged behind the windscreen wipers. And today . . . nothing!'
'Treachery. Everywhere.'
'Tell you what. We'll return to the station, with all possible haste, and run a check on the National Computer.'
'What do you propose to check?'
'I think we run a check on this guy Thomas Hardy. If you ask me, he holds the key to the entire mystery.'
'Wonder if he still hangs around with that guy Laurel?'

'Hello, sir. Hello, miss.'
Yvonne was sitting in the middle of the floor playing with First-Born. The game seemed to be three-card brag.
'Anything happened I should know about?' said Jill, dumping thirty-eight exercise books on the settee.
'Not exactly, miss. Except that something that should have happened hasn't happened, if you see what I mean.'
'I haven't the faintest idea what you mean.'
Yvonne nodded towards the window. Ivan was curled up in Trevor's favourite armchair, which he had moved across the room, to catch the residual shreds of northern sunlight.
'We see what you mean,' said Trevor.
'Hello Ivan,' said Jill.
Ivan blinked his eyes, emerging from a long and contented doze with the marginally bewildered air of one who didn't recall pricking his finger in the first place.

'I am tell-ing them I-van. A-bout you. A-bout how no-bod-y came to col-lect you and take you a-way.'

'Please?'

'I am tel-ling Miz Swin-burne and Mis-ter Chap-lin a-bout . . .'

The telephone rang. It was a great relief to everyone. Trevor answered it and heard the familiar tones of Big Al.

'Trev, I know what you're thinking. You are thinking: we were promised this refugee would be off the premises by the end of the afternoon and we have just come home from school at the end of the afternoon and the refugee is still here.'

'Dead right so far.'

'Who is it?' said Jill.

'Big Al.'

'Ask him about your cool friend.'

'No need. He's already telling me.'

'Trev, I hate to ask you yet another big favour after the many big favours I've asked you in the past but I'd like to ask you another big favour.'

Jill had moved closer to the telephone.

'He wants to ask us another big favour.'

'What a surprise.'

'Trev. Can you take Ivan to the border?'

'What? The Mexican border?'

'The Mexican border?' said Jill.

'Sounds great,' said Yvonne.

'No Trev, the Mexican border is in Mexico which is in North America. We'd like you to take our man to the southern frontier of Yorkshire where it meets Lincolnshire. To be exact, at the Humber Bridge. Which is a bridge. Across the Humber. His people will meet him on the other side. Obviously, once he's out of Yorkshire he ceases to be our responsibility.'

'It's all very well smuggling people over the border but what do we do for a baby-sitter?'

'I'll baby-sit,' said Yvonne.

'And it's sixty miles to the Humber Bridge.'

'The Humber Bridge is not in Mexico. I know that for a fact even though I'm English and not Geography,' said Jill.

'On the other hand, Trev, the traffic will be very light after sundown.'

'What's sundown got to do with it?'

'Sundown?' said Jill.

'I am sure you will appreciate that these operations are best carried out under cover of gloom. Trev? Are you there?'

Jill took the phone from Trevor.

'Al?'

'Trev? Your voice has changed. It has assumed an upward cadence. And very pleasing too.'

'This is Jill Swinburne speaking, Al, and I would like you to explain, simply and unambiguously, what you are asking of us.'

'Ah. Mrs Swinburne. A pleasure, as always, to be speaking to you again. And I know exactly what you are thinking. You are thinking: we were promised this refugee would be off the premises by the end of the afternoon, and we have just come home from school and . . .'

'Heigh ho.'

'Another day gone.'

'The streets rendered clean.'

'Old-age pensioners may sleep securely in their beds.'

'And sheep may safely graze.'

Joe and Ben were in the CID office, soothing their stress levels with cheeseburgers, coke and the late racing results.

Suddenly, Joe frowned.

'There's something strange about my desk.'

'I see no strangeness.'

'Somebody has been rearranging my garbage.'

'There's no respect for people's garbage any more. I blame the lack of violence on television.'

Joe scrutinised his desk more closely. It was stacked high with files and documents, some of them so venerable they related to felons and footpads who had long ago paid their debt to Society and whose descendants were now successful property speculators in Van Diemen's Land. Perched atop of the tallest heap was a clear white envelope. The cleanliness was a vital clue.

'An envelope with a note attached,' said Joe.

'Tell me what it says. I love having notes read to me, especially if they're boring.'

Joe read the note: 'This was handed in at the desk by some nutter. Suggest you refer it upwards.'

Joe tore open the envelope. Inside was an audio-cassette and another note. 'Yet another note. More processed words.'

They examined the note.

'I THINK THE FORCES OF LAW AND ORDER SHOULD KNOW WHAT IS STILL GOING ON IN A ONCE RESPECTABLE AREA THUS UNDERMINING OUR BRITISH WAY OF LIFE AND SUBSTANTIALLY REDUCING PROPERTY VALUES.'

'I fancy this is the same loony that left us the video-cassette yesterday,' said Joe.

'It all falls into place. He intended to leave *this* under our windscreen.'

'But he arrived just too late.'

'Saw us driving away.'

'Gave chase.'

'Pulled up, breathless.'

'And took a 97 bus with all possible haste.'

'In order to hand this in at the desk.'

'Knowing with total confidence that we would immediately refer the matter . . .'

'Upwards.'

Inspector Hobson placed the cassette and the note side by side on his desk, exactly one inch apart, so that the space between them formed a straight line on the central axis of his room. He thought of it as one of his little endearing quirks.

'Handed it in at the desk?'

'Seemingly, sir,' said Joe.

'It appears to have factors in common with the video-cassette we passed on to you yesterday, sir.'

'Anonymity.'

'Technology.'

'The accompanying notes both written on a word processor from, let's not mince words, the bottom end of the market.'

'The word "STILL" on the second note, underlined in green.'

'I don't recall any green underlining on the first note,' said Hobson.

Ben was equal to his superior's challenge.

'The exception that proves the rule, sir. I would guess the green ink is a cunning ruse to throw us off the scent.'

'We sniff a *modus operandi*,' added Joe, leaving space for his partner to elaborate further.

'Double-check with forensics, throw in some house-to-house inquiries and we could have ourselves a result here.'

Hobson held up a hand, like a weary traffic cop, keen to avoid a snarl-up of cheap jargon stretching as far as the M25.

'Leave it all on my desk.'

'Thank you, sir.'

'Thank you, sir.'

'A good day's work.'

In his heart of hearts the Inspector did not consider it a good day's work. He thought it a sloppy and irrelevant day's work. But he had learned, slowly and doggedly, that a well-timed sliver of praise was the best way to rid himself of his turbulent detectives. He was unable to explain this phenomenon, but found some small comfort in its reliability.

After they had gone, he stared at the cassette and the note. Then he broke his rule of a lifetime. He decided to leave them until later.

Gloom descended upon Hotspur Street, more or less at the hour recommended by the manufacturers. Under its benign cover, Trevor, Jill and Ivan left the house, swiftly and discreetly. Yvonne, with babe in arms, dented the discretion by calling down the path:

'Good-bye I-van. First-Born, say good-bye to I-van.'

First-Born gurgled and allowed his right arm to be flapped up and down, in the style traditional among babies bidding farewell to departing refugees.

'We'll give you a lift home when we get back,' said Jill.

'Take your time, miss. I can watch the late night horror.'

'Be quiet and get in the van,' said Trevor, conscious of Big Al's instructions about operational security.

The yellow van drove off along the street. The Unfrocked Bank Manager watched and wondered: was it too dark for his video-camera? He recorded it anyway, for what he devoutly hoped would be an avenging posterity.

The great highway of the M62 was built to link the giant ports and colliding cultures of Liverpool in the west with Hull in the east. It enabled imports and exports to travel freely in any chosen direction, enriching mercantile adventurers and digging a trade deficit deeper than the Grand Canyon. Container trucks the size of country mansions roared along its length, with cargoes of Tyne coal, road-rail, pig-lead, firewood, iron-ware and cheap tin trays. Ivory, apes, peacocks, sandalwood, cedarwood and sweet white wine travelled on more southerly routes.

Trevor was driving east, into a gloom now solidifying into a formidable blackness. He reached into the glove compartment for a cassette.

'How about a little music?'

'Bix?' said Ivan.

'Cool,' said Jill.

Beiderbecke's staccato lyricism sang them past Exit 32, to Pontefract and Knottingley, at the precise moment that Mr Wheeler rose to address the audience gathered in the hall at San Quentin High School.

It was, by any standards, one of the sparser assemblies in the history of human congregation. Twelve people and the caretaker's dog were scattered around the room. The headmaster scanned their faces, hoping to glimpse a nominal teacher or even an identifiable parent. On casual scrutiny most of them seemed permanently exempt from breeding and rearing on the grounds of age, infirmity and apathy. It was essentially an audience that had come in for a warm and the possibility of a free cup of tea. But Mr Wheeler had already cancelled the arrangements for tea, confident as ever they would find sustenance in his rhetoric.

'My friends. The school is facing a crisis. Education is facing a crisis. It may be said that our nation is facing a crisis. And certainly, nobody can be in any doubt that the whole world is facing a crisis.'

He waited. Speakers at party conferences received rounds of applause, even standing ovations, for more mundane oratory. But this was not a party conference. This was San Quentin High, graveyard of grandiloquence, abattoir of ambition.

'Let us at this stage ignore the world. Let us consider the school.'

A politician of great renown had promised the voters of the Humber Delta their very own bridge in the 1960s and it turned up ten years later, setting new standards in swiftness where political pledges are concerned. It united the mighty conurbations of Hessle, population 13,590 the last time anyone counted, on the North Bank, and Barton, population 9,030, on the South Bank. The bridge arrived with a kit comprising a Royal ceremony and an RAF fly-past timed with exquisite military precision to drown out the blessing from the neighbourhood Archbishop. A high-flying economist with a full set of capped teeth predicted a dramatic rise in the interflow of Tyne coal and cheap tin trays, leading remorselessly to great prosperity for the local peasantry. In the event, the main result was increased communication between Hessle and Barton as the people sampled each other's fish-and-chips and draught bitter. It was progress of a kind.

Nobody needed the bridge and everybody loved it at first sight. An itinerant Yorkshireman, leaving his heart in San Francisco, also left stickers reading SECOND BIGGEST all over the Golden Gate. Gift horses had rarely trotted as far as the Humber Estuary and hitherto most of them had turned out on close examination to be Trojan. But now the people looked at what they had been given and said: it is good. We have our very own Concorde and we will try to keep it nice. The only marginal whinges came from Sunday dog-walkers who pointed out that modern technology, in designing a suspension bridge three miles long, should have been able to run to a grass verge and saplings at ten-yard intervals.

The towers rose, a hundred times higher than kites, then disappeared in low cloud as Trevor drove the van towards the toll booth. The vergeless road-way stretched ahead in a slow curve, like a Tony Nicholson away swinger, towards a black horizon called Lincolnshire.

'Have you got any money?' said Trevor.

'I didn't bring my handbag,' said Jill.

'Hello,' said Ivan.

By the time they realised that between them they could not raise the one pound and fifty pence toll, the van was at the head of a small traffic jam: a lorry-load of pig-lead, several cars bearing revellers heading south in search of haddock and frolics and a solitary, enigmatic milk-float.

Jill was aware of the control tower looming over the scene, its bank of television monitors shining bright in the darkness, men moving slowly but purposefully behind glass, a Mission Control staffed by unfrocked bank managers. Whatever she, Trevor and Ivan did, it would be seen to be done.

Trevor manipulated the van out of the traffic stream, with a helpful commentary from the waiting drivers:

'Why don't you sell that thing and buy a van?'

'Get thissen a wheelbarrow, sunbeam.'

'Take your time, petal, I don't go on my holidays till July.'

'Bloody onion.'

He completed an untidy, gearbox-grinding U-turn and did his best to park quietly and inconspicuously. He and Jill helped Ivan climb from the back of the van. Despite the language barrier, Ivan seemed to have grasped the essence of the situation: he would have to walk across the bridge. Indeed,

Jill reflected, there had been time enough for him to translate half a dozen chapters of *War and Peace* while they had been doing their quick and discreet drop.

She pointed a finger towards the south.

'Ivan,' she said, 'your people will meet you on the other side.'

Ivan smiled, nodded and shook hands, first with Jill, then with Trevor.

'Goodbye, sir. Goodbye, miss.'

He picked up his bag and set off walking. The mist wrapped itself around him, eager to welcome foreign visitors with chill dankness. Perhaps he was walking towards comradeship and safety, but he looked like a spy walking into the cold.

'This reminds me of a film,' said Trevor.

'*A Bridge Too Far*?' said Jill.

'No.'

'*Bridge Over The River Kwai*?'

'No.'

'*Flying Down To Rio*?'

'That's probably it.'

Ivan was out of sight. Their day's work was done. It was time to go home.

In the school hall at San Quentin High, Mr Wheeler had almost finished his speech.

'But at the end of the day, or perhaps I should say the end of the evening . . .'

The headmaster thought this was a joke. The audience disagreed. Mr Wheeler continued, impervious to the numb and drowsy silence.

'The school must raise several thousand pounds as a matter of urgency. I cannot do this on my own. The solution must come from you. My colleagues on the staff. The parents of our children. I need your input, your ideas, your enthusiasm, your dedication, your inspiration. I will hear contributions from the floor.'

He sat down and waited for the tidal wave of inspiration. A

man stood up at the back of the hall. He was wearing corduroy trousers, a donkey jacket, woolly hat and big boots.

'Yes, sir?' said the headmaster.

'Got to go. I'm on nights this week.'

The man clumped his way from the hall. The rest of the audience followed. There had been no mention of a cup of tea so there was no compelling reason to stay. The caretaker's dog woke up, had a pee on the piano, scratched itself and went back to sleep.

Mr Wheeler gathered up his notes, placed them neatly in a cardboard folder and put the folder in his briefcase. His day's work was done. It was time to go home.

It was time for Inspector Hobson to go home too, but he was hesitating, irked by a sense of duty no bigger than a man-made audio-cassette. It was not his style to leave things until later. He had not won his early promotion and spectacular PhD by dumping responsibility in an overflowing tray indelibly marked TOMORROW. That was for other people. Hobson was a Now Man.

He loaded the cassette into the appropriate orifice of his wall and pressed the PLAY button on his remote control. He heard a deep voice, recorded in the lowest fidelity since Thomas Edison's, resembling an elderly cleric mumbling in a catacomb.

'I realise that the video-cassette I previously sent to the authorities might not make total sense. My problem is that I have to be extremely circumspect because of my position in the local community, which is why I cannot give you my name and address. However, I am concerned that you should be made aware of the activities of two people living in our street. One male, one female, living in a state of adultery, with an illegitimate child, even though they are both teachers and thereby entrusted with the cream of our youth.'

'Teachers?' said Hobson, and made a note.

'I believe their house to be a nest of vipers and a den of corruption. You may observe on my video-cassette a small yellow van. A somewhat dirty yellow van I might add.'

'A small yellow van?' said Hobson, and made another note.

Jill drove Yvonne home in the van. At the au pair's request, they had waited until the late-night horror movie was finished. They were all keen to see how the President of the United States eventually conquered the Killer Mucus from Mars.

'Thump it,' said Yvonne.

'High explosive Vick,' said Trevor.

'Talk to it nicely,' said Jill.

Eventually a little boy sang a hymn and the mucus oozed away towards the outer galaxy ready to re-group in time for the sequel. Yvonne's work was done. It was time to go home.

When Jill returned, there was cocoa on the table while Duke Ellington and John Coltrane played 'In A Sentimental Mood'. The music was elegant, beguiling and gentle. They had no trouble in hearing the doorbell.

Jill opened the door, with Trevor in attendance.

'Oh look,' he said.

Ivan stood on the doorstep, bag in hand.

'Hello, sir. Hello, miss.'

4

Charity Begins at Home but It Isn't Compulsory

'Hello, sir! Hello, miss! The au-pairing starts now!'

There was no reply. Since the living room was empty the silence was inevitable. Yvonne sat down and waited. She guessed Trevor and Jill were upstairs in the middle of their usual early morning panic. The standard ingredients were changing First-Born's nappy, finding Trevor's clean underpants and a territorial dispute about the bathroom. Yvonne was happy to wait for the tide, as and when it flowed in.

'Hello, miss!'

Ivan flowed in from the kitchen with a cup of tea.

'Hel-lo I-van,' said Yvonne, smiling. 'Why are you still here? You were sup-posed to be smug-gled ac-ross the bor-der.'

'Please?'

He obviously had no idea what she was talking about. Yvonne was unconcerned. She had tried concern a couple of times in her life but it wasn't her style. It made more sense to drift with the tide, being careful not to sign anything.

The West Riding of Yorkshire vibrated with galloping footsteps on the stairs. Then Jill entered at maximum velocity, as if pursued by a bear.

'Morning! Leave space! We're running late!'

'Hello, miss,' said Yvonne as Jill rushed into the kitchen.

There were more footsteps on the stairs and Trevor dashed into the living room, the same bear apparently on his heels.

'Morning!' he said, in transit to the kitchen.

'Hello, sir.'

Trevor and Jill almost collided in the kitchen doorway. It resembled an under-rehearsed Ben Travers farce. Jill was smiling and suddenly calm.

'Ivan. You made tea.'

'Tea. Good. Cool,' said Ivan, raising his cup in a gesture of international friendship.

'I need tea,' said Trevor, disappearing into the kitchen.

'Ivan making the tea means we've saved five minutes, so we'll only be ten minutes late for school instead of fifteen.'

Jill was pleased with the elegance of the equation.

'Why is Ivan here? I thought you were smuggling him over the border?' asked Yvonne.

Jill explained.

'We took Ivan to the Lincolnshire border. We came back here. We watched the end of the horror movie. I took you home. I came back here. The doorbell rang. We found Ivan in the porch.'

'It's a good place to stand if you're going to ring the doorbell.'

'I'll go and see Big Al at lunchtime. Ask him to arrange some more arrangements,' said Trevor, arriving with mugs of tea for Jill, Yvonne and himself.

Jill took a sip.

'Ivan! This is an excellent cup of tea!'

'Ah. Tea. Listen.'

Ivan got up from what had already become his favourite chair, since it occupied one point of a golden acoustic triangle with the twin speakers of Trevor's cool music system. But this was not a musical moment. Ivan was about to make a speech. He frowned, arranging the words in his head. His concentration would have done credit to Marcus Antonius limbering up for his Forum speech. But Ivan's subject was not power politics, but how to make tea.

'One for sir. One for miss. One for maiden. One for Ivan. One for pot.'

'A fifteen-word sentence!' said Jill.

'You've just won a clay pipe!' said Trevor.

'Please?' said Ivan.

'Oh look. A beckoning digit.'

Trevor and Jill were walking from the van to the school entrance when Trevor spotted Mr Carter at the staffroom window, making mystic signs with his index finger. The coded message was: come on up, you're missing a treat.

'Perhaps Mr Bickerstaffe's come back,' said Jill.

'And I bet he's having another nose-bleed.'

They were wrong. There was no sign of Mr Bickerstaffe or his blood in the staffroom. The reality was much more alarming. Mr Wheeler was making a speech.

'Before I come to my main purpose, may I point out that everyone standing between me and the door is technically, legally, contractually and, worst of all, morally, late.'

With a calculated swirl of his academic gown, the headmaster turned on the offenders. Over half of the staff found themselves morally condemned. Trevor and Jill were at the end of the line and therefore at the top of the list for whatever sanctions lay in wait. It was their accustomed position in the academic order of San Quentin High and they never worried about it.

'But that is not the main thrust of my presence here this morning.'

'It's a bit early for thrusting,' said Trevor to Jill, who pretended not to hear.

'Last night,' said Mr Wheeler, doing his best to hold all forty-eight teachers with a glittering eye, 'I organised, as you are well aware, a meeting of parents and teachers in the school hall to discuss fund-raising. Our school is dying for lack of resources.'

He scanned the room for examples. He picked those who always came first to mind, for reasons he tried not to think about.

'Mr Chaplin is trying to teach woodwork without . . .'

He hesitated, trying to remember how woodwork was taught.

'Wood?' suggested Trevor.

'Without wood. Precisely. Mrs Swinburne is trying to teach English Literature without . . . er . . .'

'*Tess of the D'Urbervilles*?' said Jill.

'Books, Mrs Swinburne, books!'

Maybe he was vague about woodwork but he knew how English Literature operated. His attention switched to Mr Carter.

'And Mr Carter is trying to teach . . . to teach . . .'

He could never remember what Mr Carter taught, let alone what he taught it with.

'History, headmaster.'

'Of course. Mr Carter is attempting to teach history without . . . er . . .'

'Bloodshed,' said Mr Carter, eager to come to the rescue.

'Indeed, Mr Carter. Without bloodshed.'

Mr Wheeler was in no mood to allow mere logic to get in the way of his accelerating rhetoric.

'We have a needlework room without needles. A playing field without balls. A gymnasium without horses.'

'My kingdom for a horse,' murmured Jill, relishing the lurch into surrealism.

'Indeed yes, Mrs Swinburne. You talk of kingdoms and our kingdom is indeed at stake. And *I* take the initiative. I accept my role as spiritual leader of this community. And how many members of my staff attended my meeting? Not one!'

Mr Wheeler consulted a list.

'I have here a piece of paper bearing the names of those present. There were seven people claiming to be parents. Two apparent prowlers. And a man trying to sell cavity wall insulation. But . . . and I use the word advisedly . . . but not one member of staff. I require full explanations from all of you.'

'I had a recurrence of my malaria,' said Mr Carter. 'As you know, I was a district officer during the twilight of the Empire.'

'We couldn't get a baby-sitter,' said Trevor.

'Oh look. A man telling the truth,' said Jill, but her comment to Trevor was drowned by voices raised in a crescendo of overlapping excuses:

'It was our family therapy night . . . pre-menstrual tension . . . the dog had diarrhoea . . . mid-menstrual tension . . . the gazebo caught fire . . . post-menstrual tension . . . the SAS sealed off our street . . .'

Mr Wheeler yelled above the cries of the mob.

'Explanations in writing! By four o'clock!'

With one climactic swirl he was gone. The room fell silent and Mr Carter beamed.

'Well done everybody! We've had apathy before. We've had mild insurrection. But we've never scored one hundred per cent.'

'Does he really expect written explanations?' said Jill.

'Of course he does,' said Trevor.

'Are you going to give him one?'

'Of course not. Nobody else will. Why bother?'

'The hundred per cent syndrome, Mrs Swinburne,' said Mr Carter. 'The hundred per cent syndrome.'

The day had started well.

Later, in surprising accord with the headmaster's speech, Jill found herself trying to teach English Literature.

'Now according to my sealed orders from Whitehall, I am supposed to enlighten you about the eternal mysteries and cosmic significance of our shared heritage.'

'Do you mean English, miss?' asked Sharon.

'Yes, I mean English. On the other hand, we don't have more than three copies of any book written during the last five hundred years . . .'

'Please, miss, we've got a few more Tesses of the D'Urbervilleses, miss.'

'Have we?'

'Yes miss.'

Jill looked around the room.

'Hands up . . . anybody with a copy of *Tess*?'

She counted. Nine hands went up, each holding a

shiny-bright paperback edition of the book. Nine between thirty-eight. One between four-and-a-quarter. Approximately. They were limping slowly towards the truth and the light.

'Excellent. Where did the books come from?'

'Shops, miss,' said Sharon.

It was an obvious explanation. A supplementary question fluttered across Jill's mind but she shooed it away.

Joe and Ben sat at their desks in the CID office. They had considered doing some house-to-house inquiries about Thomas Hardy but the wind was blowing from the north-west, with a hint of rain. It was a day when a detective should sit at his desk and ponder the deeper realities of investigation.

'I don't understand how an overworked police force can be expected to cope with urban stresses and a rising tide of crime . . .'

Joe passed the thought to his partner for adornment.

' . . . when we are also expected to grapple with an ever-increasing mountain of paperwork.'

They stared at the heaps of paper on each of their desks. They were proud of them. Eighteen months of devoted neglect had gone into their making. They looked at what they had made and it was large.

'Mindless Bureaucracy,' said Joe.

'Everywhere you look.'

'No. Not everywhere. Running in the four thirty-five at Ripon.' Joe handed his partner a copy of the *Sporting Life*.

'Beaten by a head the last time out,' said Ben.

'But it's been dropped in class.'

'I know the feeling.'

The door opened with a precise, military click of the latch and Inspector Hobson marched in.

'Good morning, men.'

'Morning, sir.'

'Morning, sir.'

'Catching up with paperwork?'

Hobson took four smart paces across the room into the detectives' territory, in which time the *Sporting Life* was transmuted into several sheets of computer print-out indicating the regional crime rate had risen, continued to rise and was unlikely to diminish.

Hobson's men had done their practice.

'I don't understand how an overworked police force can be expected to cope with urban stresses and a rising tide of crime . . .' Joe began.

' . . . when we are also expected to grapple with an ever-increasing mountain of paperwork,' Ben continued.

'My office,' said Hobson, leaving the room.

The detectives spent a little time debating the meaning of their commanding officer's closing words. My office? Was it a statement, a question, a cry for help? They agreed he was probably thinking of redecorating and needed their advice about curtain material. They decided to make the trek to his office to find out. It would be a little harmless fun to ease the long day's journey into overtime.

'I've been glancing through your reports,' said Hobson.

Ben clicked his heels, hoping to make a good impression. The effect was dulled by his plain clothes sneakers.

'Nothing untoward, we trust, sir?'

'Not as such. But I am intrigued by some of the details.'

'It's our infinite capacity for taking pains, sir.'

'Tell me about these book thefts.'

'We're experiencing a small rash.'

'More in the nature of a mild acne,' added Joe, keen to place the larceny in a proper context.

'Mainly from bookshops.'

'*Tess of the D'Urbervilles*?' queried Hobson.

'We're doing some follow-up inquiries on that one,' said Ben.

'Good.'

Hobson immediately regretted his hint of approval. Joe delved into the pocket of his fashionably cut designer jacket and found his notebook. The notebook bothered Hobson, as did the jacket. Its cuffs were neatly and permanently rolled up and they never fell down. Hobson had tried rolling up the cuffs of his own jacket strictly in the privacy of his own home, and they always fell down. What was worse, they held the wrinkles so people could tell what he had been up to. It was all part of his alienation from a world full of secrets. The secrets were trivial and absurd – jacket cuffs, Rugby League, the legends of Sir Leonard Hutton and the early recordings of Pink Floyd – yet knowledge of them somehow represented the true measure of a man. On that scale, Hobson was two feet tall and shrinking daily.

Joe read from his notebook.

'*Tess of the D'Urbervilles*. Follow-up inquiries. Written by Thomas Hardy, 1840–1928. Set in so-called Wessex. Actually an alias for Dorset.'

'Somewhere down south,' said Ben.

'Thank you both. I have read the book.'

The detectives were impressed.

'O or A level, sir?' asked Joe.

'For fun.'

'Fun?'

'Good,' said Joe, before returning to his notebook.

'The thieves also took two volumes of the *Alphabetical Guide to Sexual Behaviour*. *A to K* and *L to Z*. Which seems to us pretty comprehensive. Have you read them, sir?'

'Certainly not!'

'Nor have we,' said Ben, 'though we like to think we have a reasonable working knowledge of the alphabet.'

Joe closed his notebook and slipped it into his pocket. The detectives waited. It was Hobson's turn to serve. The inspector fiddled with a ball-point pen then put it down in its designated tray in case he was betraying something unseemly from his subconscious.

'Does it strike either of you that these inquiries might be considered on the trivial side?'

'Absolutely, sir.'

'No question about it.'

'But,' said Ben, 'it could just be . . . could just possibly be . . . the tip of an iceberg.'

He passed the ball to Joe.

'The tip of an iceberg that turns out to be a tiny, apparently insignificant piece of a very large jigsaw puzzle. You could say we're playing a hunch. Sir.'

It was their favoured method when criticised by superior officers: instant agreement followed by a barrage of second-rate cop-show dialogue. The jacket cuffs were an oblique part of the strategy though Hobson did not know it. He never watched cop-shows.

'I take the point you are making about icebergs and . . . jigsaw puzzles. But try not to be too obsessive.'

Joe found his notebook and made a note.

'Noted, sir.'

'And now, moving on . . . I have been studying the anonymous video-cassette you brought in.'

'With what startling results, sir?' said Ben.

Hobson played a short, staccato, tuneless melody on his computer keyboard. The screen lit up and was filled with an array of printed information. In its midst were two names, underlined:

CHAPLIN, TREVOR

SWINBURNE, JILL

'As all of you know, I do not like acting on information received anonymously.'

'But you'd like us to act on it,' said Joe.

'What I have in mind is a very careful surveillance operation. I have to rely on your total and absolute discretion.'

'No problem,' said Ben. 'It's the better part of our valour, sir.'

Within the hour the detectives were parked outside Paddy Lynch's Chip 'n Chicken Tandoori Trattoria, nibbling kebabs and working out the prettiest route to Hotspur Street.

Ben glanced out of the window.

'These people whom we are under orders to observe with

tact and discretion. Am I right in supposing that the man Chaplin, Trevor drives a yellow van?'

Joe looked in his notebook.

'Chaplin, Trevor, yellow van. Yes. It checks out positive.'

'I spy with my little eye something beginning with yellow.'

Trevor's van was waiting for the lights to change at a pedestrian crossing recently installed to cope with Paddy Lynch's late-night drunken revellers; though since the relaxation of the licensing laws late-night revelry tended to start in the middle of the afternoon.

The lights changed and Trevor's van moved along the street, passing close to the unmarked police car. The detectives compared the van's colour, design, demeanour and registration number with the information supplied by Inspector Hobson. It was, in their professional parlance, the van in question. There were, nonetheless, other considerations, as Joe pointed out:

'It is very difficult for a police car to chase a yellow van discreetly. Car chases and discretion are, in my view, mutually incompatible.'

'I concur. Also it's lunchtime.'

'So all things considered . . . I saw no yellow van.'

'Neither did I.'

Trevor was on his way to the park to see Big Al about arranging some arrangements for the peaceful disposal of Ivan. He was half-listening to the local radio station, waiting for the sports news and the latest information about an international footballer's groin strain. The information was vital to Trevor and even more so to the footballer and his groin.

While he waited for the sports news to arrive, Trevor gritted his teeth against the prattling of the presenter, a self-elected expert on popular music with an accent marooned halfway between Todmorden and Tamla Motown. Suddenly he heard something to relax his teeth.

'And here's some hot jazz news for the wrinklies in our

midst. All you elderly swinging hipsters and flipsters, tonight's the night at the newly-opened Village Vanguard.'

'The Village Vanguard?' said Trevor.

'Which historians tell us is an old-established venue in New York but I am here to tell you it happens once a week in what some of you may know better as the Singing Room of the Limping Whippet in Canal Street. So get yourselves down there, park your wheelchairs and walking frames and you'll hear music like this.'

'Pin-headed fartface,' said Trevor.

But he listened to the music: a vibraphone solo with the lilt of Lionel Hampton, the majesty of Milt Jackson and the grandeur of Gary Burton. He would need arguments at that level of bullshit to persuade Jill into an evening at the Limping Whippet. She always claimed that the average vibraphone player sounded like a long-term prisoner banging on the bars of his cell; but Chaplin, Trevor, a normally taciturn man, could speak with tongues when his music was at stake.

He arrived at the park to find Big Al and Little Norm playing yet another end in their apparently eternal game of bowls. Al's voice boomed across the green:

'Trev! That is exceedingly well timed. You have arrived at a moment of high drama in this epic encounter. Little Norm will remember with advantages the feats he did this day.'

'I won't, will I?'

'Sorry, Al. I haven't time to watch the match. I'm missing lunch as it is. It's about Ivan. Your refugee.'

'Ah. Did it go well? The border crossing?'

'It went fine. We dropped him off at the Humber Bridge, exactly as planned.'

'Them arrangements was well arranged,' said Norm.

'Rather better than your syntax, Norm, if I may say so.'

'Then he turned up on our doorstep at midnight.'

'Ah.'

'Ah.'

Al and Norm fell silent as they pondered the unexpected

frailty of their organisation. Unusually, Norm was the first to reach a conclusion.

'It's what I've always said.'

'What have you always said, Norm?' said Al.

'Once you're over the Yorkshire border you can't trust nobody.'

Al was unimpressed.

'Everybody knows that. But the fact remains. We have to reach an accommodation with people of foreign blood. Mere tribalism is retrogressive. The planet's future depends on an understanding of that fact.'

'But what are we supposed to do with Ivan?' asked Trevor, keen to terminate Al's planetary reflections.

'You could give him a cup of tea.'

'There's no need. He makes his own tea. He's getting quite settled.'

'Did he say what happened? Across the border?'

'Al. He doesn't speak any English.'

'Yes. Point taken. No English. Limits communication, does that. What do you think, Norm?'

'What you need is some alternative arrangements.'

'Dead right. On the nose as usual, Norm. We need some alternative arrangements.'

'Can we have them fairly soon?' asked Trevor.

Al's attention reverted to the game of bowls, which had been lying dormant during the discussion. He bent down and played his shot. The wood ran smoothly across the green in a graceful arc and came to rest against the jack: they nestled together like a Madonna and child posing for a Florentine painter. Al straightened up.

'The alternative arrangements shall have top priority, Trev. And what is more, when I give a thing top priority I am no slouch. As you can see by that last shot. Beautiful game, bowls. Simplicity, elegance and a touch of the unknown.'

'I'll see you,' said Trevor.

Jill sat in the dining hall of San Quentin High, contemplating the three main elements of her cheese salad: lettuce, tomato and – by logical elimination – cheese. Surely they should be green, red and yellow respectively? What combination of market forces and factory breeding had produced the subtly varied shades of puce on her plate? As for the mayonnaise, she tried not to think about it. It was the first time she had seen neurosis in molten form.

'Mrs Swinburne?'

Mr Carter loomed over the table, carrying his tray. His food was giving off steam, or possibly fumes.

'I know,' said Jill. 'May I sit with you and kindle my desires?'

'May I?'

'Anything to take my mind off the salad.'

It was their traditional dining hall greeting, formalised and ancient as the Pyramids or the twelve-bar blues.

'Where is your paramour today?' said Mr Carter, sitting down.

'The father of my child?'

'They are, I believe, one and the same person.'

'If I told you, you wouldn't believe me.'

'Belief doesn't come easily to an old man, Mrs Swinburne.'

'Very well. I'll tell you. Mr Chaplin has gone to the public park. There he will seek out two men on the bowling green. One large man. One small man. They will give him instructions about the swift disposal of a foreign refugee called Ivan.'

'Thank you, Mrs Swinburne.'

'I said you wouldn't believe me.'

'I believed all of it. Except the bit about the bowling green, which I find highly unlikely.'

Mr Carter's right hand twitched, as if his fork had been struck by lightning.

'My mashed potato. It made a noise. I do believe it groaned.'

'Think of its prospects. Wouldn't you groan?'

The unmarked police car crawled to a halt almost opposite Number 17, Hotspur Street.

'Does this strike you as discreet?' said Joe.

'Ish.'

'Bless you.'

'I mean this is discreet-ish. Rather than discreet. May I suggest, with respect, that you back up a few yards?'

'All right. It'll be good practice in case I ever take my driving test.'

Joe reversed the car into a more discreet position for maintaining surveillance over Chaplin, Trevor, Swinburne, Jill, and their house.

Ivan watched the manoeuvre from the window of Number 17.

'Is ev-ery-thing all-right I-van?' said Yvonne. She was sitting on the floor, trying to teach First-Born the rudiments of three-card brag.

'Yes. Good. Cool.'

'Fine.'

Ivan moved away from the window.

'Tea? Yes? Good?' he said.

'Cool.'

Ivan went into the kitchen. Yvonne heard him filling the kettle.

'First-Born! You've been chewing the aces again!'

Mr Wheeler had spent the lunch-hour in his study, sacrificing food and drink to the selfless task of raising money for his besieged kingdom. He had a telephone, a list of names and a prepared text.

'We are contemplating a wide range of fund-raising activities . . . raffles, tombolas, bring-and-buy sales . . . and you, Mr Carew, as a leading, may I say pre-eminent member of the retail greengrocery trade in our area, came immediately to our minds as a possible benefactor, knowing of your public spirit and long-standing concern for the young people in our community. Mr Carew? Mr Carew?'

The headmaster hung up the receiver. Clearly Mr Carew the Greengrocer was not sensitive to the needs of scholarship. Mr Wheeler put a cross beside the name Carew on his list. So far he had thirty-four crosses, no ticks and no passes. It would be good to have a tick before the end of the lunch break.

The next name on the list was Mr Prendergast the Ironmonger.

'Good afternoon, Mr Prendergast, we haven't had the pleasure of meeting face to face so may I introduce myself? My name is Wheeler. I am headmaster of the . . .'

Again the headmaster hung up the receiver, disappointed by the brusque response at the other end. Did Mr Prendergast not realise the intimate correlation that existed between secondary education up to and including sixth form level and ironmongery in all its manifestations? Apparently not.

He put a cross beside the name Prendergast and moved down the list to Mr Flynn, Fast Food. He was not hopeful about Mr Flynn; but his empty wrappers were a primary component of the garbage that fringed the playing fields of San Quentin High. The man might even have a conscience. If so, it would be a lonely organism in these parts. But Mr Wheeler was a resolute man. He had seen both versions of *Henry V*.

Mr Flynn's Fast Food Dial-a-Dinner number was 222-222. The local radio commercials used the slogan: 'Tous les deux for your cordons bleus.' Somehow the locals had worked this out and Mr Flynn had achieved prosperity and celebrity, with a yacht and half a football club to prove it.

The headmaster had got as far as dialling 222 when he was distracted by a clanking and grinding from the school drive. He replaced the receiver immediately. Bizarre noises demanded investigation and, as often as possible, sanctions or punishment.

Looking out of the window he saw an ancient lorry trundling towards the main door of the school. It looked as if it had driven directly from the Victoria and Albert Museum via a television mini-series about the General Strike.

Mr Wheeler strode out of the main entrance as the lorry came to a lurching halt. The driver, a fresh-faced man wearing a cloth cap, greeted him like an old friend.

'Now then sunbeam! Where do you want it?'

'I am not a sunbeam and I have no idea what you are talking about.'

'This is San Quentin High, isn't it?'

'That is not the school's correct name.'

'But this is it, isn't it? San Quentin? This is where you want the timber.'

'Timber?'

The driver climbed down from the cab and walked around to the back of the lorry. Mr Wheeler followed reluctantly. Communication with the lower orders was his Achilles heel: one of many. Had he been born a centipede, he would still have had several Achilles heels to spare.

The lorry-driver pointed at his load.

'There. Look. See. Timber. Like, wood. Comes from forests, mostly.'

'Thank you, I know about timber's origins.'

'I was told to deliver it here. I was told you needed some wood. Well this is it. The wood.'

'But the only possible use we have for wood is in woodwork.'

'So that must be it, petal.'

Mr Wheeler noticed a small yellow van enter the drive. It did nothing to ease his anxiety.

'I cannot accept this delivery without a note from the office at the Town Hall.'

'Sorry pal. No notes. No paperwork. None of that. I'm not even a proper lorry-driver.'

'You're not?'

'No. I'm a gravedigger, me. By vocation and profession. They all know me. Charlie the Gravedigger. Life and soul of the Municipal Cemetery. Not that there's much competition, like. Little bit of soul. Not a lot of life. Not down there.'

Mr Wheeler tried again to secure a foothold in the conversation.

'You're a gravedigger?'

'That's what I said, flower. This load of timber is me doing a favour for my brother.'

For the first time in his years of office, the headmaster was grateful to see his woodwork teacher.

'Mr Chaplin!' he cried, as Trevor parked his van. 'Do you know anything about this?'

Trevor walked across to the lorry and glanced at its contents.

'Yes. It's a load of timber.'

He looked at the driver.

'Hello there! How you keeping?'

'Can't grumble. Little and often.'

'You two know each other?' said Mr Wheeler.

'Yes,' said Trevor. 'I used to pop down his cemetery. The odd errand of mercy.'

'We had some nice chats, didn't we? Right good laughs.'

He and Trevor chuckled at the memory of their right good laughs.

'Were you expecting a load of timber, Mr Chaplin?'

'You know me, Mr Wheeler. I never expect anything. So if something turns up, that's a bonus.'

Trevor inspected the load more closely.

'There's some good stuff here. Some nice bits of oak. Haven't seen oak since I was at training college.'

'So where do you want it?'

'We keep timber round the back.'

'Right then. Round the back it is.'

Charlie and Trevor were suddenly aware of a mushroom cloud of doubt hovering around Mr Wheeler's head, shrouding his mortar-board.

'Round the back, Mr Wheeler?' asked Trevor.

The headmaster was in spiritual turmoil. He had never before authorised a transaction without a note from the office. On the other hand a double-locked drawer in his desk contained a list headed: PROBLEMS. There were 174 problems on the list and no ticks. A nod of the head and he could return to his study and put a tick beside problem 95: WOODWORK SUPPLIES.

'Round the back,' he murmured, in case God or anyone

from the office was listening. He would make the tick in pencil. He could always rub it out later.

'Hop in, sunshine,' said Charlie to Trevor. 'I'll give you a lift round the back. It's a pity to walk.'

'Especially on a nice day like this.'

Trevor climbed into the cab.

There was a grinding of gears, then the lorry lurched into forward motion. Above the noise of its ancient but reliable engine, Charlie's voice, full-throated and nasal, echoed across the campus, singing: 'On The Sunny Side Of The Street'.

It was his favourite song: music to dig by and to live by. It had never betrayed him yet.

5

Constables of the Watch

In the middle of the afternoon Yvonne took First-Born to the shops to buy bread and milk. The police surveillance team took due note.

'Young woman with pram left premises at . . .'

Joe paused to check his watch.

' . . .ten past three.'

'Call it fifteen-eleven hours,' said Ben. 'It has a nice ring of authenticity.'

'Do you think we should follow her?' said Joe, completing the entry in his notebook.

'No. She'll be going to the park.'

'You reckon?'

'It's what you do with babies. My brother's got one. He takes his to the park. They throw stones at the ducks. It's all part of the great Cycle of Nature.'

'Is that right? So what do ducks throw stones at?'

'Worms.'

San Quentin's day ended with the usual combination of bangs, whimpers, letters of resignation and murmured incantations over wax effigies of the Minister.

Jill walked into the staffroom to find Trevor slumped in a battered armchair. Its upholstery had been leaking for years and Trevor looked more like part of the leak than a separate entity.

'What's wrong with you?' said Jill.

'I'm shattered. That's what's wrong with me.'

'Have you been doing something unseemly?'

'I didn't have any lunch. Then I had to unload half a ton of timber. Then I had to teach proper woodwork, on account of having some wood to teach it with.'

'Proper woodwork teaching?'

'Yes. Planing and sawing and chiselling and hammering and sand-papering and fetching the first-aid box. It gets you in the arms. I'm out of condition. My body's become attuned to diagrams of trees.'

'There, there.'

She sat on the arm of his chair and stroked his brow.

'I do wish you wouldn't do that, Mrs Swinburne,' said Mr Carter, as he entered the staffroom. 'Public displays of affection always fill me with . . . how can I best describe it?'

'Jealousy?' said Jill.

'Nostalgia?' said Trevor.

'Bile.'

'Good. In that case I'll do it again.'

And she did.

'There, there. I won't let that nasty Mr Carter hurt you.'

Trevor smiled and stood up, suddenly recharged in body and soul.

'Thank you. I feel better now. Let's go home.'

'I thought you were shattered?' said Jill.

'I've just remembered something to unshatter me.'

He headed for the door. Jill collected up her statutory thirty-eight exercise books and followed him.

In the corridor she asked him, 'Where did it come from?'

'Where did what come from?'

'You said you'd unloaded half a ton of timber and you'd been teaching proper woodwork with proper wood. Where did it come from?'

'Off the back of a lorry.'

'Young woman with pram returned to premises at ten past four. What's that in authentic police jargon?'

'Call it sixteen-eleven hours,' said Ben.

Yvonne let herself into the house while the detectives reviewed their afternoon's work.

'The way I see it,' said Joe, 'this kid with the pram leaves the house just after three o'clock and comes back just after four o'clock.'

'I'd call that a pretty good day's work.'

'Just about wraps up the entire investigation.'

'Tie it in pink ribbon and pass it to Interpol.'

'What time's our next appointment?'

'Four thirty-five.'

Driving home, Trevor and Jill discussed the unexpected but welcome arrival in their midst of quantities of timber and Tesses of the D'Urbervilles. They agreed there was a hint of the unorthodox in the sudden appearance of these teaching aids but since San Quentin High subsisted on various brands of abnormality the proper professional response should be the Chaplin Syndrome: Don't Worry About It.

Then Trevor made a sudden lurch into the personal. Jill recognised the symptoms: the scratching of the nose and the shuffling in the seat. They generally indicated he had chopped down a cherry tree and was working up to a guilty plea. It always took him a little time to build up a head of confessional steam.

'You know how you're always going on at me . . .'

'Trevor. I never go on at you.'

'You always do it nicely. You go on at me. But nicely. Very nicely indeed. But you do go on at me about not being a cabbage. About maintaining interests outside the home.'

'Yes. That's true. I do go on at you about that. Nicely.'

'You usually go on at me when you're going to a meeting about ozone layers.'

'All right. We agree. I go on at you about maintaining outside interests. Now. Will you stop going on at me about me going on at you? And move on to chapter two?'

'Chapter two is you also go on at me, still very nicely, about *sharing* our outside interests.'

'That's usually when I want you to come with me to a meeting about ozone layers and you want to stay in to watch a football match on television.'

'Or snooker. Sometimes it's snooker.'

'Football. Snooker. It's all cabbage to me.'

'Well. I've been thinking about it. And I agree.'

Jill looked at him, baffled but intrigued.

'I'm not quite sure what you're agreeing with.'

'I'm agreeing we should go out more and not be cabbages, and share each other's interests. I think I should come to a meeting with you and learn about ozone layers. And I think you should come out with me . . . and learn about jazz.'

'Ah.'

This was it: the sixty-four thousand dollar confession. She should have guessed it was jazz. She peered out of the window, checking the side-streets for men with saxophones.

'Do I take it there is a jazz band lurking somewhere in the vicinity?'

Trevor shrugged his shoulders.

'I haven't checked the exact details but . . .'

'When?'

'Tonight. Nine o'clock. The Limping Whippet. Canal Street.'

Time was also of the essence in the police car discreetly parked not quite opposite Number 17, Hotspur Street.

'Twenty-five past four,' said Joe.

'Call it sixteen-twenty-six hours.'

'I'm talking about the real world. We have an appointment.'

'Sorry, partner. The real world. I'd forgotten about that.'

'Time we were moving.'

'Fancy a count-down?'

'Why not. We haven't had a count-down for ages. You start.'

'Five.'

'Four.'

'Three.'

'Two.'

'One.'

'Zero!' they cried in unison, then almost leaped out of their trendy plain clothes as, right on cue, a fist banged loudly on the roof of the car.

'Now then lads!'

Big Al nodded through the window at them. He was perched on his bicycle and leaning against the car. He and the police force had a firm but gentle understanding based on the traditional Northern precept: you leave me alone to scratch my back and I'll leave you alone to scratch yours. It served them well enough. Everybody kept his hands to himself but, by the same token, everybody's back ended up scratched.

Ben wound his window down.

'Good afternoon, sir.'

'Just maintaining a discreet surveillance, are we?'

'We're not empowered to divulge that information,' said Joe.

'Nation's security at risk. Usual thing,' said Ben.

'Bollocks,' said Big Al.

The three men smiled. The exchange had confirmed the continued strength and depth of their mutual understanding.

'In point of fact,' said Joe, 'we're about to leave. Another pressing appointment. Top priority.'

'Don't tell me. You're going to back a horse. The four thirty-five at Ripon is it?'

Joe glanced at his partner. Ben nodded, seeking to imply, silently, that there was no point in trying to withhold information from Big Al, since he already seemed to know everything.

'OK, guvnor, it's a fair cop. We're planning to invest half-a-crown each way on a horse called Mindless Bureaucracy,' said Joe.

'Any profit to go to bona fide charities, preferably those devoted to old people and non-violent dogs,' Ben added.

Al stared at them, aghast.

'Mindless Bureaucracy? Don't waste your money, lads. The jockey's bent. Let me see your paper.'

He reached into the car for the *Sporting Life*, where it rested in the glove compartment on top of a list of stolen cars. The paper was already open at the right page.

'Look, see? Same race. Solidarity. You'll get ten to one at least. Put your helmets on it.'

The detectives knew better than to argue with Al in matters of metaphysics and turf.

'Thank you, sir,' said Joe.

'May we give you the right time before we go?' said Ben.

'No need. Save it for another occasion.'

The car drove away down Hotspur Street. Al waited until it was out of sight, then parked his bicycle outside Number 17.

Minutes later the police car was parked outside the premises of Warner Brothers, Turf Accountants (Outer Limits) Ltd. As Joe and Ben were walking towards the betting shop, a small yellow van drove past.

'Did you see a yellow van?'

'Yes. Did you?'

'Yes.'

'It's a funny old world, the world, isn't it?'

They went into the shop.

Big Al cycled away down Hotspur Street in a northerly direction. It was his favoured compass bearing.

Minutes later the small yellow van arrived from the south and parked outside Number 17 with no thoughts of discretion. Jill and Trevor went into the house, dumping coats, books and themselves in the living room. Yvonne was alone.

'Where's everybody?' said Jill.

'First-Born's asleep in his manger. Ivan's upstairs in his room. And I'm here.'

'Very neat.'

'And you just missed Big Al.'

'Has he arranged some arrangements?' asked Trevor.

'He left some messages, if that's what you mean.'

'About Ivan?'

'Just a second. I've got to concentrate and get them right.'

Yvonne sat on a settee, concentrating. Jill and Trevor sat

either side of her, also concentrating. Al's messages tended to be on the lateral side of elliptical: in a translation by Yvonne there could be a severe shortage of logical footholds.

'Right. Got it. Listen. There are two messages and a map.'

'That's nice. I like maps.'

'Be quiet, Trevor.'

'Message number one. Will you please take Ivan to the Lancashire border. He says he realises it's against his better judgement, it being Lancashire, but would you do it just the same.'

'But there's hundreds of miles of Lancashire border. Which bit of the Lancashire border?' said Trevor.

'Message number two. Please look at map.'

Yvonne retrieved the map from Level Four of First-Born's model multi-storey car-park. She handed it to Trevor.

'I see,' said Jill. 'Men look at maps. Women don't look at maps. Men's work, is that it?'

'Mr Chaplin says you don't understand maps, miss. He says you have trouble with left and right, let alone north and south and stuff like that, miss.'

'That's all quite true, Yvonne.'

Trevor studied the map, oblivious to the dialectic.

'It's not too bad. X marks the spot. Up beyond Haworth. We can be there and back in just over an hour if the traffic's OK.'

'When is all this supposed to happen?'

Yvonne lapsed into another bout of concentration, emerging to announce, 'Two messages and a map and a footnote. I've given you the two messages and Mr Chaplin's got the map. Then Big Al said there was a footnote. Time is of the essence. That's the footnote.'

'It's all amazingly clear by Big Al's standards.'

'Are you going to ask her about baby-sitting?' said Trevor.

'You ask her. You're a big grown-up man.'

'Do you want me to baby-sit? Yes. That's all right, miss. Are you going somewhere nice?'

'The Singing Room of the Limping Whippet in Canal Street.'

'What for?'

'To hear some red hot jazz music. And stomp the night away.'

'Oh. That stuff.'

'Do you mind?' said Trevor. 'You're speaking of the music I love. Yvonne, has anyone ever explained jazz to you? Properly?'

'No sir.'

'Make an excuse and leave,' said Jill.

'No problem, miss. If I get bored I stop listening. They have heavy metal on Mondays.'

'Pardon?'

'At the Limping Whippet.'

'Please. We go to border? Now?'

The three of them broke off their discussion of the state of the nation's music to see Ivan standing in the doorway of the living room. He was wearing his coat and had packed his bag.

'Quick cup of tea and then we'll be off,' said Trevor.

'I think. We go. Now.'

Though Ivan was standing still, there was an unmistakable urgency in his stillness.

'Time is of the essence,' said Jill.

'We go. Now. Back way.'

Ivan walked into the kitchen and stood beside the back door.

'I'll drive the van round to the back,' said Trevor.

'This is beginning to feel important,' said Jill. 'Did Big Al say anything else we should know about?'

Yvonne spooled back the tape in her head and slipped once more into concentration mode.

'Two messages and a map and a footnote. Yes. And a question. A question for Mr Chaplin. Was the timber all right?'

Trevor was already on his way to the front door, ignition keys in his hand. Jill called after him.

'Was the timber all right?'

'Yes. Terrific. Who wants to know?'

'Big Al.'

'What's it got to do with him?'

They realised simultaneously the answer was probably: everything. But before they could pursue it to a logical – or, more likely, an absurdist – conclusion Ivan reappeared in the living room.

'We go to border! Now!'

He spoke with Lithuanian passion and urgency. There was no evidence that he was Lithuanian but it had started as Trevor's guesswork and was now embedded in the mythology.

They departed in the late afternoon by way of the ginnel that ran along the back of Hotspur Street. Jill sat in the front of the van with Trevor. Ivan crouched in the back.

'Which way's Lancashire?' said Jill.

'Left at the beer-off,' said Trevor. 'Let's have the radio on. They'll tell us about broken traffic lights.'

Jill switched on the radio in time to catch the fag-end of the sports news. She sat quietly. Whatever the feminist ideologues might say, it was quicker and easier not to stand between Trevor and the sports news. She heard but did not understand:

'And here's the result of the Stewards' Inquiry into the four thirty-five at Ripon. First, Solidarity at twelve-to-one. First past the post, Mindless Bureaucracy, the seven-to-four favourite, was disqualified. The result in full – First, Solidarity at twelve-to-one . . .'

The yellow van turned left at the off-licence and headed west, towards Lancashire.

Minutes later, the police car returned to Hotspur Street. Inside the car there was great rejoicing. Joe was ecstatic.

'Twelve-to-one. Isn't that the sweetest sound you ever heard? Twelve-to-one.'

'Yes. That's a lot of helmets in anybody's language. Thank you, Al.'

They raised imaginary glasses in a toast to their omniscient tipster.

'Meanwhile, back at our official duties . . .'

The detectives looked at Number 17. The street wisdom concealed within their sloth told them that the yellow van that should have been parked outside was not parked outside; that the departure of the yellow van should have been observed and recorded in the admittedly unlikely case that it might turn out to be evidence; and all that being so, they had better think of a good story and quickly.

'It seems to me,' said Joe, 'in the absence of first-hand observation, what we need is fair-minded speculation.'

'Let's attempt a reconstruction. I always enjoy reconstructions.'

'Right. Eyes down. Here we go. Suspects come home from school, arriving at twenty to five. That's sixteen-forty.'

'Plus VAT. Sixteen-forty-two.'

'They go into the house. They say to themselves: my word, I'm quite exhausted by a hard day's teaching. I could murder a cup of tea.'

'And some ginger nuts.'

'And some ginger nuts.'

'But guess what? There's no milk!'

'Catastrophe!'

'There's a short domestic quarrel about who forgot to get the milk. And then it's off to the supermarket they go, at or about ten to five.'

'Sixteen-fifty-one. Yellow van leaves house.'

Joe completed the entry in his notebook.

Ben looked over his shoulder.

'A constructive word in your ear, partner?'

'Is always welcome.'

'In your report. Don't mention the ginger nuts.'

'I haven't.'

Joe closed his book and slipped it in his pocket.

'I wonder where they've really gone?' he said.

'Does it matter? People are entitled to their privacy.'

The mist was hanging over the moors beyond Haworth. Jill rubbed at the condensation on the window of the van.

'It's weird. I can almost imagine that I can see them,' she said, peering out.

'See who?' said Trevor.

'The Brontë Sisters.'

'Huh?'

'The Brontë Sisters. Trevor, you do know who I'm talking about?'

'Course I do. The Brontë Sisters. Patti, Maxene and LaVerne.'

It was one of the gentle but spiky moments that marked the boundaries of their relationship. He had long ago perfected the device of a flip response when he was wrong-footed intellectually. Jill had once asked him whether he knew anything about Havelock Ellis. He had responded:

'You bet. The finest full-back who ever played for Stockport County.'

'Trevor! He was a pioneer in our understanding of sex.'

'I don't wonder. Have you ever been to Stockport?'

He often found himself making jokes to cover his ignorance of people, places and events when, on reflection, he realised he knew all about them in the first place. But generally he played safe and played the game. As far as he was concerned, Tom Paine was a tenor player with the early Count Basie band, Garibaldi was a sweeper with AC Milan and Germaine Greer was in his class at school and he was once given a hundred lines for pulling her pigtails.

He parked the van in a rocky lay-by.

'Is this it?' said Jill.

'According to Al's map. This is the spot marked X.'

They got out of the van. A long road stretched out ahead.

'Lancashire that way.'

'Let me see the map.'

Jill examined the map.

'This doesn't look at all like what I see around me.'

'Obviously. Everything's bigger than it is on a map. Look. All you've got to do is pretend you're flying very high in an aeroplane and there's the world down below and . . .'

'Trevor.'

'Yes.'

'Knock it off.'

Still a little uneasy, Jill stared along the road. It seemed long and uncertain, with little prospect of joy at the other end.

'I suppose I thought there'd be a sign saying: Lancashire this way.'

'They took them all down in the Wars of the Roses. To confuse the enemy. But take my word. Lancashire is in that direction. Definitely.'

Jill knew that when a man from the ancient Kingdom of Northumbria used the word definitely, it was better not to argue. He might be wrong but it was better not to argue. In any case, they were immediately distracted by a strange tapping noise.

'What's that?' said Trevor.

'You're the noble peasant.'

'I'm not.'

'You know where Lancashire is.'

'If you want the honest truth, the countryside scares me stiff. It's full of weird noises I don't understand. This is one of them.'

Then they heard the voice.

'May I come out please?'

'Ivan!' said Jill.

'I'd forgotten about Ivan. All this talk of maps. And talking through my feelings about the countryside.'

Trevor opened the rear doors of the van.

'Sorry about that, Ivan.'

'Is cool.'

Ivan climbed out of the van with his bag. He stamped his feet on the grass verge to restore sufficient circulation for the journey ahead.

'Ivan,' said Jill, 'your people will meet you on the other side.'

It was already a familiar script. She felt like a character in a soap opera that had outlived its natural time-span. She murmured to Trevor:

'Do you get a feeling of *déjà vu*?'

'No. I've seen it all before.'

Ivan shook hands, first with Trevor, then with Jill.

'Goodbye, Mr Chaplin. Goodbye, Mrs Swinburne.'

'You've learned our names!' said Jill.

'I learn . . . fastly. With much . . . pace. Yes?'

Trevor pointed along the road.

'Lancashire. You can't miss it.'

'Thank you.'

Ivan picked up his bag and started the long walk towards the frontier.

'He's a nice man,' said Jill, 'but I do hope we never see him again.'

'It reminds me of a film.'

'Which one?'

'I can't remember what it was called.'

'Charlie Chaplin. He walked along a lot of roads.'

'Not Charlie Chaplin. More modern than that.'

'I need more clues.'

'A man. Walking along a road. And he gets attacked by an aeroplane.'

Jill nodded and smiled.

'Alfred Hitchcock. Cary Grant. *North by North-West*.'

'Good. That narrows it down to three.'

Mind at rest, Trevor opened the door of the van.

'Let's go home. The sooner we get home the sooner we can go out again.'

Jill was still watching Ivan. He was almost out of sight, masked by moorland mist. She was haunted by the fear that he would be walking for ever, like his doomed predecessor.

'If I say the name Heathcliffe to you, what does it convey?'

'Easy. Desperate Dan's dog.'

'Trevor!'

'Or else the bloke in *Wuthering Heights*.'

'Time to go home,' said Jill.

They were back in Hotspur Street soon after half-past six, a fact dutifully recorded by the surveillance team.

'Yellow van returned to premises at eighteen-thirty-three,' said Joe, completing the entry in his book.

'Empty-handed,' said Ben. 'They didn't buy much at the supermarket.'

'An entirely justifiable reaction against recent price rises.'

'Maybe it was all a bluff. Maybe they just wanted us to think they were going to the supermarket.'

'You mean . . . there could be more to this than meets the eye?'

'Or less. It can work both ways.'

While the detectives pondered their dilemma, Yvonne stood beside the living room window, keeping them under surveillance.

'They're still here.'

'Who?' said Trevor, who was hanging up his jacket in the hall.

'The police.'

'The police?' said Jill, who was watching the kettle in the kitchen.

They joined Yvonne at the window.

'They've been here all day. I was going to tell you before you went to Lancashire but I didn't have time on account of you not having time on account of time being of the essence.'

'A street like this one, they could be watching anyone,' said Jill. 'There's the unfrocked bank manager. There's Mr Frobisher. He's got one job, two wives, three cars and double glazing. There's the fat man with horn-rimmed glasses. He had a Tory poster in the window at the last election.'

'There's that feller that dresses up as a Scoutmaster,' said Trevor, who was getting the hang of the game.

'Trevor. He *is* a Scoutmaster.'

'It's still highly suspect, showing your knees like that.'

'Your problem is you're homeophobic.'

'I'm not. I'm heterosexual. And when I was a kid I was strict chapel.'

'Ivan thought they were watching here,' said Yvonne, trying hard to bring the meeting to order. 'He stood here, getting all twitchy. Then he went upstairs to his room. That was after he'd made the phone call.'

'They can't have been watching Ivan,' said Trevor.

'Explain,' said Jill.

'Because if they were watching Ivan, they wouldn't be here now. Ivan's in Lancashire. So if they were watching Ivan, they'd be in Lancashire as well. Watching him. 'Cos that's where he is.'

'Phone call?' said Jill.

'Yes. He made a phone call.'

'I hope he reversed the charges,' said Trevor. 'It's a long way to Lithuania.'

'It wasn't a long distance call. Well I don't think it was. He talked in English.'

'I think Ivan's English is better than he pretends,' said Jill.

'But miss, I don't mean he talked good foreign English. I mean he talked proper English English. Like an English man.'

'What sort of English English? Like Mr Chaplin? Like me? Like you?'

Yvonne gave the question prolonged and serious thought: comparative linguistics had never been high on her personal syllabus.

'Well. Like. He spoke a lot posher than me. A lot posher than Mr Chaplin. Not as posh as you, miss. But a bit south country. Yes. Definitely Southern.'

'Southern?' said Jill.

'He won't last five minutes in Lancashire,' said Trevor.

6

A Hot Time in the Old Town

Dusk settled over Hotspur Street like a disapproving frown. Five of the nine street lamps flickered into half-light. The police surveillance continued; but the detectives shuffled, scratched themselves and agreed decision time was approaching.

'It seems to me,' said Ben, 'that we need guidance from on high.'

'A very good place to seek guidance, in my experience,' said Joe.

Jill stood by the living room window. She watched the plain clothes policeman as he walked along the street, making no apparent attempt at concealment. Despite her jaunty jests about Mr Frobisher and the unfrocked bank manager, Jill knew the policemen were watching Number 17. Once your names were on the police computer you were likely to be watched at any time of day or night, with or without cause. Her paranoia generally arrived with the dusk.

Yvonne was also in the living room, her ear pressed to the intercom.

'Mr Chaplin tells very funny stories, miss.'

'Switch the volume up. Let's both listen.'

They heard Trevor's voice from First-Born's bedroom.

'Once upon a time there was a little boy. He lived in Washington, in America, which is a long way from where we live. The little boy's name was Edward Kennedy Ellington. Can you say that? Edward . . . Kennedy . . . Ellington.'

First-Born gurgled.

'Very good. Now although that was the little boy's proper name, everybody called him the Duke. They called him that because he was a very snappy dresser. When the Duke was still very young he learned to play the piano. His piano teacher in Washington was called Mrs Clinkscales.'

'Does it go on for very long?' said Yvonne, turning the volume down.

'Hours and hours and hours and hours.'

'Does it work?'

'It works when he does it to me.'

In the bedroom, Trevor continued with his story.

'Shall I tell you some of the tunes little Duke Ellington wrote when he grew into a big man? All right then. I will. And pay attention because I'll be asking questions before you go to sleep. He wrote "Mood Indigo", "Creole Love Call", "Black and Tan Fantasy", "Ring Dem Bells" . . .'

The telephone rang. Inspector Hobson picked up the receiver and held it to attention, parallel with his ear.

'Hobson.'

'Sir.'

He recognised the voice of Joe or Ben. He had trouble distinguishing them face to face. On the telephone it was impossible, especially when they traded accents or drifted into stage Irish, Peter Sellers Indian or, as on this occasion, brisk professional detective-about-town.

'How's it going in Hotspur Street?'

'Superficially, quiet and uneventful, sir. A few comings and goings, both pedestrian and vehicular. All observed and fully recorded. On the other hand, as you well know, sir, in the world of criminal investigation, superficiality is only skin deep.'

'What precisely are you telling me?'

Hobson suspected he was being told absolutely nothing.

'Absolutely nothing, sir. But we fancy there could be developments under cover of darkness. No hard evidence. You could say we feel it in our bones.'

'Quite.'

He tried to convey icy scepticism. There was no apparent impact on his junior detective.

'Our view, sir, is that it would be circumspect if we were to maintain our surveillance a little longer. Do we have your authority to do that?'

'Yes. You have my authority.'

'Bearing in mind that this will involve a purely nominal amount of overtime, sir.'

'Overtime?'

Hobson was too late. The line went dead. Once more his men had dug a hole, then stood back to watch in wonder as their commanding officer had jumped smartly into it, heels together and eyes front.

'Knickers,' said the Chief Inspector.

Trevor had almost finished his bedtime story.

'The Duke's most famous saying was: you are very beautiful, very gracious, very talented, very generous and I want you to know that I do love you madly. Remember that, baby, and it will serve you well.'

Jill pushed the door open.

'We are supposed to be going out tonight. To broaden my mind.'

'And we'll all live happily ever after.'

Trevor kissed his fingertips and brushed them gently against First-Born's cheek.

'Tomorrow night we'll have the story of Count Basie, the Kid from Red Bank.'

'Ignore that silly man,' said Jill. 'Tomorrow night I'll tell you the story of the blue whales.'

First-Born smiled as Jill tucked him in. He knew whichever way it went – Basie or blue whales – he was on to a good thing.

The detectives had made the same discovery.

'We have his authority to maintain the surveillance?' said Joe.

'Yea, even unto the overtime claim.'

'Inspector Hobson really is the commanding officer of our dreams.'

'Oh dearie me.'

'What's wrong?'

'I spy an incident.'

They looked across the street at Number 17. Trevor and Jill were leaving the house. Yvonne was waving them off from the doorway.

'I see the suspects, Chaplin, Trevor and Swinburne, Jill, going out, leaving the baby-sitter in charge at . . .'

Ben checked his watch.

'. . . just gone half-past eight.'

'Twenty-thirty-three,' said Joe, recording the information in his notebook.

'Do we follow them?'

'It's dark. We might bump into something.'

'Try this. They might be going somewhere nice.'

'A table for two in a secluded rendezvous?'

'A dimly-lit opium den?'

'A temple of erotic pleasure?'

'Well. You don't win medals for maintaining surveillance on a baby-sitter.'

There was the usual traffic jam on the inner relief road so Trevor drove to Canal Street by the old tram route. It was lined with ancient mills and warehouses, now being transformed by keen-eyed speculators into pottery boutiques and executive apartments. Whether there were enough executives to fill the apartments and buy the pottery was an awkward question and anyone asking it was accused of bad taste and talking down the boom. Jill, who had preached her fill on the subject, had a more immediate concern.

'What sort of music are you going to make me listen to tonight?'

'Jazz.'

'Obviously. But what kind of jazz?'

'What kinds do you know about?'

'I know three kinds. Hot. Cool. And what time does the tune start?'

'It's a guy called Frank Ricotti. He plays all three.'

'Thank you, Trevor. May I ask another question?'

'If you never ask, you never learn.'

'Why is that police car following us?'

'No idea.'

'But you have noticed?'

'Been following us since we left the house. It's the same one that's been watching the house all day. According to Yvonne.'

'You're *not* worried?'

'No.'

It was a quality in Trevor that she found perplexing and, though she rarely admitted it to him, irresistible. She also enjoyed the explanations.

'Why are you not worried, Trevor?'

'Because if they were *really* following us, they'd be more subtle. They'd do it so we didn't notice.'

'So if they're not really following us, why are they behaving in such a way that it looks as if they're following us?'

'They could be young policemen practising following people. They've got to learn somewhere. Follow innocent people and learn how to do it, ready for when they've got to follow criminals and villains and such.'

'You've got to do better than that.'

'All right. They're jazz freaks. They're going to the same place as us.'

'It's a more sensible theory than apprentice policemen brushing up on their following.'

'Well anyway, what's the problem? We haven't done anything wrong.'

'What about Ivan?'

'Ivan's safe in Lancashire.'

'Isn't that a contradiction in terms? Safe in Lancashire?'

'Ivan is only a problem if he's done anything wrong. And he likes Bix Beiderbecke and Duke Ellington, which proves he's OK because people who like Bix and the Duke obviously wouldn't do anything wrong. Therefore, there is no problem.'

'Trevor Chaplin, you are an amazing man.'

'Yes.'

'Is that your solution to everything? Stay cool?'

'There's no better place to stay.'

The Limping Whippet was a pub in the grand tradition. In the 1960s, breweries across the land had improved most pubs of this kind by demolishing them and rebuilding them in laminated plastic. The Limping Whippet had survived. This was not because of a sudden plague of sensitivity in brewery boardrooms; it was simply that no building contractor was prepared to set foot in the No-Go area around Canal Street, especially if he valued his wheelbarrows, cement mixers and workforce. All three categories tended to disappear without trace minutes after arriving in the street.

In the style-conscious 1980s, the brewers once more laid waste to their kingdom. They ripped out the laminated plastic of the 60s and embraced their customers with post-modern, hi-tech, Victorian-facsimile theme interiors. You couldn't order a pint without tripping over a designer's concept.

Throughout all this progress the Limping Whippet had stood alone, resolutely unmodernised. Now its time had come. It was buttressed on all sides by preservation orders, the Real Ale lobby was campaigning for the restoration of sawdust on the floors and an alternative poet was preparing a slim volume of the graffiti from the lavatories.

The Singing Room lay at the back of the pub, within spitting distance of the canal, a dimension checked each night by the regulars. Its ceiling was veneered with the stains from a million Woodbines and the room was haunted by the cheerful echoes of a century of cheap music; from 'A Boy's Best Friend Is His Mother' to 'I Did It My Way' and beyond, if it is possible to conceive of such a beyond.

Trevor and Jill had followed the chalked signs reading: JAZZ THIS WAY. Now they sat at a table near the stage. Six middle-aged men with beer bellies were dismantling their musical instruments.

'Who are those large men?' said Jill.

'The support band,' said Trevor. 'Mickey Mouse music.'

Jill was about to demand an explanation when a breathless man wearing a parody of a tuxedo rushed on to the stage, blew into the microphone and announced:

'And let's hear it again for Sid Norris's New Orleans Rhythm Kings from Batley!'

The fifty people in the audience took no notice. The breathless man blew again into the microphone and carried on, undeterred.

'Thank you very much, folks. I always enjoy a nice frenzy. Well. Now. On with the cool music. In a few minutes, tonight's big attraction. From London, England, the Frank Ricotti All-Stars. Providing the train was on time. Unless they're driving. I'll just go and check. Thank you.'

'It's Mr Pitt,' said Jill.

'That figures,' said Trevor.

Jill remembered Mr Pitt as a junior employee in the Town Planning Department. He had then taken what he himself described as a lateral promotion at less money and became a local registrar of births, deaths and marriages. Trevor had met him in that role, while investigating the apparent death of a barman called John. He no longer remembered why he was doing such a thing. The key revelation had been Mr Pitt as a loyal and undeviating keeper of the jazz faith. He could sing the complete recorded works of Charlie Parker, note for note. It was, as they both acknowledged, a remarkable gift, made the more precious by being totally useless in a materialistic world. Nobody would give you a job singing Charlie Parker solos, least of all in local government. If the Gospel according to St Matthew, chapter 5, verse 5, were ever granted legal status, Mr Pitt would inherit the earth. As it was, he seemed blissfully content with the Singing Room of the Limping Whippet.

'Mrs Swinburne! Mr Chaplin!'

Mr Pitt saw them as he left the stage in search of his missing All-Stars.

'Mr Pitt! From the Town Planning Office,' said Jill.

'And the Registrar's?' said Trevor.

'Formerly of both.'

'Formerly?' said Jill. 'Does that imply yet another sideways career move?'

Mr Pitt smiled.

'Yes. I accepted lateral promotion into compulsory redundancy. Please go, they said, and handed me some money.'

'A golden handshake?' said Jill.

'Not very golden, Mrs Swinburne. It would be more accurate to say they lightly dusted my palm with iron filings. So I decided to invest my capital. Open a jazz club. This is it. Do you like the artwork?'

At the back of the stage, a frayed off-white sheet was fastened to the wall with drawing-pins. Painted on the sheet were the words: TONIGHT – JAZZ AT THE VILLAGE VANGAURD.

'Great,' said Trevor.

'Is that how you spell vanguard?' said Jill.

'You are the first person to spot it, Mrs Swinburne. I've decided to call it this week's deliberate mistake. From next week we'll have prizes.'

'Forgive my asking,' said Jill, 'but is all this likely to be viable?'

'Oh yes. Bearing in mind it's only once a week. Every Tuesday. Is it Tuesday? Well, whatever night it is.'

He did a quick calculation on his fingers.

'But yes, totally viable. I shall be able to keep going for six weeks before the money runs out. If that's not viable, then I don't know what is. Excuse me. I think the orchestra has arrived.'

He headed towards the back of the room.

'Well. You certainly know how to give a girl a good time.'

'Would vodka help?'

'It never does any harm. Just a minute. Who's driving?'

'Ah.'

Trevor brought out a ten-pence piece.

'Call.'

'Heads.'

'Heads it is.'

Trevor walked across the room to the bar. He ordered a large vodka-and-tonic, a pineapple juice on the rocks and two bags of crisps. Jill was right. He knew how to give a girl a good time.

'What flavour crisps?' said the barmaid.

'Potato.'

Joe and Ben walked into the room.

'What manner of place is this?' said Ben.

'I always thought of it as the Singing Room of the Limping Whippet,' said his partner.

'It still looks like the Singing Room of the Limping Whippet.'

'Mutton dressed as mutton.'

'This place used to be full of sailors and harlots. What became of sailors and harlots?'

'They went out as credit cards came in.'

A fat and hairy New Orleans Rhythm King from Batley walked past them, carrying a tray loaded with twelve pints of bitter. It was the band's fee.

'Splendid sight,' said Joe. 'It gives me an idea.'

'Who's driving?' said Ben.

Joe brought out an ancient Irish coin of the realm.

'Call.'

'Shamrocks.'

'Shamrocks it is.'

They walked across the room to the bar and ordered a pint of best and a Tizer with an olive in it.

Jill raised her glass in a toast to her co-hab.

'Love and peace.'

'Stay cool.'

'Oh look.'

'What?'

'They've brought the sweet trolley.'

Trevor turned to see what she was talking about. A slim, dark-haired man was wheeling a vibraphone on to the stage.

'That's not a sweet trolley. It's a set of vibes. Frank Ricotti plays vibraphone.'

'You didn't tell me he was a vibraphone player. I always think a vibraphone player sounds like . . .'

Trevor helped her finish the sentence.

'. . . like a long-term prisoner banging on the bars of his cell.'

'I'm sorry,' said Jill, 'but that's what I think.'

'I made the effort and learned about cholesterol. The least you can do is make the effort and learn about vibraphones.'

His voice was low, his logic impeccable and his gentle passion as deep as the lost city of Atlantis.

'All right. I'll try.'

They offered each other crisps by way of a peace pact. Trevor's attention switched to the stage where the All-Stars – a pianist, a drummer, a bass player and their leader – were tuning their instruments.

'Oh look,' said Jill.

'You already did that. You saw a tea trolley.'

'This is something else.'

'What?'

'Two policemen, keeping us under surveillance.'

Trevor turned to look. Joe and Ben were leaning on the bar, drinks in hand.

'So? They've probably dropped in to collect their protection money. The music's going to start.'

His attention reverted to the bandstand.

'Music or no music, as soon as I've finished my nice vodka, I shall go across to those men and ask them. Have you been watching our house? Did you follow us here tonight? Are you keeping us under observation? And if so, why?'

There was no reply.

'Trevor?'

She turned to see Trevor, fingers to lips, as Mr Pitt returned to the microphone.

'Hello, good evening and welcome, jazz lovers, to the Village Vanguard, for this, the high spot of the evening. The

Village Vanguard is proud to present, all the way from London, England, here to soothe your savage breasts, the Frank Ricotti All-Stars!'

The audience applauded. There was a degree of musical expertise in the room that calculated there was a better chance of finding a decent band in London, population ten million, than in Batley with a population of forty thousand and a Second Division Rugby League team.

The music began. It sounded like water cascading down a rocky hillside, with occasional sideways spurts. Trevor was instantly entranced. Jill was not.

After thirty-two bars of music she murmured to Trevor, 'What time does the tune start?'

'They've played the tune. Now they're improvising.'

Again he put his fingers to his lips, tenderly and lovingly; but the coded message was please shut your goddammed mouth, oh precious jewel of the whole wide world.

She tried very hard. She concentrated but found herself thinking: when I am fully concentrated I shall be one-tenth my normal size but retaining all my natural juices. The notes from the music seemed to be flying in several different directions at once and she couldn't catch any of them. She glanced at Trevor. He was happily marooned on a magic carpet en route from seventh heaven to cloud nine. It might be days before he returned to Planet Earth.

She thought about Planet Earth, the policemen at the bar, the tropical rain forests, the policemen at the bar, new nappies for First-Born, the policemen at the bar, *Tess of the D'Urbervilles* and the policemen at the bar.

She finished her drink, got up and crossed to the bar.

'Excuse me,' she said to the detectives, 'may I have a word with you?'

'Our pleasure, ma'am,' said Ben, with a polite bow, 'we are here to assist the public at all times.'

'Shhh!'

The angry hisses came from all sides, a quadrophonic reprimand from the devout. Somebody tapped Jill on the shoulder. She turned to see Mr Pitt holding up a hand-written notice. It said:

PLEASE BUTTON ALL LIPS WHILE ARTISTES ARE CREATING.

Then he turned the notice round. On the back was written:

FOLLOW ME.

They followed him down a narrow corridor, squeezed past a rusty bingo machine and an unconscious New Orleans Rhythm King, and found themselves in a back yard facing the canal.

'This is the designated conversation area,' said Mr Pitt.

'Charming,' said Ben.

Mr Pitt conducted them to a table with a parasol advertising Pernod.

'You have a nice view of the water. Perfect for exchanging finely-tuned thoughts by the light of the moon.'

Jill and the detectives sat down.

There was no sign of the moon. Much of the yard lay beyond the reach of the lights from the pub. As her eyes became used to the semi-darkness, Jill managed to identify a broken swing, a row of overflowing dustbins and a pile of sacks in a corner that could have been last night's forgotten drunks.

'Beautiful,' said Mr Pitt.

'Is it?' said Jill.

'The music,' said Mr Pitt.

'Of course. The music. Yes. Very cool.'

'I can see Mr Chaplin's been educating you, Mrs Swinburne.'

'I'm given to understand that's what our relationship is all about.'

'Excellent.'

Mr Pitt smiled at the three of them.

'I gather all this is a beer garden and children's play area that never caught on. But we must all seek to rise above our environment, don't you think? Excuse me. I must go about my business.'

He disappeared into the gloom.

'Very pleasant spot,' said Joe. 'Lovely view of the harbour and the fishermen mending their nets.'

'Are you following us?' said Jill.

'A leading question, you might say.'

'Your car has been parked outside our house all day. We drive here this evening. You follow us. We pay our modest entrance fee to listen to the cool music and you are in the room too. We can, I think, be forgiven for thinking you are keeping us under surveillance.'

The detectives looked at each in silent consultation.

'Well?'

They reached a silent consensus.

'Mrs Swinburne,' said Ben, 'given the choice between truth and lies, which do you prefer?'

'Truth. I'm sentimental, I know, but that's what I like. Truth.'

'This is an unexpected turn of events,' said Joe.

'But we'll try to handle it,' said Ben.

'Bearing in mind there's very little we can tell you.'

'Because of official secrets, confidentiality, Habeas Corpus and Magna Carta.'

'Bollocks,' said Jill.

'Fair comment.'

The detectives spoke in unison. Here, they realised, was a woman made of sterner stuff than they were used to. The slick double-act might fool superior officers and the poor in spirit but confronted with Swinburne, Jill, they could well be forced to take the giant step into plain speaking and honesty. It was the coward's way out; but they could live with cowardice.

Ben took the initiative.

'As we've said, there is very little we can tell you. Especially if you insist on the truth. But let me tell you what I can tell you. We have been watching the house. We did follow you here. We did sit in the same room, listening to that strange music.'

'Thank you,' said Jill. 'I already knew all of that. In fact, I think you'll find I already told you what you've just told me.'

'Excellent. So there's no room for misunderstanding. We see everything in the same way. Shall we go home now?'

'I need to know why you are doing these things.'

'Why?' said Ben.

'Why?' echoed his partner.

'We really are into the murky waters of confidentiality, the minute you ask the question why, Mrs Swinburne.'

'All right. Let me guess. You are following us because our names are on the police computer. Yes?'

'It is just possible.'

'And you are following us because you are carrying out orders. Yes?'

'That too is also just possible as well.'

'Very well. Give me the name of the officer who gives you the orders and I'll take it up directly with him. I am not frightened of senior police officers.'

'Nor are we,' said Joe.

'We have a lot in common,' said Ben.

'Tell me his name.'

There was another silent consultation between the police officers. A startling and stunning possibility arrived in their minds simultaneously. Here, in this faraway failed beer garden and kiddies' playground, with modern jazz hanging on the chill night air, faced with a tough woman asking awkward questions, they had found a well-tried solution to their dilemma. They would refer it upstairs.

'The name is Hobson,' said Joe.

'Sergeant Hobson, BSc?' said Jill.

'Detective Inspector Hobson, PhD.'

'I know him well. I shall speak to Inspector Hobson and his PhD.'

'We wish you joy of the experience. He certainly supplies us with many a merry laugh.'

Jill stood up. Time had passed and she ought to make the effort to hear at least one tune, so Trevor could explain it on the way home.

'Mrs Swinburne. We have one last request,' said Ben.

'A hearty breakfast?'

'No, not that. Though we do appreciate your friendly wit and cheerful badinage. No, it's rather more important. May we follow you home after the concert? You and Mr Chaplin in your yellow van? Us in our motor car?'

'Whatever for?'

'It's an accountancy problem.'

'We will go home. We will take our baby-sitter home. We will go to bed. None of that requires a police escort.'

'But you will have total security from footpads and highwaymen,' said Joe, 'and our responsibility, with luck and ingenuity, will creep over the witching hour of midnight. Thus making it much simpler for the accountancy department of the constabulary to calculate our overtime.'

'Forgive the badinage, but after midnight, do they pay you in pumpkins?'

'Mrs Swinburne,' said Ben, 'we are the pumpkins.'

He turned to his partner.

'Shall we go listen to the music? It hath a dying fall.'

The detectives got up from the table and walked across the beer garden into the pub. Jill was following them when she became aware of a movement in the shadows.

Mr Pitt was playing an imaginary saxophone, fingers dancing across invisible keys, body swaying in time to the music from his very own Village Vanguard. The Ricotti All-Stars were playing a slow blues. Jill had absorbed enough education from Trevor to know a blues when she heard one. It was a long way from the Mississippi Delta to the Blackwater Canal in downtown Leeds but the blues had made the trip, and Mr Pitt was playing along with them.

He noticed Jill watching him. He carried on playing his silent improvisation.

'We must all find our fantasies the best way we can, Mrs Swinburne.'

'Indeed we must, Mr Pitt.'

'At least I know where to look for mine. Imagine. I can do this for six whole weeks.'

'And then?'
'Who knows?'
'Another sideways career move?'
'I've always lived my life sideways. It's the best way of avoiding what lies ahead.'
The music changed key and Mr Pitt swayed into a fresh bout of highly-charged invention. Jill said no more. It was polite to button your lips while artistes were creating.
She stood at the back of the Singing Room until the set was over. Then she returned to their table to discover Trevor had left it, and was enjoying a one-sided conversation with Frank Ricotti, who was packing away his sweet trolley.
'Did you ever work with a tenor player called Sam Bentley?' said Trevor. 'I met him on a North Sea ferry going to Rotterdam. He was supposed to be going to Rotherham but he didn't hear his agent properly on the phone.'
'Trevor. We have a child, a baby-sitter and a police escort waiting outside.'
'A police escort?'
'That's cool,' said Ricotti.

At one o'clock in the morning they sat down in the living room with toast and marmalade and a pot of tea. They had taken Yvonne home and waved good night to their police escort.
'Did you enjoy the music?' said Trevor.
'I cannot tell a lie. I missed most of it. I was talking to the policemen and watching Mr Pitt's fantasies.'
'So do you want me to explain anything? We could talk through vibraphones if you like.'
The doorbell rang before she could think of an answer.
'I'll go,' she said.
'I expect it's the police. They forgot to say "evening all".'
'It might be Ivan.'
'I'd forgotten Ivan. I bet he likes vibraphone players. I'll sort out some Lionel Hampton and Milt Jackson.'
Jill decided it would be easier to answer the door than wait for a translation. Trevor was delving into his record shelves

when she returned to the room. The man with her was, as far as Trevor was concerned, a total stranger.

'That's not Ivan,' he said.

For once Jill seemed uneasy and on the edge of embarrassment.

'Trevor. This is Peter.'

'Hi, Peter.'

'My ex-husband.'

'I'll get another cup.'

7

Is He the Lodger?

While Trevor waited for the kettle to boil, he thought about Peter. There was very little to think about. All he really knew about him was that he existed, had once been married to Jill and she had thrown him out. Even this he had learned at second hand: a school staffroom conspiracy with the main ingredient a discreet vow that they should all be very kind and considerate towards Mrs Swinburne at this time of trauma. Trevor had seen little visible evidence of trauma but had offered her a lift to school in his yellow van. Public transport was no fit place for people with traumas, visible or otherwise.

The daily lifts became a routine, and the routine begat social trimmings, culminating eventually in pleasurable adventures under the duvet, gently initiated by Jill and lubricated by a bottle of Frascati. To this day Trevor had no idea whether Frascati was the name of a town, a grape or a factory, but he was grateful nonetheless. When his old attic flat was demolished in the cause of a still unbuilt ten-lane highway, he had moved into 17, Hotspur Street where, in the fullness of time, they had begotten First-Born. Strictly speaking, the begetting took place in the honeymoon suite of a hotel in Edinburgh, but that was a mere geographical whim in the great Cycle of Reproduction.

During their years together, they had talked many things through. As jazz and football were to Trevor, so was talking through to Jill. Like muesli and fresh vegetables, it was essential to everybody's well-being. But now Trevor realised with a slight shock that they had never talked through Peter. They had never even talked about him. Talking about was altogether quicker than talking through: once through became involved, it took much longer because pain barriers had to be confronted and transcended. That was why Trevor didn't like talking things through. He disliked pain. It hurt.

The kettle boiled and he still knew nothing about Peter. He carried the tray into the living room to hear the question:

'Is he the lodger?'

'Don't be silly. It's Trevor,' said Jill.

Trevor put the tray down on the table.

'Sorry to keep you waiting,' he said. 'I decided to make a fresh pot of tea. Also, I didn't know whether our visitor qualified for a cup and saucer, or a mug. I took a gamble on the cup and saucer.'

Peter smiled.

'Most people take one look at me and say: mug.'

Trevor took one look and decided: yes, they probably do. This man who thinks I'm the lodger smiles too much and combs his hair diagonally forward even though he isn't going bald. Pound to a penny he goes to a unisex hairdressers' called Peter, Paul and Mary.

'Whereas I take one look at you,' said Jill, 'and I say, what the hell are you doing here?'

'Found myself back in the North. I thought I'd come and say hello.'

'At one o'clock in the morning?'

'I telephoned earlier. Somebody told me you'd be in after midnight. Sounded like a young kid.'

'That was Yvonne.'

'I see.'

Trevor watched them. They were sparring edgily. He could imagine them having rows. He would intimidate this man with politeness. He handed Peter his cup of tea.

'Milk? Sugar?'

'Both, please.'

He handed Peter the milk and sugar with the old world courtesy of a tenth generation family retainer.

'We only stock brown sugar. It's better for your cholesterol levels and E numbers.'

'Still saving the Planet Earth, are we, dear?'

'It's the only one we've got,' said Jill.

You are unquestionably a mug to call her dear, thought Trevor. It could easily have been your first mistake.

Peter stirred his tea, thoughtfully.

'So who's this kid Yvonne who answered the phone?'

'Our baby-sitter,' said Trevor.

'Baby-sitter?'

'Bright kid. Used to run protection for 5C.'

'But she hasn't looked back since she was deported from Holland,' Jill added, as a supplementary testimonial to the standards of neighbourhood child-care. In reality, Peter's concern was much more basic: teetering on the edge of the primeval.

'If you've got a baby-sitter, that means . . . there must be a baby?'

'Without a baby, it's an expensive luxury,' said Trevor.

The ex-husband stared at Trevor: a long, slow gaze of the type patented by Humphrey Bogart in Hollywood *films noirs* of the 1940s. To achieve the full effect, he should have stared in black-and-white.

Peter began his question. 'And are you . . .?'

But was unable to finish it. At the factual level he simply needed confirmation that Trevor was father of the child. At the emotional level, he needed reassurance that it was all a terrible mistake, a clerical error, a genetic oversight. During the brief and turbulent years of their marriage, he and Jill had practised and perfected birth control so they could pursue respective careers in merchant adventuring and secondary education. At the time orginally pencilled-in for procreation, Jill had achieved the ultimate in birth control by throwing him out of the house. Now he had returned to the house, where lived a baby that should have been his.

Jill knew what was in Peter's mind. Of all the seed in all the loins in all the world, she had chosen Trevor's. Admittedly, it had been a mistake: an afternoon of careless rapture in the honeymoon suite of an Edinburgh hotel. They had not intended to go to Edinburgh, nor were they on their honeymoon; but the story so far was too convoluted. She took refuge in simplicity and truth.

'Yes,' she said, 'Trevor is the father of my child.'

'And Jill is the mother of my child,' said Trevor, moving a little closer to her, to avoid any misunderstanding about the parentage in question. Peter found himself confronted by what looked alarmingly like a happy couple.

'Are you married?'

'No,' said Trevor, 'we're probationary co-habs.'

'Significant others.'

'Spousal analogues.'

'Where did you learn that one?' said Jill.

'One of your feminist magazines. I was looking for the sports page.'

Peter realised these two shared an easy intimacy of a kind he had never experienced, either with Jill or any other woman. He wondered how it was done. Perhaps he should have read the feminist magazines at the proper time.

He relaxed into tea and small talk.

'So . . . how are you?'

'Fine,' said Jill. 'I'm a little tired but I get these occasional waves of exhaustion at one o'clock in the morning. Especially when I've had a full day's work at school, a return trip to the Lancashire border, a night out at the Village Vanguard and brief encounter with a couple of policemen.'

'Policemen?'

The word caused Peter a momentary twitch.

'We're under surveillance,' Trevor explained.

'Under surveillance? Why?'

'It's a secret. They're not allowed to tell us.'

Increasingly, Peter felt like an alien from outer space: adrift in downtown Albania without a phrasebook. His head was full of policemen, analogues and babies and they wouldn't keep still.

In the middle of a long yawn, Jill asked, 'By the way, which five-star hotel have you booked into for tonight?'

'I haven't. I was hoping . . .'

'There's nobody in the refugee room tonight,' said Trevor. 'There was, but we took him to the Lancashire border. That was before we went to the Village Vanguard.'

'You call it the refugee room?'

'Yes.'

'Still running a home for waifs and strays?'

'We have strolling vagabonds, too,' said Jill. 'There's no shortage.'

'Don't you mind?' Peter asked Trevor.

'I don't mind anything. Except injections and spiders. The last one was OK.'

'The last injection or the last spider?'

'The last refugee. He was from some place like Lithuania and he liked Bix Beiderbecke.'

'Who?'

Trevor and Jill slid into another well-oiled routine.

'Bix Beiderbecke. The first great white jazz musician.'

'Cornet player.'

'Drank himself to death.'

'His playing sounded like bullets from a bell,' said Jill, completing the ritual incantation.

Peter shook his head.

'Sorry. I've never been into jazz.'

Trevor shrugged.

'It isn't compulsory.'

Half an hour later, Trevor and Jill were reading in bed, cosily back to back, like bookends. It had become one of their most precious moments, a time for the soul to catch up, a time for the blues to slide from a minor into a major key, a time to anoint the scar tissue of the day with healing balm.

Trevor asked the inevitable question.

'Why did you marry a bloke like that?'

'May I tell you tomorrow? Or the day after? Or a week on Friday?'

'But he's never heard of Bix Beiderbecke.'

'Trevor. I realise that makes him a non-person. A total failure as a human being. A traitor to the Planet Earth.'

'True.'

'But may I remind you, *I* had never heard of Bix Beiderbecke until I met you.'

'But that's you, and you're different. You just needed somebody to explain jazz to you.'

'Trevor!'

He fell silent. He knew a firm whisper when he heard one.

'Have I to shut up?'

'Yes please. I've had a lot of excitement and I need five minutes of absolute peace. Read your football annual. There's a good boy.'

'It isn't a football annual.'

He held up the book for her inspection.

'Doctor Spock,' he said, proudly.

'My apologies.'

'I'm hoping he's going to explain how he got his pointed ears.'

Jill refused to be drawn into a surreal debate about ears. They settled back into their reading positions, Siamese bookends joined at the hip in parallel pursuits of wisdom. Within minutes, Doctor Spock and an old copy of *New Statesman* (incorporating *New Society*) sang them to their rest.

'Morning, miss. Morning, sir.'

'Morning, Yvonne,' said Jill, on her way from the kitchen to the dining room table where a pile of exercise books lay inert and unmarked.

'Morning, Yvonne,' said Trevor, on his way from the kitchen to the hallway with a slice of toast in his mouth.

'Oh, Yvonne,' said Jill, 'there'll be a strange man wandering about again.'

'Has Ivan come back?'
'Not yet.'
'Pity. I like Ivan.'
'This one's called Peter. He's my ex-husband.'
'Good. It'll be interesting to have a look at him. See what you got rid of.'
'Telephone.'
'Follow the wire, miss. I think it's in the kitchen.'
Jill and Trevor disapproved of cordless phones, symbolising as they did terminal yuppiedom and a giant step on the road to the destruction of the Universe. Instead, they had an ordinary phone on an extension lead long enough to exercise a pedigree greyhound. It was possible to use the phone in any part of the house, including the loft; it was equally possible to lose the phone in the same places, where it became buried under layers of life. The local telephone engineer who came to fix things whenever they gave way under the pressure of privatisation usually arrived with a consultant archaeologist.
By the time Jill had disinterred the phone, Trevor was in the living room, leafing truculently through the *Guardian*.
'They don't publish football results in this paper. They *hide* them. The sport should be on the back page. Everybody knows that.'
'It's summer, isn't it?' said Yvonne. 'There aren't any football results in summer.'
'Any football results will do. Even Australian. I've been keeping an eye on Wollongong.'
Yvonne swiftly changed the subject.
'So what do you think of him, sir?'
'Who?'
'The ex-husband?'
'I've seen better.'
They became aware of Peter standing in the doorway. He smiled, apparently oblivious to the verdict passed upon him.
'Good morning, everybody.'
'Morning,' said Trevor.
'And this must be the amazing Yvonne.'

'Yes. This is the amazing Yvonne,' said Yvonne.

'Where's Jill?'

'Kitchen.'

Peter went into the kitchen. Trevor looked at the amazing Yvonne.

'What do you think?'

'I agree with you, sir.'

Peter arrived in the kitchen in time to hear Jill say:

'I'd like to speak to Inspector Hobson, please. Swinburne. Jill Swinburne. I think you'll find he'll be very happy to speak to me.'

'Hi,' said Peter.

'Do you mind? As you can see, I am on the telephone and it is somewhat confidential.'

It was only twenty past eight but Hobson, as Jill had calculated, was at his desk, bright-eyed, on the case and well into his second floppy disc. He also gave the impression that he was happy to hear her voice. Perhaps he was.

'Mrs Swinburne! What a delightful surprise!'

He listened briefly, then smiled.

'Thank you very much, that's very kind. You heard about my PhD?'

Then he had second thoughts and frowned.

'*How* did you hear about my PhD?'

In the living room, Peter sought reassurance from Trevor. He should have known better.

'I couldn't help overhearing. Jill's on the phone to a guy called Inspector Hobson.'

'He's an old family friend.'

'Is that Inspector, as in police force?'

'Yes. We do a bit of informing on the side.'

'You do?'

'They don't pay very much, but it buys little luxuries like bread and milk and swaddling clothes. It all helps, teachers' salaries being what they are.'

'But Jill used to think the police were all fascist pigs.'
'She still thinks that. But Inspector Hobson is a special case.'
'And what do you think?'
'Me? I don't think. It drowns out the sound of the music.'

Driving to school in the little yellow van, Trevor was silent. Jill guessed the inner meaning of the silence.
'You don't like Peter very much, do you?'
'Not very much.'
'Because he's never heard of Bix?'
'More than that.'
'Tell me.'
'It's difficult to put into words.'
'Try. Come on. Get in touch with your true feelings.'
Trevor got in touch with his true feelings.
'I think he's a shifty bastard.'
Jill said nothing. It was hardly a spirited defence of her ex.

As soon as he had finished his telephone call with Jill, Inspector Hobson sent for Joe and Ben. His message was waiting when they arrived at the station soon after ten.
'Alas! Up before the Beak again,' said Joe.
'On the carpet.'
'Once more unto the fitted broadloom.'
'Put the cuffs on, Inspector, it's a fair cop, we'll come quietly.'
The detectives drank their morning coffee, scanned the office tabloids, then made their way to Hobson's office.
Hobson had decided to experiment with firmness.
'You disobeyed my orders!'
His men did not crumple under the weight and fury of his accusation. They had served their time under senior officers who were genuine, sixty-four carat, vindictive psychopaths. They would accept no imitations, least of all from the South of England, even with the garland of a PhD.
'What specific orders had you in mind, sir?' said Joe, gently implying: tell us where it hurts and we will kiss it better.

'The surveillance, dammit!'

'Ah.'

'What *were* my orders? Do you remember? Purely for the record and without reference to your notebooks?'

Ben snapped to attention.

'To maintain surveillance on Number 17, Hotspur Street, with specific reference to the people who live therein, specifically, Swinburne, Jill and Chaplin, Trevor, and specifying any journeys undertaken by same in the van, yellow, registered in the name of the said Chaplin, Trevor.'

'All of which we have done, sir, to the best of our ability,' Joe added. 'Our notebooks are available for inspection.'

'And *how* were you supposed to conduct your surveillance?'

It was a trickier question, but they gave it their best endeavours.

'In a manner befitting the best traditions of the force?' Joe suggested, leaving space for Ben to embellish:

'Bearing in mind a continuing need to gear our efforts to the changing context of the 1990s?'

Hobson broke in sharply. He could see the twenty-first century looming and it would be every inch as long as the real thing.

'The key word was discretion! Maintain surveillance with discretion!'

'Ah.'

'Ah.'

'Yet Mrs Swinburne telephoned me this morning. She is coming to see me at lunchtime and she is demanding a full explanation.'

Joe decided to spill the beans, though not all of them: a nominal amount, sufficient to nourish a negotiating position.

'Mrs Swinburne is a strong, brave and resourceful woman. She blew our cover, sir.'

'How did she blow your cover?'

'Would you like the short version or the long version, sir?'

It was an impossible question. It was meant to be. Hobson realised he was once more over a barrel. He still had no idea how it was done; but he knew, beyond all reasonable doubt, that if he looked down, he would see it: the barrel. The short version or the long version? A classic barrel.

'Make it the short version.'

'Over to you, partner,' said Joe.

Ben repeated his heel-clicking routine and reported.

'Sir. The short version is that Mrs Swinburne walked up to us, confronted us, face to face or, strictly speaking, face to faces, since there are two of us. She asked us two questions. Are you watching the house? Are you following us? And we felt, in the circumstances, we should tell the truth. It was, in our estimation, at the specific time in question, what you, sir, would have wished.'

Hobson thought: if this is the short version, thank God I didn't ask for the long version. Hobson said:

'You told the truth?'

'As I say, it was our interpretation of what we deemed would have been your response.'

'The truth.'

'Yes sir.'

'Yes sir.'

'It also happens to be our own chosen preference.'

Hobson frowned, seeking a toe-hold on one of the most glacial concepts of his career: that these two should have the remotest awareness of the existence of truth, let alone the will or the ability to put it into practice.

'You told Mrs Swinburne the truth,' he said, playing for time.

Joe nodded.

'As we've told you on many occasions before, sir, we are old-fashioned policemen. Boys in blue. Bobbies on the beat. Your friendly neighbourhood coppers. That's us.'

In case the Inspector was in any doubt about who they were, the detectives gave a few examples.

'We are George Dixon and Fabian of the Yard,' said Ben.

'We are Sherlock Holmes and Biggles,' said Joe.

'Sherlock Holmes and Biggles weren't policemen,' said Hobson.

'But they were men of honour, sir,' said Joe.

Hobson knew he was beaten. All he could remember about honour was that Falstaff had called it a mere scutcheon: not much use as a tool for debate and discipline, especially with these two. He dismissed the detectives, instructing them to resume their normal duties.

Over their second cup of coffee, Joe and Ben were, as usual, in total unanimity.

'Inspector Hobson is a well-meaning man.'

'Yes. He deserves better than us.'

Trevor Chaplin used a modified Shavian approach to the teaching of woodwork, inspired by the great man's dictum: he who can, does. He who cannot, teaches.

Trevor's version ran: those who can should be encouraged, and those who cannot should be kept away from anything sharper than a ruler as a security measure on behalf of their digits. In the former category was Gary, younger brother of a leading local Hell's Angel. Gary had a genuine flair for woodwork, probably inherited from his father, a celebrated housebreaker and famous for his neatness. He might well steal your worldly goods but he always left the place tidy. It was widely expected that Gary would inherit the family business.

As he strolled between the work-benches, Trevor's commentary echoed this approach: 5 per cent encouragement, 95 per cent prevention of bloodstains on the floor.

'Well done, Clint. If you keep improving you'll soon be right up there with the mediocrities . . . Gently does it, Elvis, that stuff took three hundred years to grow and you've destroyed it in five seconds . . . Don't worry about hitting your thumb, Jason, you'll find there's a spare one on your other hand.'

Trevor stopped.

Mr Wheeler was staring at him through the glazed upper panel of the Woodwork Room door. He looked like a model who had failed an audition for Franz Hals. You could hear the painter saying: I'm looking for a Laughing Cavalier – when I want a Surly Scholar, I'll let you know.

Trevor realised the headmaster wanted to speak to him: there was a slimy beckoning behind the eyes.

He turned to his class.

'I am going to speak to the headmaster in the corridor. If I'm not back in five minutes, start a small fire.'

Mr Wheeler checked that nobody was listening in the long, empty corridor. His academic gown was, according to Mr Carter, lined with paranoia.

'Mr Chaplin. I'll come straight to the point. Have you had any more thoughts about wood?'

'Thoughts about wood?' said Trevor, vaguely. The headmaster may have gone straight to the point, but it remained totally invisible.

'Yes. Thoughts about wood.'

'No more so than usual,' said Trevor, trying hard to think of thoughts about wood. 'I mean, I like wood. I like it very much. Wood has been very good to me. It's my bread and butter.'

'I do not mean wood in general. I mean wood in particular.'

'Some . . . special piece of wood?'

'The wood that arrived at the school yesterday. On a lorry. Driven by that peculiar man.'

'Charlie the gravedigger?'

'I have telephoned the office. They have no knowledge of the wood. Officially, we are not due for any supplies of wood until the middle of next term. So. What is your conclusion, Mr Chaplin?'

'Yesterday was our lucky day?'

It was the wrong answer but at least Trevor could see the point. In the world according to Wheeler, nothing could exist without a note from the office. In the beginning God created the heaven and the earth but he, too, must have had a note from the office.

'Where did that wood come from, Mr Chaplin?'

'Charlie's lorry.'

'And before that?'

'No idea.'

'Mr Chaplin. It is essential to the smooth running of the school that I know where that wood came from. Would you please speak to your friend, the gravedigger, and clarify the situation?'

'If I see him. I don't get down the cemetery all that often but . . .'

The five minutes were up. The Woodwork Room door opened and Gary stepped into the corridor, bristling with youthful urgency.

'Please sir, Mr Chaplin, sir, can you come quick, sir, we think Jimmy Dickenson's cut his arm off, Mr Chaplin, please, sir.'

'Would you excuse me, Mr Wheeler?'

'Yes. But remember what I said. I need a full explanation. On paper!'

The headmaster and his gown swirled away down the corridor, as if propelled by a wind of self-righteous indignation.

Life was altogether calmer in the Woodwork Room.

'All right,' said Trevor. 'Hands up the boy who's cut his arm off.'

'Nobody has really, sir,' said Gary. 'We just reckoned you'd had enough of old fartface.'

'You shouldn't really call the headmaster fartface. Should you?'

It was not a rhetorical question. Trevor needed a second opinion. Gary provided it.

'We only do it behind his back, sir.'

'Well, that's probably all right. As long as you do it with respect.'

Trevor sat in the San Quentin dining hall, contemplating his meal. He had chosen Today's Special: its components were the left-over bits of Yesterday's Special, blended with artificial colouring additives, spiced with twenty-four matters arising from previous meals and baked in a pie. Trevor prodded the crust with his fork. It felt ten times thicker than the earth's, but was less fragrant.

'May I sit with you and, as is our long-standing tradition, kindle my desires?' said Mr Carter, approaching Trevor's table.

'Mrs Swinburne isn't here but why don't you sit down anyway, and see how you get on?'

'The bi-focals, Mr Chaplin, the bi-focals.'

Mr Carter adjusted his spectacles and sat down.

'In the absence of Mrs Swinburne, I shall place my erotic fantasies on a low light.'

'Probably the best place for them.'

They stared in awe at Mr Carter's plate. It bore a small mound of grey substance which quivered when wafted.

'Does it have a name?' said Trevor.

'I ordered loaves and fishes, but apparently they arrived without the instruction manual. This appears to be a chemical theory that doesn't work in practice.'

'Just another day.'

They poked the food around their plates in a mood of gentle inquiry and exploration, being careful not to eat any of it.

'Comfort me with trivial gossip, Mr Chaplin. Yesterday, you went to the bowling green in connection with Ivan the refugee. That is what I was told.'

'It's all true.'

'Do I infer that today, Mrs Swinburne has also gone to the bowling green in connection with Ivan the refugee?'

'No. That's all sorted out.'

'Excellent. I do worry so much about the refugee problem.'

'Ivan's safely over the border in Lancashire. We've got Peter staying with us instead.'

'Peter?'

'Yes.'

'Who is Peter? What is he? Another refugee?'

'No. Mrs Swinburne's ex-husband.'

Mr Carter adjusted his bi-focals, switching focus from his food to Trevor.

'Don't tell me. Let me guess. Mrs Swinburne has gone to have in-depth discussions with her ex-husband? Talking things through? The state of his desires, perhaps?'

'No. She's gone to the police station.'

'Does that relate to Peter, the ex-husband? Or to Ivan the refugee?'

'Nothing to do with either of them. She's gone to find out why the police have been watching the house.'

'The police have been watching your house?'

'I think they call it a twenty-four-hour surveillance in the trade.'

'But why?'

'She's gone to find out. She'll ask them. They'll tell her.'

Mr Carter pushed his plate away and out of his life. He took out a handkerchief and cleaned his spectacles.

'Do you realise, Mr Chaplin, that cleaning my bi-focals is likely to be the most exciting event of my day? Why are my days, compared with yours, so unspeakably tedious and boring?'

'It's probably because you're not in touch with your true feelings. Or the opposite. It can work both ways.'

Jill parked the yellow van outside Sherlock Road Police Station in a space marked ACC. She assumed the letters stood for Assistant Chief Constable. If challenged, her defence plea would be that she thought the letters stood for Anyone Concerned with Children. She would, if provoked, flutter her eyelashes like a helpless woman. Though an ardent feminist, she could play dirty if need be.

It was a new building. The design consultants had left their fingerprints all over it. Blue lamps and Victorian porticos were out. Corporate imagery had crawled everywhere. It looked like the last defiant gesture of a bankrupt airline.

Joe and Ben stood either side of the doorway, like a pair of caryatids, but less animated. They flickered into life when they saw Jill.

'Mrs Swinburne!' said Joe. 'How are you this bright new morning?'

'It is not morning. It is lunchtime. I am here. I would rather not be here. I would rather be at school, such as it is.'

'You would rather be at San Quentin High?'

'But it's lunchtime,' said Ben. 'We hear alarming tales about the school meals. Words like foot and mouth, dysentery, cholera.'

'That's all part of the master plan at Whitehall. A vital element in the National Curriculum. Kill off some of the kids, there might be enough books to go round.'

'You're short of books?'

'You're short of books?'

The replies came simultaneously from either side of the doorway. The effect was oddly stereophonic.

'Yes. We are short of books. We are short of everything. Books, pens, pencils, windows, goalposts, running water and oxygen. But who am I to argue with the master plan? Now, if you will excuse me, I have an appointment with Inspector Hobson, who is going to assist me with my inquiries.'

The door was marked PULL. She pushed it. It opened. She had guessed right. She left the detectives in the doorway, pondering their brief encounter. They were dedicated ponderers.

'They are short of books,' said Joe.

'Let them eat cake.'

'I am speaking as an investigating officer. Twice in the past week we have proceeded with all haste to the scene of a crime. In both cases, the relevant felony was the theft of books.'

'As I recall, both volumes of the *Alphabetical Guide to Sexual Behaviour* and *Tess of the D'Urbervilles*.'

'Precisely.'

'But it's a nice day. The sun is shining in a clear blue sky. Why don't we just live and let live?'

They resumed pondering mode: should their day be one of investigation or contemplation? Choices – all the time choices.

'I have a sneaking fancy for a spot of community policing,' said Ben. 'Call me sentimental if you like but . . .'

'Burger, kebab, pizza or the chippy?'

'Do sit down, Mrs Swinburne,' said Hobson.

The shiny black leather chair was two sizes too big for her and had a tendency to swivel in several different orbits at the same time. If you shuffled, it made rude noises.

'You seem to have done very well for yourself, Inspector.'

'One can't complain.'

'A PhD. Nice big office. Your own computer terminal. As many floppy discs as you can eat.'

'We can only combat the crime wave by using modern technology at its most sophisticated.'

'Like posting a couple of dummies outside my house for a whole day?'

Hobson leaned forward, picked up a pencil and reached for a note-pad.

'You see them as dummies, Mrs Swinburne?'

'Approximately, yes.'

'How fascinating. I can't decide whether they are very bright men pretending to be stupid, or very stupid men pretending to be bright.'

'Have you considered bone idle?'

'Bone idle?'

He made a note on his pad.

'Thank you, Mrs Swinburne.'

'So why were these two stupid, bright, bone idle policemen watching my house?'

'I've known you a long time, Mrs Swinburne, so I will tell you the truth.'

'Does that imply that if you'd only known me a short time, you would tell me lies?'

'Of course not.'

There was a hint of petulance in Hobson's reaction. The lower lip trembled. The twelve-year-old boy peeped over the parapet. What's more, he knew his lollipops were in jeopardy.

'Let's try again, Inspector. Remember I teach English. I believe we should use the language with accuracy and precision.

I know you think so too. I'll ask you again. Why were those men watching my house?'

Hobson took a deep breath and reached out for the maturity appropriate to his rank.

'We were given information about your house.'

'Don't tell me. Let me guess. Anonymous information?'

'There was . . . a degree of anonymity.'

'The unfrocked bank manager across the street.'

'I'm not in a position to say.'

'It wasn't a question. It was a statement. He sits in his window watching all the neighbours, but especially Trevor and me. The milkman says he's got a video-camera. Is that right?'

'A video-camera?' said Hobson, with an air of innocence suggesting he had never heard the words video or camera and was only on nodding terms with the indefinite article. As far as Jill was concerned, it was a guilty plea, with no mitigating circumstances.

'Is that it? He's been zooming in on all our most intimate moments and he's sent you a copy? True or false, Inspector? We've known each other a long time, so you will tell me the truth.'

'All right.'

The protective layers of the inspectorate lay shredded at his feet. He was twelve years old but doing his best to be brave, and a credit to his parents.

Jill resisted the temptation to say, there, there.

'Tell me all about it,' she said.

Hobson resisted the temptation to call her Mummy, and told her all about it.

'We were sent an anonymous video-cassette. Technically it was not of a very high quality, but I was able to identify Mr Chaplin's yellow van. It showed, that's to say it appeared to show . . .'

He hesitated, like an apprentice jockey seeing Beecher's Brook ahead of him on the course. Jill gave him a helping hand.

'It appeared to show . . .?'

'It appeared to show a number of young girls going to your house. And a number of middle-aged men.'

'I can explain all that. The young girls came to the house because I was interviewing prospective au pair girls. The middle-aged men came to the house because Mr Chaplin and I have reached a degree of maturity and we have many friends who have also reached a degree of maturity.'

She thought: Big Al? Little Norm? Ivan the refugee? Peter the ex-husband. A degree of maturity? With luck, Hobson wouldn't probe too deeply on the subject.

In the event, the pale suggestion of a smile appeared on the Inspector's face.

'You were interviewing au pair girls?'

'Yes. Except that sounds a bit twee. We needed a child-minder.'

'You have a child?'

'Yes. The generation yet unborn has been born. The Swinburne-Chaplin line will continue. Not only that, our baby is forty-nine millionth in line of succession to the throne.'

'My congratulations. To you both. To all three.'

'Thank you.'

Hobson's smile was now broad and apparently genuine. Jill noticed his teeth had been capped, probably to match the decor in the room.

It was time to remove the smile.

'What did you *think* was going on, Inspector?'

'I had no preconceptions, Mrs Swinburne.'

'Young girls? Middle-aged men? What was your theory? Did you think I was running a disorderly house? We've known each other a long time. Do you really see me as the madam of a high-class brothel? Or a low-class brothel? Or even, God forbid, a middle-class brothel?'

Hobson remained silent. Now he was six years old. His parents had never told him about brothels.

Jill zapped up the decibels, as she used to with 5C, in their primitive heyday.

'You're not supposed to sit there and think about it! You're supposed to say: No, of course I didn't think you were running a brothel, Mrs Swinburne.'

'Of course I didn't think you were running a brothel, Mrs Swinburne.'

'Therefore, the whole business is a total nonsense and my house will no longer be under surveillance.'

'I have already given orders to that effect.'

'Good.'

It was game, set and match to Swinburne. They had both known it would end this way. It always did. Now it was time for a morsel of plaintive justification.

'It isn't easy sitting behind this desk, Mrs Swinburne.'

'You should try sitting behind mine. You've got a computer. I haven't even got a power point.'

'And yet . . .'

'And yet . . .?'

'I have an impeccable career record and academic credentials without parallel in the history of the force. I have confidential information at my fingertips. I have men and women at my command, who will obey orders without question. I have legal status and the backing of the judiciary. But one thing defeats me.'

'Something in your childhood perhaps.'

'Nothing to do with my childhood.'

'Whatever it is, you must feel free to confess it, Inspector.'

'The dark, impenetrable, tantalising mystery. The psychology of . . . Yorkshire!'

She could not help him. Nobody could help him. It was time to go back to school. She let herself out of the office quietly.

As Jill crossed the entrance lobby she heard Hobson's voice calling after her.

'Mrs Swinburne! Before you go . . .'

The Inspector caught up with her, and held out his hand.

'I'd like to give you this.'

Jill examined this. It was a five pound note.

'What is it? A deposit on some perversions in a gymslip?'

'Will you use it to buy a present for your child?'

She took the money.

'Thank you, Inspector. Please forgive my unworthy thought. I knew not what I was doing.'

Though a cheerful and guiltless atheist, she still found a slice of Authorised Version a useful ploy in an emergency.

'To know you is to forgive you, Mrs Swinburne.'

Next stop red roses and a Barry Manilow LP, thought Jill. There was a door marked PUSH. She pulled it open and left.

8

A Horse for My Kingdom

As a driver, Jill was of the slow-and-steady school, as was the little yellow van. With the aid of ten-star, lead-free petrol and a following hurricane, it occasionally aspired to thirty-five miles per hour, falling short by a furlong or so. Pedestrians and the ozone layer could breathe easily when the van was on the road.

Even so, the strange lorry was a nuisance. It should have been a comfortable ten-minute drive from the police station to San Quentin High, and it was, until Jill got stuck behind the lorry. It seemed to know in advance which way she was going: left at Wilkinson Road, right at Eccles Street, left at Crosland Avenue, right at Baker's Way. The names reflected the ebb and flow of political fortune in the Nation; most of the streets were drab, and achieving greater drabness by the minute.

The lorry was trundling along at a steady fifteen miles an hour, but compensated for its sloth by vast emissions of noise and fumes. Since there was nothing else to look at, Jill looked at it. It was heavily laden with boxes and strange devices, banners and flags. It looked like a life-size Battle of Agincourt self-assembly kit. Wasn't there a mob called the Sealed Knot, thought Jill, who fought battles for charity at weekends? Maybe they operated in midweek too, as therapy for shift-workers and Chinese waiters? Was this a battle in search of a field?

The lorry turned in at the entrance to San Quentin High. Jill kept her distance in the van, to avoid the smoke.

Occasional sparks flew where the lorry's rear end dragged along the tarmac. Combustion was a real possibility. In the midst of the smoke, sound and fury, a man's voice was singing 'Stranger In Paradise' in a bold, baritone voice.

Jill parked the van and watched as the lorry pulled up outside the school's main entrance. Elderly trucks, like Rolls Royces, park where they damn well please. She saw Mr Wheeler engage in conversation with the driver. He matched Trevor's description of Charlie, singer of songs, digger of graves, driver of lorries.

'What is all this?' said the headmaster.

Charlie climbed down from the cab and contemplated his load.

'Well, sunbeam, at a casual glance, it looks to me like there's some footballs, some hockey sticks, some boxes of books, some flags and a horse.'

'A horse?'

'Yes. A horse.'

Wheeler peered at the lorry, in search of a horse.

'I see no horse.'

'Not a proper horse with hooves on its legs. A vaulting horse. You use them for vaulting over. In gymnastics. Like that little Russian lass, in the Olympics. Olga wotsit.'

'And the flags?'

'Aye, them's flags all right.'

'But what are they for?'

'Corner flags for football. You stick them in the ground where the white lines meet. No kicking allowed, outside of the white lines.'

Jill walked slowly and quietly towards the school. The headmaster had his back to her. It was her preferred configuration.

'Do you have a list of these items?' said Mr Wheeler.

'Certainly, I've got a list, petal. There's some footballs, some hockey sticks, some books, some flags, a horse . . .'

The headmaster interrupted, sharply.

'May I see the list?'

'Course you can't. It's in my head. I learnt it. By heart. Mentally.'

'Mrs Swinburne!'

Jill had almost made it through the main door, but the headmaster had spotted her through his rear view antennae.

'Mr Wheeler?'

'I require Mr Chaplin!'

Trevor was in the staffroom, playing darts on his own. He often filled the space between lunch and woodwork practising a 149 finish – treble 20, treble 19, double 16. It was a small, personal obsession and harmed nobody.

'Trevor. Mr Wheeler requires you.'

'Tough.'

'Immediately, he requires you.'

'What for?'

'He probably wants to kindle his desires,' said Mr Carter, from a deep sleep in an armchair that wore its upholstery on the outside.

'He's just like all the others,' said Trevor.

By the time Jill and Trevor reached the main entrance a small crowd had gathered. The kids always enjoyed seeing their headmaster disconcerted; total public humiliation was even better. They watched and hoped.

'Now then, sunshine. How you doing?' said Charlie, seeing Trevor.

'Can't grumble. What's the problem?'

'Me, I can't see no problem, myself, personally. All I can see is some footballs, some hockey sticks, some books . . .'

'Books?' said Jill.

'And a horse.'

'A horse?' said Trevor.

'A vaulting horse. You use them for vaulting over. In gymnastics like that little Russian lass. Olga wotsit.'

'Korbut,' said Trevor.

'Wasn't that *The Two Ronnies*? Used to enjoy that, me. *The Two Ronnies*. Tell you another programme I liked. *The Ascent of Man*. Right good programme, that was. Made you think deep thoughts, if you get my meaning. Dead philosophical it was.'

'Did you ever see *Jazz 625*?' said Trevor.

'Mr Chaplin!'

'Yes, Mr Wheeler?'

'This is not a forum for television criticism. This is a lorry, laden with mystery. I require an explanation.'

'It's none of my business,' said Trevor. 'Most of it's PE equipment. That's not my department. That's Mr Bickerstaffe.'

'I am aware of that.'

'And he's not here. I think it's his day at the clinic.'

'Is Bickerstaffe the nutter?' asked Charlie.

'Mr Bickerstaffe has been under considerable professional and domestic stress,' said Mr Wheeler, defensively.

'I've got nothing against nutters, sunbeam. Me, I've had some really good times with nutters.'

Jill peered into one of a dozen cardboard boxes stacked on the lorry.

'What sort of books have you brought?'

'You name it, petal, we've got it.'

Charlie opened one of the boxes and held up a hand full of samples.

'We've got *Hamlet, Prince of Denmark*. *Julius Caesar, Prince of Rome*. *King Lear, Prince of Darkness*. *Two Gentlemen of Verona*. *Three Sisters*.'

'*Tess of the D'Urbervilles*?'

'Oh aye, we've got a whole stack of *Tesses*. You'll find them in that box marked "A Pure Woman".'

'Thank you. That's excellent,' said Jill, checking the contents of the box.

'This is not excellent!' said Mr Wheeler.

'I keep bringing you all this educational gear. It's got to be fairly good, hasn't it?'

'But where is it all coming from?'

'Don't ask me, flower. I'm just doing a favour for a friend.'

'And I am not a flower!'

The headmaster's gown flared like a lowdown umbrella as he wheeled to face Jill and Trevor. Staffroom wisdom had long ago determined that as his central problem: he was a Wheeler but no sort of dealer.

'Mr Chaplin. Mrs Swinburne. Shall I tell you what is in my mind?'

'If you think it would be helpful,' said Jill.

'I believe this could be stolen property.'

'Where would you go to steal a vaulting horse?' said Trevor, reflectively. It was an interesting metaphysical problem.

'Do you have any evidence that this is stolen property?' asked Jill.

'I have the evidence of my own senses. I have spoken to the office several times. We are not due to receive any supplies of books, PE equipment or wood in the foreseeable future. Yet supplies of such equipment continue to arrive. Let me put this question to you directly, Mr Chaplin. How would you feel about teaching woodwork, knowing the wood to be stolen?'

'It doesn't strike me as much of a problem.'

'It doesn't?'

'No.'

Charlie intervened.

'And while we're on the subject, petal, I am not a thief. I am but a humble gravedigger helping out.'

'I am not casting aspersions on you, personally.'

Charlie moved a step nearer to Mr Wheeler.

'I wouldn't advise it, son, on account of I have been known to punch people, personally, when provoked by aspersions.'

The headmaster edged away, in the direction of Trevor and Jill.

'My concern is purely and simply the morality of my staff.'

'If it's a moral question,' said Jill, 'I would like to say, on behalf of Mr Chaplin and myself . . .'

Trevor interrupted her.

'I'll speak on behalf of Mr Chaplin.'

It was his first interruption in the history of their relationship. It was a moment for the annals. And it was his turn to wheel. He turned on the headmaster.

'I'll tell you this, Mr Wheeler. It's a lot easier teaching woodwork with wood than without it. If you don't believe me, try it.'

'I am not unsympathetic . . .'

'I don't want sympathy. I want wood.'

'I do see your point of view . . .'

'And I'll tell you something else for nothing. I am now a father. I have a child. And if the only way I could give my child a decent education was to steal . . . there'd be no messing about. I'd go ahead and steal!'

Trevor's speech was received in silence, followed by applause, followed by cheers from the now large crowd in the playground, from staff and students looking out of windows, from local voters attracted by the possibility of a fight. It was a memorable ovation. Sir Leonard Hutton or Sir Laurence Olivier would have relished it, and asked for the supplier's name and address.

Jill was proud of him.

In the van, on the way home, she said so.

'That was a wonderful performance, Trevor.'

'What was?'

Trevor was already planning ahead: a walk to the park, a bedtime story, a Thelonious Monk tape to listen to while he prepared the evening's soup.

'I will steal for the sake of my child's education. It was terrific.'

'That wasn't a performance. That was true. I was in touch with my feelings, like you taught me.'

'All the same. I was still very proud of you, Trevor.'

'Knock it off.'

Trevor shuffled, and changed the subject.

'How did you get on at the cop shop?'

'Inspector Hobson has already called off the dogs.'

'How is he?'

'The same.'

Trevor shrugged. That was OK. He was wary of change. He had never forgiven Miles Davis for going electronic. He glanced in the driving mirror. Nobody was following them, apart from the early contenders of the rush hour.

'Good,' he said. 'All we have to do now is kick your ex-husband out of the house and then we can get back to . . .'

'Abnormal?' suggested Jill.

'That'll do nicely.'

Trevor and First-Born chatted as they meandered through the park on their way to the bowling green.

'I made a speech on your behalf today, son,' said Trevor.

'Is that right?' gurgled First-Born.

'Told them I would steal to give you a good education.'

'That's really cool, Dad.'

'Got a round of applause. Just like at the end of a Johnny Hodges solo. The audience clapped and cheered.'

'Man, you must have been really steaming.'

Trevor smiled. He understood every nuance of First-Born's gurgling. He was delighted to have his son's approval. One or two passing dog-walkers, hearing the conversation, looked a little perplexed, but no more than that. People who take babies and dogs for walks in the park know it as the best short cut to dreamtime. One day Trevor had seen a small, bald man having an animated discussion about the future of the British Film Industry with his Irish setter.

Big Al and Little Norm were playing bowls.

'Mr Chaplin must have been buying cornflakes again,' said Norm.

'That's a bit oblique, Norm. I would suggest he is merely taking his child for a walk.'

'The last time we saw him with his pram, it was full of cornflakes.'

'You have a remarkable memory for the trivial, Norm. You must be very good at that esoteric game.'

'What game?'

Big Al ignored the question and greeted Trevor with customary zeal as he parked the pram beside the bowling green to give First-Born a good view of the games in progress.

'Now then, Trev. How's the good earth treating you?'

'Fine, thanks. And you?'

'Me? I'm an oasis of tranquillity. I can't speak for my brother.'

'We're in the middle of a game,' said Norm, as Al sat down beside Trevor on an elderly wooden bench, erected in 1932 in memory of an alderman whose name had worn off.

'We have played part of our game, Norm. We will sit here and converse with our friend and comrade, Trev. We will then play the other part of our game. Thus, everything will be made whole.'

Trevor and, more abundantly, Big Al, already occupied most of the bench. Norm perched uneasily on one end, with two-thirds of a buttock left over.

Al turned to Trevor.

'Now. Does your very welcome presence here today indicate that you wanted to see me?'

'Yes. Couple of things I need to clear up.'

'Fine. But before we get on to that . . . has everything arrived?'

'Everything?'

'Wood, footballs, hockey sticks, corner flags, a selection of fine literature and a horse.'

'Yes. They've all arrived.'

'Which being so, secondary education can resume normal transmission.'

Trevor nodded. It was as suspected. Indeed, it was more or less a ground rule in the moonstruck outer limits. Whenever the inexplicable happened, the explanation lay in two short words: Big Al.

'If there's anything else you need, just let it be known,' he said.

'We can get most things,' said Norm.

'The education of our children is a sacred responsibility. It cannot be entrusted to time-serving politicians. Especially those whose social judgement and emotional development have been permanently warped by the public school system.'

It sounded like Al's last word on the subject, though much of what he said sounded like last words: terminal judgements nested in every syllable.

'Education isn't the problem,' said Trevor. 'Mr Wheeler is the problem.'

'I've met Mr Wheeler. Not one of the world's great headmasters, I'd say, at a cursory glance.'

'Agreed.'

'But Mr Wheeler is nevertheless giving cause for anxiety?'

'He thinks, because none of the stuff's come through the office, he's got it into his head it must be stolen.'

Big Al and Little Norm were shocked by the suggestion.

'Stolen?' said Al.

'Knocked off?'

'As in breaking and entering?'

'Yes.'

'How do you go about nicking a vaulting horse?' said Little Norm. 'I wouldn't know where to pick it up.'

'In addition to which, it would not fit under your coat, Norm. Nor would it fit under mine, and it is no mean coat, as anyone will tell you. A formidable garment.'

Al frowned. He was clearly upset by the slur on his integrity and his coat.

'Is your headmaster aware that stealing is a criminal offence?'

'Yes. I think that's why he's worried.'

'Doing criminal offences is an extremely reckless form of behaviour, Trevor. I am not a reckless man, as all three of us know.'

'Should I tell him that? Big Al is not a reckless man?'

'Would it keep him happy?'

'Nothing would keep Mr Wheeler happy.'

'All right. Noted. Happiness is out of the question. Should

we therefore try to keep him at bay? Should that be our aim? At bay? So you and your colleagues can get on with your primary task of educating the young?'

'Keep him at bay. I like the sound of that.'

'Paperwork. Is that the answer?'

'Documents,' said Trevor. 'Things in triplicate that he can sign.'

'We need invoices and chits, Norm.'

'And receipts?'

'Yes, Norm, receipts as well.'

'And affidavits? We can do affidavits.'

'Affidavits will not be necessary, Norm. Invoices, chits and receipts will suffice.'

Big Al stood up.

'We will now complete our game of bowls.'

As he and Trevor were leaving the park, First-Born said:

'Wow! Big Al sure is some kind of dude. A cat of infinite zest, right?'

'Right on, babe,' said Trevor.

While Trevor and his son were at the park, Jill settled down to mark thirty-eight essays on *Tess of the D'Urbervilles*. The text she had given the class ran:

'There are two men in Tess's life: Alec D'Urberville and Angel Clare. Both are male chauvinist wimps. Write two sides of your exercise book examining their maleness (if any), their chauvinism, and their wimpishness. Compare them with other male chauvinist wimps you have read about, eg Hamlet, Nicholas Nickleby, Mister Toad, Jim Dixon, Mowgli, Sherlock Holmes, Pooh Bear, Jimmy Porter or any male character from Evelyn Waugh. Do *not* write about members of your family. Yet. I'll tell you when.'

She opened Sharon's book. Her essay began:

'Rarely, if ever, in the history of Western European Literature, has a novel been dominated by such a right pair of shits.'

Jill put a tick in the margin. Sharon was getting the idea.

'Tea,' said Peter, emerging from the kitchen with a tray.

'Just like old times.'

They sipped their tea, remembering the old times, when she would do her marking and he would make tea, on the rare occasions he was home, instead of out and about, making deals. The tea generally turned out as lousy as the deals.

Jill sipped her tea. It was still lousy.

'Some things don't change. You still can't make tea.'

'And you're still collecting lame ducks.'

'It takes one to know one.'

Then she reflected: which lame duck did he mean? There had been plenty. She always responded to a quack for help.

'You don't mean Trevor, do you?'

'Certainly, I mean Trevor.'

'Don't be fooled. He might have been a lame duck once upon a time but he can walk unaided nearly all the time now. Sometimes breaks into a run.'

'I'll take your word.'

'You'd better.'

Again they fell silent, aware of the ghosts around them: a marriage that had seemed a good idea when they were aged two score years between them, and a hollow parody a decade later. They were a handsome couple in the wedding photographs, but the album was made of cheap cardboard.

'Why did you come here?' said Jill.

'I told you. I was in the area. I thought it would be nice to see you. Would you believe me if I said . . . I wanted to know you were all right?'

'No. I wouldn't believe that.'

'What would you believe?'

'I naturally assumed you wanted to borrow some money.'

Peter said nothing.

'Good. That's settled,' said Jill.

'It isn't just the money.'

'You want to borrow the van as well?'

'Can't you give me the benefit of the doubt?'

'Too many doubts, Peter. I ran out of benefits years ago.'

She remembered the benefits that never accrued, the doubts

that accumulated: the greetings card business that would fill the world with love at popular prices; the garden centre that would transform the environment with interest free credit; the solar heating system that would guarantee warmth to the shivering multitudes of the planet, or your money back.

'We're not talking about a *lot* of money,' said Peter.

'We're not talking about money at all. Not until Trevor's home.'

'What's it got to do with him?'

'We don't have secrets from each other.'

'If you want to lend me some money, you need his permission? Don't give me that. You're supposed to be emancipated.'

'I'm an emancipated mother. Trevor's an emancipated father. Between the two of us and First-Born, we could easily be mistaken for an emancipated family.'

They had argued themselves into a cul-de-sac that Jill knew by heart. Peter believed the phrase emancipated woman equalled selfish cow. Jill believed the opposite. She had wasted several years trying to explain why.

At the beginning, she had hoped for better things. Peter the twenty-year-old had proclaimed an attractive and charming independent spirit. He had a good line concerning his life-style.

'It is the proper condition of mankind to be self-employed.'

Jill, who hated the global mega-corporations who were ruining the planet, found it an attractive proposition. It was only later she discovered first, that Peter had stolen the line from a television interview with a Tyneside writer and second, that he couldn't actually do anything. He was energy in search of a natural gift, and natural gifts had he none. Inevitably, he dealt himself into the small-scale capitalist hyena game. The problem was the other players: genuine hyenas with good overdraft facilities and several generations of blood-lust behind them. By comparison, Peter was a stuffed teddy bear.

And even now, with frayed paws and a missing ear, the teddy bear was coming back for more. His resilience had nobility of a kind; but not enough to make her sign a cheque.

'I don't fancy my chances,' he said.

'Neither do I.'

They had talked it through. Money was no longer on the agenda. But the talking was not finished. Teddy bears are not exempt from jealousy; it runs deeper and stronger than avarice, even in the softest of toys.

It was Trevor's turn for the bedtime story.

'Are you lying comfortably?'

'Cool and laidback, Dad. Hit me with the soothing anecdotes,' cooed First-Born.

'Then I'll begin. Once upon a time, in a town in America called Davenport, Iowa, there lived a little boy. His name was Leon. Leon Bismarck Beiderbecke. That's a funny name, isn't it?'

'Crazy,' said First-Born.

'That's why we're taking our time giving you a name. There are more wrong names than right names, and you'll tell us soon enough what your right name is.'

'I'm working on it.'

'Well, the people in Davenport, Iowa, figured it was a crazy sort of name so they didn't call the little boy Leon. And they didn't call him Bismarck. They called him Bix.'

'Not a bad name. It could be a contender.'

'When Bix was fifteen, his brother Charles bought a gramophone and some records. That's how young Bix first heard jazz. It was a record by the Original Dixieland Jazz Band and it was the most exciting thing Bix had ever heard in his life.'

Downstairs in the living room, Peter was listening to the story on Big Al's intercom.

'Do you ever listen to this stuff?' he asked Jill, who was setting the table.

'What stuff?'

'Your significant wotsit telling his bedtime stories. Listen.'

They heard Trevor's voice, enlarged and distorted by the intervening technology.

'Now the Original Dixieland Jazz Band had a cornet player

called Nick LaRocca. Bix listened to him and said: that's what I want to do.'

Jill switched off the intercom at the switch marked SWITCH.

'Why did you do that?'

'It's private.'

'It's potty.'

'If we don't share our passions with our children, how will they ever learn to be passionate?'

'Do you tell him bedtime stories as well?'

'Naturally. Alternate nights.'

'Great women of our time.'

'Yes. Emma Goldman and Sylvia Pankhurst and Billie Holiday. As a matter of fact, Trevor told *me* the Billie Holiday story so I could pass it on.'

'It's the looniest thing I ever heard.'

'Peter. If, God help us, you ever had a child, what would your bedtime stories be about? Bright young men looking for the pavements made of gold?'

'No longer bright. No longer young. And fading in the straight,' said Peter.

He looked at the silent intercom.

'But all the same . . .'

'All the same what?' said Jill.

This was it: green-eyed monster time. She was ready for it. She had spotted it when it was still around the corner.

'I never thought I'd find you shacked up with somebody like him.'

'Tell me. What is so unremarkable about Trevor?'

'Well, for a start, he dresses like a closing-down sale at the Oxfam shop.'

'Yes. That's true.'

'And he's a woodwork teacher.'

'So?'

'A bit boring, isn't it? It even sounds boring. Woodwork teacher. Not many woodwork teachers make history.'

'Name one war that was started by a woodwork teacher.'

Peter realised he would get nowhere once politics had been introduced to the debate. He changed tack.

'And I can't imagine him being sensational in bed.'

'He's funny. Which is more than you ever were.'

'So that's the big secret? Sexually, he's a barrel of laughs?'

Had the intercom not been switched off, Peter and Jill would have realised that Trevor had finished his bedtime story. He was now sitting at the foot of the stairs, listening to an intimate discussion about himself. He had considered coughing loudly and bursting into the room; but he was only human and though a modest and reticent man, the subject of Trevor Chaplin could be fairly interesting, as long as it didn't go on for too long. So he listened to Jill.

'I'll tell you the big secret. You won't know what the hell I'm talking about but I'll tell you anyway. I like to watch crappy old black-and-white movies on the telly. Trevor doesn't. So he'll read a football annual or sit with his headphones on listening to Bix or Duke or Bird.'

'Bird?'

'Charlie Parker. Don't you know anything?'

That's my woman, thought Trevor: you listen when I talk. And you remember at least half of what I say. Nobody ever did that before. You are very beautiful, very gracious, very talented and I do love you madly.

Peter was less beguiled.

'OK. So he's listening to that weird music and you're watching a crappy old movie. What happens next? What's the big deal that makes him into Superman?'

'It's very simple. Some of the movies make me cry. When the dog doesn't come home. Or the hero walks into the sea. Or the telegram arrives and the woman says to the telegram boy . . . I'm sorry, there's no answer. At that moment, I reach out and Trevor is already handing me a kleenex. He knows, five seconds ahead of the moment, when I need to cry. That, I have to tell you, is the most precious gift known to humanity.'

Even Trevor was impressed. He almost reached for a kleenex.

'Is that where I went wrong?' said Peter.

'What?'

'Sluggish with the paper hankies?'

'Start with that and work outwards. You might emancipate yourself. You might turn into a proper man.'

'A proper man? Like Trevor?'

'Like Trevor.'

Trevor's modesty wilted under the strain. He stood up, coughed loudly and went into the living room.

'Oh, good, you've set the table.'

'Yes. Everything's ready.'

'Wine in the fridge?'

'Yes.'

Trevor explained to Peter:

'We always have wine on a Friday night. To celebrate Friday night.'

He called to them from the kitchen.

'The casserole smells great. I need five minutes to fiddle with my soup and then we'll be under orders.'

As they sat down to eat, Jill outlined the system to Peter: 'Trevor does the starter, I do the main course and we draw straws for the pudding. On alternate nights.'

'And sometimes we do the opposite,' added Trevor by way of clarification.

'Unless we're on a crash diet.'

'Or a health kick. Have you ever tried fibre and metabolism?'

'I can't say that I have,' said Peter.

'Works like a charm. You'll never want to eat again.'

Peter looked down at his soup bowl.

'Am I allowed to ask what this is?'

'Iced cucumber.'

'Eat it while it's cold,' said Jill.

'It's dead easy to make,' said Trevor, 'providing you've got a cucumber. Like the good book says, first catch your cucumber.'

He was halfway through the recipe when the doorbell rang.

'Jehovah's Witnesses?' said Jill.

'Pound to a penny it's cavity wall insulation.'

'It might be your friends the police,' said Peter as Trevor got up from the table.

It was none of those people. Trevor answered the door and, after a brief doorstep murmuring, returned to the room with Ivan, holdall in his hand, a careful smile on his face.

'It's Ivan. Home from Lancashire.'

'Did you say home?' said Jill.

'Sorry. Back from Lancashire.'

'Hello, sir. Hello, miss,' said Ivan, a little shyly.

'Ivan?' said Peter.

'A passing refugee.'

Jill stood up, in challenging mode.

'Except you're not, are you? We've been told you speak English. According to our informant, you speak very good English. Not just foreign English but English English.'

'Ivan?' said Peter, again.

'It's a perfectly common name,' said Jill, with a touch of impatience. 'It shouldn't be that difficult to learn.'

'And it makes introductions easier. Peter, this is Ivan, a refugee from Lithuania except he isn't. Ivan, this is Peter, Jill's ex-husband.'

'We know each other,' said Peter, standing up, hand outstretched.

'You do?'

'We shared a cell on Dartmoor.'

'No sweat. There's enough soup for four,' said Trevor.

9

Personal Devotions

Jill demanded an assurance from both her visitors that neither of them had been in prison for crimes of violence.

'It's just my funny little way,' she said. 'Some people say Grace, I like to know I'm not breaking bread with hoodlums.'

'You have our word, Mrs Swinburne,' said Ivan with a show of casual English elegance, 'violence has never entered our lives except by way of Channel 4 News.'

'Yvonne's right. You speak very good English English.'

'It's one of my best impressions. The educated Englishman.'

'Which means, presumably, that you're *not* . . .'

'Quite so.'

The meal, by consent and acclamation, was memorable. Trevor, opening the first bottle, said, 'We think this is an amusing little wine.'

It amused them so much, they drank three more bottles, and celebrated a whole month of Fridays. Tales of Old Dartmoor jostled for attention with tales of San Quentin High and it was difficult to spot the difference. Ivan confessed that he had several other names, and had difficulty in remembering which was his real one. Peter had known him as Edward.

'And of course, officially I was number 774232.'

'But your best friends called you 77?' said Trevor, trying to remember which music-hall comedian first used the joke.

'Knock it off,' said Jill.

'However, since the majority of you know me as Ivan, why don't you call me Ivan?'

'Any chance of a little truth to go with the name?' asked Jill.

'Truth? Is there such a thing as truth?'

'House rule. No metaphysics on a Friday. We've had a nice meal, several bottles of amusing wine and Trevor's going to make coffee.'

'Am I? Yes. Of course I am.'

'Let's start with a few simple facts. Like what were you both doing in prison?'

'I was doing six months,' said Peter.

'What was the charge?'

'Basically it was on account of Christmas cards.'

'Closed on account of molasses,' said Trevor.

The other three stared at him.

'It's in a W.C. Fields film. After the blind man's wrecked the shop. Fields puts up a sign saying: closed on account of molasses.'

He chuckled, snug with the memory and the fine juices of central France.

'Don't worry about him,' said Jill. 'When he drinks wine in large quantities, he starts free-associating.'

'No I don't. It's just these funny things come into my head.'

'Knock it off, father of my child. Sit quietly with your bottle and listen to Peter. He's going to tell us about his criminal record.'

'It was dead simple,' said Peter. 'A mail order Christmas card business. My partner designed and printed the cards. I handled publicity and distribution. Top of the range. We only advertised in the glossy magazines and colour supplements. You might see one of our ads. There was just a hint that some of the profits would go to charity, so that might encourage you to place an order and send a large cheque.'

'Don't tell me, let me guess. The cards never arrived?' said Jill.

'Right. The cards never arrived. Technically it was a breach of contract, according to the lawyers. Also a crime, according to the lawyers. But it wasn't my fault.'

'What a surprise.'

'My partner let me down. All the time he was supposed to be doing my Christmas cards, he was moonlighting for somebody else.'

'Making Christmas cards?'

'Forging passports. That was his original trade. Forgery.'

The story continued. The scam had been exposed on a regional television programme, and Peter arrested two days later. His partner made himself a passport and moved swiftly to Spain. In essence, it was the same story Jill had heard many times before: a small-scale, half-baked, quick turnover enterprise, with seeds of disaster sewn into the lining, and somebody else to blame at the moment of terminal shambles.

She hoped Ivan's confession would be more original.

'So my ex-husband's a cheapskate con man. What are you?'

'I rob banks,' said Ivan, quietly, not wishing to attract too much attention.

'There is a house rule about pickaxe handles and stocking masks.'

'I use nothing more lethal than a computer keyboard.'

'You can give somebody a nasty bruise with one of those,' said Trevor.

'I gave you my word, Mrs Swinburne. No violence. I am a pacifist, in principle and practice.'

'Listen, folks,' said Peter, 'I think you should realise this man is something very special indeed. It was a privilege to share a cell with him. He's an aristocrat among bank robbers. He is to robbing banks by computer what Einstein was to E equals MC squared.'

'If you're as good as all that, how come you ended up in Dartmoor?' said Jill.

'It was negotiated.'

'Huh?'

'I could have avoided the prison sentence, but I refused to tell them. So I served the prison sentence. Two years less full remission for impeccable behaviour.'

'What do you mean? You refused to tell them? What did you refuse to tell them?'

'How I did it.'

'I know,' said Trevor.

'Just drink your wine, there's a good boy.'

Trevor persisted. He knew.

'If Ivan told them how he'd done it, they'd be able to get the money back. But he didn't tell them how he'd done it. So they didn't get their money back. I bet I'm right.'

Ivan smiled and nodded.

'A very cool diagnosis. And partially correct.'

'Only . . . partially?' said Trevor, a little disappointed and with a perceptible lurch over the word 'partially' so that it came out resembling 'parishly'.

'The pleasing aspect about robbing banks by computer is this. You place a series of bugs in the system and they do the work for you. I take a stroll, I read a book, I listen to Bix, or Duke, or Bird, and all the time I am robbing banks. I am robbing banks as I sit here.'

'Forgive me if this sounds rude,' said Jill, 'but have you ever considered a sideways career move into honesty?'

Ivan smiled, as to a child who has asked where babies come from.

'Mrs Swinburne. I have looked at the system. You have looked at the system. Is it a system we should support? Or one we should subvert?'

He had backed her into a political corner, and a tricky one. She guessed they were in total agreement about the system. Global capitalism was very kind to capitalists but kicked the living shit out of the globe. Her response – feeble as it was – had always been strictly democratic. She voted neatly and regularly, signed peitions, marched in demonstrations and had once failed to win a seat at a local by-election on an immaculate deep green ticket.

Subverting the system by theft was a new idea – or maybe an old idea in new clothes? Perhaps computer theft from the international banking system was the hi-tech equivalent to the storming of the Winter Palace during the Russian revolution? On the other hand – and there were always dozens of other hands in these debates – wasn't the received version of the storming of the Winter Palace invented by Eisenstein for the movie? She had read somewhere that the real thing was a pretty dull and mundane affair. She had read something similar about the Relief of Mafeking. That was the trouble with history: it wouldn't keep still. Nor, though he was a contained man, would Ivan.

He reminded her of what Trevor had said about Chinese food: the more you eat, the more you have left. The more Ivan explained about himself, the less she understood.

She had drunk too deeply of the wine to indulge in prolonged ideological debates. She would save them for later. She took temporary refuge in a giggle.

'You think the system is funny?'

'No. I am thinking that earlier today I was at the police station, giving a solemn assurance to a senior officer that nothing untoward ever goes on in this house. And here we are, entertaining a couple of ex-cons. No offence meant.'

'Not merely an ex-con but an operational bank robber,' said Ivan.

'He is robbing banks even as he sits here,' said Trevor.

'When are you planning to leave?' said Jill.

It was Trevor's turn to giggle.

'The Bank Dick,' he said.

'Huh?' murmured his companions, with varying degrees of curiosity.

'It's a film. A talking picture. With W.C. Fields.'

'Ah,' said Jill, penetrating the foggy logic of her spousal analogue. 'I expect that's the film where he puts up the sign saying: closed on account of molasses.'

'No,' said Trevor, vaguely. The grape had taken its toll. He was like a dormouse in search of a teapot.

It was clearly time to clear away, stack the dirty dishes in the kitchen and go to bed.

'The weekend starts here!'

At the crack of ten-thirty, Trevor pulled back the bedroom curtains.

'Don't do that,' said Jill. 'The light hurts my eyes.'

She pulled the bedclothes over her head.

'I'll go make coffee and boil up a cauldron of muesli.'

He was always like this on a Saturday morning. She knew what would happen next. She covered her ears.

Minutes later the explosion shook Hotspur Street as the 1948 Dizzy Gillespie Big Band roared its fanfare across the neighbourhood.

Ivan was trying to make a telephone call. It was not easy with John Birks Gillespie, born Cheraw, South Carolina in 1917, applying a blow-torch to your aural perception. Trevor noticed his discomfort.

'Sorry, Ivan. It's my Saturday morning tape. All the flag-wavers. Dizzy, Lionel Hampton, Count Basie, Charles Mingus. Sod-the-neighbours music. It blows the cobwebs away.'

'It's fine,' said Ivan.

'Trying to call the bank? Don't waste your time. They never work weekends.'

Trevor tweaked up the volume, then galloped up the stairs in time to the music, carrying First-Born's breakfast.

'Room service!' he cried.

'What kept you?' said First-Born.

Across the broad acres and green swards of the West Riding, peasants and artisans allowed the breeze to blow away the week's accumulated cobwebs, while being careful to fold them neatly and leave them in a safe place ready for Monday morning. At Headingley Cricket Ground, paid-up members settled in their pavilion seats, in preparation for Yorkshire's first home match. The pitch was as flat as their vowel sounds. They looked forward with phlegmatic eagerness to another season of unrelenting dourness. They realised that by September they might have more cobwebs than they set off with; but the older Yorkshireman approaches excitement and dangerous living with proper caution.

No such restraint applied to the younger generation.

Yvonne had arranged to meet her friends, Sharon and Gary from San Quentin High, beside the sculptural feature in the Archer Street shopping precinct. Monday to Friday, Yvonne's hair was dark, neatly brushed and hung vertically, roughly in line with the laws of gravity. Today it was green, spiky and pointing at the galaxy.

Sharon and Gary were similarly transformed. Sharon's hair had turned orange, and Gary's was pink. All three were unanimous in their spikiness.

'What do you fancy doing then?' said Yvonne.

'Not bothered. What do you want to do, Gary?'

'Not bothered. What do you two want to do?'

'We could go shopping,' said Yvonne.

'We're all right for books,' said Sharon.

'We're all right for wood,' said Gary.

'What about something for yourselves?'

They headed towards the shops.

On a six-lane freeway leading from the city, a gleaming white sports car, freshly laundered, stayed resolutely in the slow lane, even though its publicity brochures stated it could accelerate from 0 to 120 mph in the time it takes to blow away a single cobweb.

Its driver was Inspector Hobson. Half a mile back he had seen a sign reading:

ROAD WORKS. TEMPORARY SPEED LIMIT. 30 MPH.

The road works had long since disappeared. Indeed, Hobson had read a memo confirming the fact soon after his return to the area. But he was not going to risk marring his day's enjoyment by a breach of the law, however technical and outmoded.

Hobson was dressed casually in grey flannels, open-necked sports shirt and blazer. He had blazers the way M & S had underpants. In his time he had attended two prep schools, two minor public schools, two colleges and two universities. He had a blazer with a badge from each of them. He took badges seriously.

Today's blazer was yet another marking the voyage of his life. It proclaimed his membership of and unswerving allegiance to the West Riding Divisional Mixed Hockey team. Though he kept his sporting prowess in low profile around Sherlock Road, he was not without pride in his achievements on the field of play. Today he hoped to lead his team to victory in the tournament ahead: the Northern Area play-offs leading to the national finals of the Robert Peel Rosebowl – one of the lesser-known sporting trophies, but a minor legend among mixed hockey players in the constabularies and crime squads of the nation.

Two coaches taking old-age pensioners to Skegness overtook him, honking their scorn. He glanced at the digital clock on his dashboard. It showed 12.19.37 . . . 8 . . . 9. Damn! It was seven seconds slow. He activated the mechanism whereby the car would calculate, by relating its current speed to the distance lying between it and its eventual destination, the time required for the balance of the journey.

The answer came out in weeks and days. Hobson frowned. He tried again. At the third attempt, the car gave him a sensible answer. By that time, he had missing his turning.

Joe and Ben had less need than most people to blow away cobwebs. Many of their colleagues argued that the detectives were solid cobweb all the way through; but they liked to move with the spirit of each passing day.

They sat in the public bar of the Swinging Hod, a pub much favoured by the building trade when building was a trade, rather than the construction and development niche in a corporation's portfolio.

They were drinking draught bitter. It was part of a campaign to stamp out lager louts. First drive lager off the market, and the louts will follow: QED.

'Today,' said Joe, 'we should devote ourselves to sport and recreation. A healthy body, a healthy mind.'

'Is that a choice?'

'I am serious.'

'OK. Let's think of some healthy sports and recreations.'

They concentrated hard. Ben made the opening offer.

'We could flight a few skilful arrows into yonder dartboard in a spirit of cheerful competition.'

'We could pass a friendly hour in Slimy Jake's billiard hall, and protect it from interior designers with rubber plants who want to turn it into a snooker centre.'

'We could dally for a while in any of half a dozen congenial betting shops, perhaps emerging a few quid ahead of the game.'

'We could do all three, probably in that order.'

And they did. The ritual, including the preliminary conversation, had not changed in five years.

Big Al and Little Norm were on their bicycles, conserving the planet's energy resources and their own. The manner of their cycling matched that of their walking. Norm's legs moved three times as fast as Al's, and still he had trouble keeping up with the big man.

'Is it business before pleasure?' he said, breathing hard.

'Certainly not, Norm. It's pleasure before business. Do I have to remind you this is Saturday? A time to replenish our souls.'

'What sort of pleasure had you in mind?'

'I was wondering about a game of bowls.'

'Makes a change.'

'No it doesn't, Norm. We play every day, except when it's raining. Which means, during the current fashion for global warming, we play every day.'

'I was joking.'

'And after our game of bowls, we will attend to Mr Chaplin and Mrs Swinburne.'

'Bin liners,' said Trevor to himself. Nobody could have heard him anyway, above the sound of the Lionel Hampton orchestra as it screamed its way through 'Flying Home'.

Trevor added bin liners to his shopping list.

'Is it always like this?' yelled Peter at Jill, who was dressing First-Born.

'No. Sometimes it's loud!' shouted Jill.

'Washing-up liquid,' said Trevor.

Ivan, who had been sitting beside the telephone, stood up and walked closer to Jill. He, too, had to raise his voice, though it seemed contrary to his nature.

'I shall be leaving you tomorrow. For good.'

'Fine.'

'Can I come with you?' said Peter, screwing up his ears.

'Kleenex,' said Trevor, which reminded him.

On the way to the supermarket, Trevor owned up.

'I have a confession to make.'

'Good. We haven't had a good juicy confession for ages. And a dozen Hail Marys should put you in the clear.'

'No, listen.'

She could tell he was serious, so she listened.

'Last night, I was on my way downstairs and I heard you talking to Peter. About me. So I sat on the stairs and listened. Not to all of it. Just some of it.'

'That was a bit sneaky.'

'I am a bit sneaky.'

'What did you hear?'

'That stuff about handing you the kleenex when you cry at the soppy bits.'

'I see. Any comments? Criticisms? Complaints?'

'No. Only, thank you. I suppose.'

'You're welcome.'

It was as close as either of them ever came to saying: I love you. They managed very well without it.

The team was on the pitch and warming up when Hobson trotted out to join them.

'What time do you call this, Inspector?' said WPC Wren, a mean defender from a crime squad in the Brontë country. 'Did you come via Bradford?'

He had come via Bradford, but had no intention of admitting it.

'One or two things cropped up.'

'Where's your stick?' said retired Superintendent Windsor,

a corpulent midfield player who retained enough clout with serving officers to keep his place in the team, despite the onset of weight and age.

'Well, that's just it,' said Hobson, shuffling as all ten members of the team became aware of his dilemma.

'Can anyone lend me a stick?'

'Did you forget it?' said WPC Wren.

Hobson considered lying, but knew it was a waste of time. These people were his team-mates, his professional colleagues and, he liked to think, his friends. They would drink a half of lager together after the game. But they were predominantly Yorkshire people, and they would spot a Southern lie as it left the vocal chords.

'I think it's been stolen.'

'Stolen? From where?' said the superintendent.

'From the boot of my car.'

'I think, Inspector, you must look to your security arrangements,' said the goalkeeper, Detective Sergeant Shastri, from Crime Prevention.

'The stick was in my bag, which has a combination lock. The bag was in the boot, which has two locks. The car has an alarm system. What else can I do?'

'You're better report it to somebody,' said the superintendent, 'but not to me. I've retired, thank God.'

'I'll lend you a stick.'

The speaker was Barbara. As a matter of policy, nobody knew her second name. She had played hockey for England and, though not in the force, once played the piano for a police choir in Wakefield. The choir had folded when the principal tenor and two of the baritones were charged with corruption. Singing went out of fashion; but the piano player lingered on. She was the star of the team.

'I'm deeply grateful,' said Hobson. One day he would pluck up the courage to ask her second name and buy her a half of lager.

The back of the van was stacked high with groceries and First-Born, who gurgled.

'He says it's a bit crowded back there. Can he come in the front with you?'

'Of course he can,' said Jill.

She lifted the child from the carry-cot, and sat him on her knee, as requested.

'Thanks Dad, that's really cool,' said the babe.

'I've got another confession,' said Trevor.

'We've done confessions. Look, it's ticked off. On the list. Confessions, bin liners, washing-up liquid, all ticked off.'

'Something else I heard you say.'

'What did you hear me say?'

She had a shrewd idea what it would be. She had a good memory for conversations, especially when she knew they had been bugged.

'Peter said to you: what was I like in bed? And you said I was funny.'

She was right.

'Well?'

'Am I?'

'Yes.'

'I don't strike me as funny in bed. What's funny about me in bed?'

'Some of your phraseology.'

He began to understand.

'Do you mean things like . . . any chance of being on the team tonight, pet?'

He exaggerated his residual Geordie accent, in the style of a craggy voice over on a beer commercial.

'Not to mention your celebrated "Howay the lads!" at the crucial moment.'

'I said that in Edinburgh, didn't I?'

'Didn't we all.'

'You're telling me,' said First-Born.

'And all that's funny?'

'In my experience, Mr Chaplin, which, let it be said, is not enormous, you are exceedingly funny.'

They smiled, sharing memories of sublime and sticky

moments, warmed by the prospect of more of the same, but different. Then Trevor started to laugh.

'Now what?'

'I've thought of a new one.'

'What have I started? Go on. Tell me.'

'Not in front of the children,' said First-Born.

'There isn't room in the van,' said Trevor.

The van turned a corner, unnoticed by Joe and Ben, as they emerged, blinking into the light, from the Owner's Risk, a pub run by an ex-wrestler called Timothy Hardaker, formerly known as the Masked Vampire. Hardaker weighed over twenty stone and had operated flexible opening hours well in advance of Whitehall legislation.

The detectives had worked well: they had played darts and snooker in a proper sporting spirit, iced with ineptitude: they had backed one winner, five losers and a non-runner, and would spend the money lost on fancy chocolates for their wives; and between them, they had reclaimed fourteen pints of draught bitter, yet another hammer-blow in the campaign against lager louts.

It was a good afternoon's work. They walked along the street singing 'Are You Going To Scarborough Fair?' in two-part harmony. It was a tender and pleasing sound. They finished the final chorus as they arrived at the bus stop.

'It's ridiculous,' said Ben. 'I've arrested people for behaving the way we do.'

'Me too.'

'Why do we do it?'

'Because we're here.'

On a distant playing field, Inspector Hobson returned his temporary hockey stick to Barbara, avoiding eye contact. He had scored three goals: one for his own side, two for the opposition. The team had lost 4–1.

At Headingley Cricket Ground, Yorkshire's brightest new batsman played a forward defensive stroke. He had scored seven runs in two hours.

'Yon lad'll be a good 'un, when he learns to control his aggression,' said the oldest paid-up member.

In the living room of Number 17, Hotspur Street, Jill Swinburne looked around her, gobsmacked. She and Trevor had arrived back from the supermarket to find their home transformed into a floral paradise: a cross between Kew Gardens and Barbra's Streisand's dressing room on a Broadway first night.

'A modest token of our affection, appreciation and admiration,' said Ivan, with a low bow.

'You call this modest?' said Jill.

'We sincerely wish it could be more.'

'If it was any more we'd have to move into a bigger house.'

'It's amazing,' said Trevor. 'It's like being up the Amazon without the creepy-crawlies. It must have taken you ages to get all these from the park.'

'Trevor!'

'Sorry, pet.'

Nobody had ever given Jill flowers in such quantity and variegation. What were those things that looked like orchids? Could they be orchids? She had no way of telling. She had led a full life but it had been totally orchid-free so far. She felt a short speech coming on. She really needed the Queen's help.

'May I say, on behalf of my apparently ungrateful consort and myself, how much we appreciate this wonderful floral display. Thank you, Ivan. Thank you, Peter.'

'Credit where it's due,' said Peter. 'It's thank you, Ivan. We used the telephone and one or two of his secret bank accounts.'

'Also there is a message,' said Ivan.

'From the florist?' said Trevor.

'No. A strange-sounding man with a strange-sounding name. Little Norm? Does that make sense?'

'Yes,' said Jill. 'It makes sense. Little Norm doesn't always make sense, but that's usually our problem.'

'He would like to meet either or both of you as soon as possible.'

'Whereabouts?' said Jill.

Trevor guessed.

'The bowling green?'

'Yes. The bowling green. That's very impressive. How did you know it would be the bowling green?'

'It's always been the bowling green, ever since it stopped being Big Al's shed on the allotment.'

Ivan had travelled widely, seen many small miracles and a few big ones, but was still impressed by the casual, everyday surrealism of Number 17, Hotspur Street.

'I shall miss this place when I leave.'

'Thank you, Ivan,' said Jill. She turned to Peter.

'And what about you?'

'I shall miss some things about it.'

'Name one,' said Jill, before correcting herself, quickly. 'No. Don't.'

'Who's coming to the park?' said Trevor.

Trevor went to the park alone.

Jill wanted to unpack, catalogue and store the groceries. Peter and Ivan agreed to baby-sit while First-Born watched a documentary on BBC2.

'No baby today, Trevor?' said Big Al.

'He's at home. Watching a documentary about pelicans.'

'Not even any cornflakes,' said Norm.

'Cornflakes?'

'Ignore him. Norm has these moments of lateral conversation. Lovely wood, Trev! When did you learn to play?'

Because he was on his own, Trevor had accepted Al's invitation to join them in a game.

'I used to play with my Dad when I was a kid.'

'A fine apprentice to a skilful sorcerer, if I'm any judge.'

Al bent down to take his shot. As he did so, Norm handed Trevor a large plastic carrier bag.

'Please don't rustle when I'm playing my shot. I lose concentration.'

Al completed his shot. Norm completed his transaction. Trevor looked inside the bag.

'Paper?'

'Invoices, chits, receipts,' said Norm.

'Requiring a signature,' said Al.

'All of them?'

'No. Just one. The master receipt at the top of the pile requires a signature. Your headmaster's, for preference.'

'Right.'

'In triplicate, for preference.'

'I'll see him on Monday morning.'

'Sooner than that, for preference.'

The sonorous repetition in Al's voice was unusual. It hinted at urgency, like the slow tolling of a bell. Trevor did not ask for whom it tolled; but the signs were that without Mr Wheeler's signature, whom would find out, and quickly.

Jill telephoned the headmaster at home. First-Born was in bed, dreaming of pelicans. The men were at the table, playing Monopoly.

'Hello, Mr Wheeler? This is Jill Swinburne . . . Yes, I'm a little surprised myself, but I'm told life is full of surprises. I wonder whether we might arrange to see you tomorrow . . .? I know it's Sunday but it is rather urgent. In the morning, for preference . . .'

Jill completed the arrangements and hung up the receiver in time to hear Ivan reading from a card, 'Go to jail. Go directly to jail. Do not pass Go. Do not collect two hundred pounds.' He replaced the card in its pile, adding, 'In the words of a very great man: so it goes.'

In bed, Jill told Trevor what the headmaster had said on the telephone.

'It really is most inconvenient dealing with professional matters on a Sunday morning, when one is preoccupied with one's personal devotions.'

'Personal devotions?'

'He goes to church.'

'Good job somebody does. Pity to waste all that bell-ringing.'

'Read your book.'

He read his book for a while, then chuckled.

'What's funny?'

'Erogenous zones.'

'That's funny?'

'I read it in one of your magazines and I thought: that's what I'll say to her in bed. I'll say . . . I am feeling erogenous in several of my zones.'

'How many zones have you got?'

'Never counted. About six, I think.'

She did something ingenious under the duvet with his pyjama cord.

'Sorry, not six, seven. No, eight. Hinny, I'm losing count. What are you doing now?'

'Personal devotions, pet. And what's more, I bet I've got more zones than you.'

They shared the delights of numeracy until, for the second time that day, fanfares of sounding brass and tinkling cymbal rang out in Hotspur Street.

10

Jolly Hockey Sticks

St Amber is one of the more demure saints in the theological archives. There is no gospel according to him. Indeed, there is no historical evidence that he ever existed. He once cropped up under Any Other Business at a Synod, but at the end of a long and demanding day. He was adjourned until the next meeting and then slipped off the agenda. In private, the liberal wing of the clergy admits Amber was probably a misprint in a mediaeval manuscript, allowed to survive on the basis that an imaginary saint would do less harm to the established church than a gaping hole in its infallibility.

The parish church of St Amber stood, gaunt and unlovely, in a suburban patch of the moonstruck outer limits, marooned between a mouldering estate of 1930s semi-detached houses and a field, officially designated as a green belt by the town planners, but brown because it had recently been ploughed. Its owners, a property company with an office in Milton Keynes, intended to plant something but were waiting for the results of a feasibility study by a firm of consultants before deciding on the precise shade of green.

The outstanding feature of the church was its bell, claimed by the neighbourhood faithful to be the loudest in Christendom. When the wind blew towards the south, it could be heard on the Channel coast. Ancient seadogs in Plymouth had been known to rush to the shore on a Sunday morning, braced and eager to repel the latest Spanish Armada.

Arnold Crosby, dispensing chemist and campanologist,

tolled the knell of parting sleep, calling the faithful to prayer, and forcing the heathen majority to hide under blankets, duvets and the *News Of The World*. A small yellow van parked nearby shook in sympathy with the vibrations of the earth's outer crust.

'What is that row?' said First-Born. 'It's too piercing, man, it hurts my ears.'

'Don't worry,' said Trevor, 'it isn't tolling for thee.'

Jill saw a familiar figure walking along the street towards the church.

'Oh look. A sinner in search of redemption.'

By the time Mr Wheeler arrived at the lych-gate outside the church, Trevor and Jill were waiting for him.

'Good morning, Mr Chaplin. Good morning, Mrs Swinburne.'

'Good morning, Mr Wheeler.'

'Good morning, Mr Wheeler.'

'I understand you have a document requiring my signature?'

'Trevor. The document.'

Trevor produced an envelope from his inside pocket.

'Shall I explain?' said Jill.

'I wish you would,' said Trevor.

They looked around, but nobody was watching. A labrador passed by on the other side of the road, but seemed preoccupied with a personal quest. Jill explained.

'The various items of equipment that have arrived at school during the last few days are the gift of an anonymous benefactor. He is a former student of the school, now a very successful businessman, who was very distressed to hear of our problems.'

She opened the envelope and handed Mr Wheeler a sheet of paper. 'This is a simple form of receipt for his files and your peace of mind.'

'Am I allowed to ask the name of this former student?'

'You're allowed to ask,' said Trevor, 'but we're not allowed to tell you.'

It was a tricky moment. All three of them had taught at San Quentin High for a decade, but at no point had the school produced a student who matched the description. It had contributed other useful elements to the body politic: Rugby League professionals, night-club bouncers, street bookmakers, croupiers and one eminent safe-blower. Tycoons of paternalistic bent were non-existent. Jill spotted the quicksand in good time.

'As he so rightly says, Mr Wheeler, if everyone knew of his generosity, he'd be besieged by all kinds of people. His life wouldn't be worth living. Think of it. All the other schools in the area, hospitals, old people's homes, orphanages, refugees, the Third World . . .'

'I do understand, Mrs Swinburne.'

Mr Wheeler reached for his fountain pen.

'If you could sign three copies . . .'

'Three copies?'

'One for his files, one for your files and one for emergencies.'

Mr Wheeler signed the three documents, slipped one into his pocket and handed the others to Jill.

'Thank you, Mrs Swinburne, I am much relieved.'

He turned towards the church.

'Perhaps you would like to join me in prayer?'

'Thank you, Mr Wheeler, but we really must get back to our . . .'

She hesitated, trying to think of something they had to get back to.

'Personal devotions,' said Trevor.

'Of course. I respect that. I wish you both good morning.'

Driving back to Hotspur Street, Trevor added his postscript to the encounter.

'Well, he may be a good, God-fearing Christian but he is also a receiver of stolen property. He is over a barrel, with a signature to prove it. Bang to rights.'

'Stolen property?' said Jill.

'Not all of it. Some of the kids decided to help out,

according to Little Norm. Bit of shop-lifting on the side. Books and such.'

'Tess?'

'I don't know any of their names.'

'Trevor!'

'He's always been an idiot, our headmaster. He'll sign anything, as long as it's in triplicate.'

'There's one born every minute,' said First-Born.

Hobson was approaching his current investigation on three fronts. His VDU glowed with impenetrable graphics, his desk was covered with computer print-outs to a depth of several inches and he was on the telephone to the Criminal Records Office, speaking to D.C. Nobbs, recently transferred, swiftly, from Traffic. Nobbs was transferred, on average, once every three weeks.

'What do we have on hockey sticks . . .? Yes, I know it should be on the computer, I am looking at the computer as I speak to you . . . Yes, I realise computers haven't really caught on in these parts . . . All that being so, I still see no reference in any of our lists of stolen property to hockey sticks . . . It is not your job, Constable, to decide what constitutes high priority . . . A hockey stick may not be a priority item to you but nevertheless, someone very close to me has had a hockey stick stolen . . . No, *not* me, Constable!'

Hobson was doodling methodically on his jotter. He took pride in his ability to doodle a straight line without the use of a ruler. He never doodled circles or curves. It may be true, as claimed by the Spanish architect, Gaudí, that there are no straight lines in Nature; but in Hobson's nature there was little else. They stuck out in all directions as he continued his efforts to extract useful information from D.C. Nobbs.

'My concern about the stolen hockey stick is purely and simply to see whether it falls into a broader pattern of such thefts . . . Thank you, yes, I have already looked under the heading Sports Equipment . . . Yes, I am aware it begins with S . . . And yes, I know it's Sunday!'

He hung up the receiver and looked at what he had doodled. On the pad was a neat, well-proportioned drawing of a gallows. He tore the sheet from the pad and shredded it immediately. Such an item could easily be misunderstood by his colleagues. Misunderstanding of his endeavours was more than commonplace; he sensed it was compulsory. He took no chances.

Trevor, Jill and First-Born arrived home to find a smell of freshly-made coffee and conspiracy.

'We are leaving you today,' said Ivan.

'We're going to the seaside,' said Peter.

'Can anybody come?' said Trevor.

'Just a moment,' said Jill. 'I'm a little confused. First you say you've leaving. Then you suggest a trip to the seaside. Are these two things related?'

Ivan explained, as he poured the coffee.

'We are going to the seaside because it's beside the sea.'

'It's the best place to keep it,' said Trevor.

'And since we are planning to catch a boat, the sea is more or less a pre-requisite.'

Jill and Trevor caught a glimpse of truth, no bigger than a man's hand.

'You're going away on a boat?' said Jill. 'Both of you?'

'I fixed it this morning,' said Peter.

A memory flickered at the back of Jill's mind, like a candle in a crypt.

'You used to have a friend with a boat. At Flamborough. You used to go fishing with him. You used to catch hang-overs.'

'That's the one.'

'Is this like when you went to the Lincolnshire border and the Lancashire border?' said Trevor.

'Very similar,' said Ivan.

'But this time,' said Jill, 'you're sailing away in a beautiful pea-green boat to start a new life across the broad ocean?'

'That's the principle.'

'Good. What time are you leaving?'

There was a shuffly silence. Jill translated it into plain English.

'I see. You are taking it for granted that we will give you a lift to Flamborough.'

'It's a nice day,' said Peter.

'Ignoring the fact that I have dozens of other things I should be doing. Books to mark, clothes to wash, the papers to read, a child to bring up, an old black-and-white movie on Channel 4, plus a whole range of personal devotions.'

'We could take the football,' said Trevor, 'and I'll make some cucumber sandwiches and we'll buy some lemonade at the corner shop.'

Jill looked around her at the three men. Between them, they had lived on the Planet Earth for over a century. At this moment, Trevor and Peter were grinning like ten-year-olds. By way of compensation, Ivan's face looked older than its natural years, unlined to be sure, but eyes fixed on a horizon well beyond Flamborough. It was difficult to decide which was the more alarming: a second childhood or a sense of destiny. But she spotted the principle that united them.

'You three are the sort of men I have always warned myself about.'

'And you are the sort of woman who inspires men to cross oceans,' said Ivan, a little unexpectedly.

'Bollocks.'

'Right on, Mum,' said First-Born.

The party left for the seaside half an hour later. Ivan carried First-Born, Peter carried the sandwiches and Trevor carried the football. The Unfrocked Bank Manager, now in total control of his video-camera, recorded the event in sharp focus and full colour.

Joe and Ben enjoyed their Sunday mornings at work. The emergency calls were few and the living was easy. The only major incidents in living memory had been complaints from the Noise Abatement lobby about St Amber's church bell and a minor fracas when a Salvation Army euphonium player in spiritual crisis had blown a rasping version of 'Colonel Bogey' while the rest of the band was playing 'Onward Christian Soldiers'. The magistrates had let him off with a caution, on condition he joined a more secular orchestra.

The detectives valued their Sabbath tranquillity and were both startled and slightly hurt when Inspector Hobson walked into the office, bearing piles of computer print-out.

'Good morning, men. Glad to see you're here.'

'Unceasing vigilance, sir,' said Joe.

'A lot of nasty things can happen on a Sunday,' said his partner.

'You only have to read the papers.'

'Which we were, in point of fact, doing.'

Hobson placed the computer print-out on the desk, on top of the Sunday papers where they lay open, displaying the current fashions in self-righteous lubricity under banner headlines Naming the Guilty Men and, on this occasion, one Guilty Horse.

'I'd appreciate a second opinion on this.'

Joe peered warily at the Inspector's gift. He fingered the corner of the print-out, like an inexperienced angler checking the pedigree of an unfamiliar fish.

'May we ask, sir, with respect, what we are looking at? And for?'

'This is a list of property reported stolen during the last four weeks. I have marked a number of items with asterisks, in red, thus.'

He showed them one of his asterisks.

'Very neat,' said Joe.

'And pertinent,' said Ben.

'All these items come under the collective heading of sports equipment. Footballs, both association and rugby, cricket balls, bats, stumps and bails, netballs, hockey sticks . . .'

'Hockey sticks?' said Joe, pouncing with the speed of light.

'Yes. Hockey sticks,' said Hobson, faltering.

It was too late. Joe had spotted another Achilles heel in the Inspector's psyche.

'Sir, correct me if I am wrong, but are we not talking to the star striker of the West Riding Divisional Mixed Hockey Team?'

'Almost right,' said Hobson.

Barbara, the piano player and former international, was the designated goal-scorer. Statistically speaking, she was their only goal-scorer in the last ten matches. Hobson put the record straight.

'I have played striker in my time, but this season I have adopted a midfield role, in the interests of the team.'

'A midfield dynamo?' Ben suggested

'I prefer to think of myself as a playmaker.'

Ben fell on Hobson's self-image with glee.

'Ah! A midfield general! Yes. We can understand that, sir. You are to the hockey field what Billy Bremner was to the football field. Or Raymond Illingworth to the cricket field. Or Lewis Jones to the rugby field. Or Napoleon to the battle-field. Or . . .'

'And somebody's stolen your stick?' said Joe, just as Hobson was warming to the catalogue of heroics.

'Yes. Somebody has stolen my hockey stick. But I am *not*, repeat *not* concerned about my hockey stick. I *am* concerned about what appears to be the premeditated and concerted theft of sports and games related equipment.'

He walked briskly to the door.

'I leave it with you. I'd appreciate some immediate action.'

He left quickly, keen to avoid any further debate, since he had no chance of winning.

To pass the time, the detectives calculated the length of the computer print-out. They decided, fully-stretched, it would reach from the police station to the nearest pub, a homely spot called the Owner's Risk. They would check it later.

Then they pondered the Inspector's words.

'The midfield general wants immediate action,' said Joe.

'On a Sunday?'

'We could wait until tomorrow. Have a dawn swoop.'

'A what?'

'A dawn swoop. They have them in London. Very trendy with the Met. I've long fancied a dawn swoop.'

'Does it have to be at dawn? My understanding is that dawn, from all accounts, is very early.'

'Point taken. We'll put dawn on ice on the back burner.'

'Let's go to the park.'

'The park?'

'Isn't it obvious?'

They realised it was obvious. They went to the park.

Like the poor and dispossessed of the area, Joe and Ben went to Big Al in time of trouble. He was a fount of knowledge, information and wisdom, happy to share these with passers-by, including officers of the law. Nothing he told them had ever resulted in an early arrest, or even an eventual arrest. But he rarely let them down when they needed an excuse, however flimsy, for a meandering and ultimately meaningless investigation. Their long-term ambition was to be suspended, permanently, on full pay, pending retirement. On the long and winding road to that happy land, they needed the comfort of pointless inquiries; this, in its turn, meant they needed Big Al's guidance.

'Hello lads!' said the familiar voice from the heart of the bowling green.

'Lovely day,' said Joe.

'Oh aye. Bliss was it in this afternoon to be alive, so I said to Norm: let's go to the park for a game of bowls.'

'Are these things valuable?' said Ben, picking up one of Al's woods.

'Priceless.'

'Really?'

'They were my Dad's. Look. They've got his initials on. You can't read them, like, but you can see where they've worn off.'

There were residual traces of initials on the bowls, but too faint to form any known alphabetical symbol. It was the closest the detectives had ever been to finding out Big Al's real name. There was no firm evidence that he was called Al, though he was unquestionably big.

'These woods are my inheritance. Along with the country estate. And the grouse moor. And the merchant bank. But mostly he left me his woods.'

'These things ever get nicked?' said Joe.

'Don't be daft,' said Norm.

'The bowling green,' said Al, 'is the last resting place of truth and honour.'

'Along with billiard halls,' said Norm, 'but not snooker centres.'

Joe lowered his voice. It was a busy afternoon on the green and though it might be the last resting place of truth and honour, confidentiality seemed appropriate to the occasion.

'Strictly between yourselves, ourselves and the police national computer . . .'

'Which narrows it down to about two million people,' said Al.

' . . . we are investigating the widespread theft of sports equipment.'

'Somebody been knocking off bowls?' said Norm, outraged.

'Not bowls. Ben . . . the list.'

Ben recited:

'Footballs, both association and rugby, cricket balls, bats, stumps and bails, netballs, hockey sticks.'

Al gave serious thought to the items in the recitation.

'Nothing pertaining to lacrosse?'

Ben shook his head.

'In which case, officers, you must look to those places where sports, games and physical recreation are required to take place by law. Even though the self-same law-makers make such activity impossible by depriving the said places of the proper resources.'

'You what?' said Joe, Ben and Norm in unison.

'Schools,' said Al.

'Let me get this clear,' said Joe. 'You are suggesting that schools need sports equipment?'

'How else can they make healthy bodies?'

'But are you seriously suggesting that a school would solve its problems by knocking off the appropriate gear?'

Even Ben found it difficult to believe.

'What school would consider solving the problems caused by expenditure cuts, rate-capping and the like, by organised theft?'

As he articulated the question, all four men realised they knew the answer.

'Ah.'

'Ah.'

'Ah.'

'Ah.'

The detectives knew where to swoop. Dawn might still be a problem.

The white cliffs of Flamborough deserve a song of praise though it presents difficulties in the rhyming department; Dover is obviously more congenial to the lyricist.

Lying about halfway down Yorkshire, on the right-hand side, the headland has touched the hem of history on at least a couple of occasions. Danish invaders had landed here, finding a degree of shelter from the natives sufficient to organise pillaging workshops prior to venturing further inland. A few centuries later, in 1779, the locals, including the now fully-integrated Danes, lined the clifftops to watch an epic gun battle between two English ships and the celebrated American pirate, Paul Jones. People still flocked to Flamborough Head at weekends, hoping to catch the replay.

Trevor left the van in a car-park at the top of the cliff, in the lee of the lighthouse. Then they walked down a steep slope to the North Landing, a bay nestling between cliffs. There were fishing boats at rest on the beach. A little later, one of them would take Ivan and Peter to their new life across the ocean.

'We'll be setting sail on the tide, in an hour's time,' said Peter. He's trying to sound nautical, thought Jill. There wasn't a sail in sight. That had always been Peter's problem. He was always trying to sound something.

Trevor held up the football.

'Anyone fancy a game? Work up an appetite for the cucumber sandwiches?'

'You're on,' said Peter.

Jill and Ivan watched as the two men explored the beach, looking for a patch of level sand among the golden hummocks. It was not one of the world's great footballing beaches.

'He's a good man, the father of your child,' said Ivan.

'I know.'

'Don't let him grow up, whatever you do.'

'I don't think there's any real danger. He tried maturity, but it didn't fit him.'

Trevor and Peter settled for a football pitch approximately five yards long and five yards wide: smaller than Wembley but easily big enough for their fantasies.

They kicked the ball idly to and fro.

'I'm Eddie Gray,' said Peter. 'Who are you?'

'Bobby Charlton. I'm always Bobby Charlton.'

He hit the ball on the half-volley, in the graceful manner of Wor Bobby's thirty-yard special against Portugal in the 1966 World Cup. The ball, imitating the action of a banana, arced away into a rocky pool.

'You kicked it. You fetch it,' said Peter.

Trevor took off his shoes and socks.

'You're very different, you and Mr Chaplin,' said Ivan.

'*Vive la différence*,' said Jill. First-Born, sitting contentedly in her lap, was testimony to the glory of celebrating differences.

'He accepts the world as it is. Whereas I form the impression that you believe something can be done.'

'About what?'

'About the Planet Earth and the way we organise it.'

'If you're getting stuck into the meaning of life,' said First-Born, 'shove me in the cot. I'm going to have a kip.'

Jill did as she was told, and confessed.

'Oh yes. I tried to change the world. I stood for the Council, as a Conservation candidate. Finished last out of four.'

'It's a start. Christ set off with twelve disciples. Karl Marx with rather less.'

'Conclusion?'

'The attempt must be made.'

'Forgive me being personal, Ivan, but you strike me as being out of the usual run of bank robbers. Not that I've met all that many.'

'Robbing banks is like any other skill. Once you master it, it's quite simple. Stealing the money is easy. Redistribution is the difficult bit. But then, it's all a game.'

'Robbing banks is a game?'

It was a startling thought. Jill enjoyed games, preferably with silly variations. She and Trevor played Rude Scrabble on a regular basis; and long ago she had been very impressed to read that John and Yoko Lennon had invented a non-competitive version of chess. All the pieces were the same colour and after a few moves the players simply forgot which side they were on and substituted love for competitiveness. It sounded like a decent game. But robbing banks was different. She couldn't see it in a Waddington's box.

'Do you have a bank note about your person? Any denomination will do.'

'I think so.'

Jill checked her pockets.

'Oh look.'

It was the five pound note Inspector Hobson had given her at Sherlock Road.

'A senior police officer gave me this to buy a present for First-Born.'

'Senior police officers can be very charming. And they have a difficult job, dealing with people like me.'

'This one's also a little stupid.'

'That too is possible.'

Ivan took the note.

'The theory of this note is very simple. You are legally entitled to take it to the Bank of England where the Chief Cashier will exchange it for gold, to the value of five pounds. See? It carries his signature. This note constitutes a contract. Now let us suppose all of us, all these people gathered together at Flamborough Head, let us all go to the Bank of England tomorrow where we will present our notes and demand our gold. Do you fancy our chances of getting the gold?'

'Not in the slightest.'

'Therefore, it is a game. International banking is a game. Money is a game.'

'And robbery?'

'I prefer to call it redistribution.'

He returned the five pound note. Jill put it in her pocket. She must remember to buy a present. Inspector Hobson might drop by on constabulary duties and it would be embarrassing to be caught without some designated building bricks.

'You're political, aren't you?' said Jill.

'Everybody's political. Most of all those people who say: I am non-political. They are *really* political.'

'Am I right? Your plan is to overthrow world capitalism? Give or take a dollar or so?'

'The hands that touch the keyboard rule the world.'

'And you start by stealing a few million?'

'We started a long time ago. You might remember the crash.'

'The stock market crash?'

Ivan nodded.

She remembered the headlines, if not the small print. Was it 1988? And how had it started? Was it Black Friday or Black Monday? The day the bubbles had burst and the yuppies fled from the temple of Mammon, clutching their portable telephones as souvenirs of their never-never land. And nothing could be heard above the sound of gravy trains crashing into the buffers, and the metallic shriek of Porsches as they were pushed through the shredder.

Jill had enjoyed every second of it: it was really good fun.

'Did you do that?' she said.

'With a little help from my friends.'

'Is that the reason they sent you to prison?'

'Yes. Well, wouldn't you, in their position?'

Ivan smiled.

'They wanted to know how we did it. But I wouldn't tell them.'

She knew by now that Ivan was serious whenever he smiled. When amused, he stayed resolutely dead-pan. He was an enigma, double-wrapped in contradictions. She remained uncertain about him. Was he a genuine, hundred carat genius, capable of overturning the New World Order of wall-to-wall game shows and burger bars, literally with his fingertips? Or was he gently, quietly, elegantly, off his nut?

It was all too cosmic for a sunny Sunday afternoon at Flamborough. She sought safe refuge in the domestic.

'Tell me something else. Was it really a coincidence? You and Peter turning up together?'

'Totally. Your ex-husband was a pleasing companion in my prison cell, but I wouldn't choose him as an accomplice.'

'I did.'

'And you got rid of him.'

'Will you get rid of him?'

'Yes. I shall do it nicely, of course. I can play the game, because I know it's a game and God, if he or she exists, is a stand-up comedian. Peter thinks everything is real. He believes in it. Therefore he's bound to fail.'

The tide was rising. The football pitch was flooded. Trevor and Peter gave way to the inevitable, abandoned football and went for a paddle at the edge of the sand. Trevor, who had grown wise in such matters, suspected Peter wanted to talk something through. He was right.

'How do you find it? Living with Jill?'

'Hard to say. I've never lived with anyone else. It doesn't bother me much.'

'I found it impossible.'

'Obviously. Or you'd have stayed.'

'I mean, I'm not trying to stir it but . . .'

Hello, thought Trevor, he's trying to stir it.

' . . . don't you ever feel you want to be master in your own house?'

'No. For a kick-off, it's her house.'

'I realise that. I'm talking about the principle.'

'The principle of being master?'

'Yes.'

'As a principle it's daft. If you're the master, you have to give orders. Otherwise you wouldn't be the master.'

'So?'

'I can never think of any orders. So I don't bother about it. I listen to the music. I stay cool.'

'Trevor!'

They turned to see Jill approaching.

'Come and eat your sandwiches before they get curly at the edges! The boat leaves in half an hour.'

'Coming,' said Trevor.

Jill turned, walked back up the sloping beach to Ivan and First-Born. The message was clear: you have two minutes to finish your men's talk.

'See what I mean?' said Peter.

'No. I do not see what you mean.'

'You give way all the time.'

'Yes. I go with the tide. Look.'

He jerked a casual thumb in the direction of the water, in case Peter had overlooked the intimate presence of the North Sea.

'That's the tide. Nobody's beaten it yet. Not in thousands of years. It's been around a lot longer than I have. It knows more than I do. So I go with it.'

Peter shrugged. He had run out of debate. The tide had beaten him.

'Well, anyway . . . thanks for looking after her.'

'It's a pleasure. Nothing personal, but I think she was probably too good for you.'

Trevor headed in the direction of the cucumber sandwiches.

Peter stood still, watching him, thinking: how come such a wimp can smack you between the eyes without trying? There was a sudden swell in the water while his back was turned. Damn! His trousers were soaking. That was another difference. Sea water would have no effect on the sort of trousers Trevor wore.

There were many tidal matters to ponder on the long sea journey ahead.

After the frenzied activity at the park, Joe and Ben adjourned to Headingley for an afternoon watching Yorkshire play cricket. In the light of Inspector Hobson's orders, they felt it incumbent to maintain a careful surveillance on the bats, balls, stumps and bails.

They watched the game for two hours. Nobody tried to steal anything.

'Frankly, my dear,' said Joe, 'I couldn't give a damn. I wish someone would steal the entire match.'

They left early, at Ben's request.

'There were signs of excitement creeping into the game. I can't handle excitement.'

'Pity,' said Ben, pointing at the windscreen of their car.

Tucked under the wipers was a small, brown paper package.

'Another mysterious object waiting upon our return.'

'The unknown video masked crusader strikes again.'

Ben extricated the package.

'This could easily be mistaken for excitement.'

'File under T for Tomorrow.'

'It might be raining tomorrow.'

Trevor, Jill and First-Born stood on the cliff-top.

The boat carrying Ivan and Peter across the broad ocean was bobbing on the waves, a mile away. They had no idea what was supposed to happen next. They had taken a policy decision not to ask.

Trevor's attitude had been firm, verging on masterly.

'If we ask too many daft questions, we'll end up rowing them all the way to Oslo or Copenhagen.'

Their educated guess was that somewhere in the North Sea, Ivan and Peter would leave the small boat and go on board a more substantial ship. Beyond that, they had no more guesses, educated or otherwise.

They waved, in the sure and certain knowledge that the voyagers would not be able to see them. Waving was often like that, but remained necessary. Two centuries earlier, the locals had probably waved at Paul Jones.

'This usually reminds us of a film,' said Jill.

'You go first.'

'*The Cruel Sea*.'

'*Mutiny On The Bounty*.'

'*On The Waterfront*.'

'*Dumbo*,' said First-Born.

That was the one. So they went home.

11

When it's Swooping Time Up North

Yvonne arrived at 17, Hotspur Street on Monday morning to find Trevor and Jill sitting at the table, having breakfast, reading their chosen bits of the *Guardian* and behaving like any normal, run-of-the-mill pair of spousal analogues.

'Hello, sir. Hello, miss. What's going on?'

'Nothing's going on,' said Jill.

'That's what I mean, miss. Where is everybody?'

'We are everybody.'

'No refugees?'

'No refugees. They've sailed away in a beautiful pea-green boat to the land where the Bong-tree grows.'

'Good. I've heard it's really nice.'

'They've gone where?' said Trevor, absorbed in the baseball results. During summer months he followed the fortunes of the Toronto Blue Jays. He had a distant cousin in Edmonton, Alberta. Edmonton was almost two thousand miles away from Toronto, but logic played little part in sporting allegiances.

'Don't worry about Bong-trees. It's a three-hour lecture,' said Jill.

'In that case, I won't bother about it.'

Yvonne went into the kitchen to make herself a cup of instant. She liked the smell but not the taste of the house coffee. In her universe, coffee was made with powder and water, and tea with bags. Jill had patiently explained to her about beans and leaves, but with no impact on her drinking habits.

Yvonne joined them at the table, added three spoonfuls of sugar to her drink and smiled.

'It's better when it's just us, isn't it?'

'A big improvement,' said Trevor.

'Mind you, I shall miss Ivan. He was nice. Are they both villains?'

'That depends on your point of view,' said Jill, still under the influence of Ivan's beguiling theories of a New World Order based on the peaceful uses of computer energy.

'Yes, they're both villains,' said Trevor, adding, 'What's more, the Jays lost 5–4 to the White Sox in the eleventh.'

They ignored him. He was used to it.

On the way to school, Trevor was in benign mood, even by his standards, where a raised eyebrow equalled emotional cataclysm.

'Yvonne's right. It's best when it's just us at home.'

'Sentimental old cabbage.'

'Yes.'

It was also like old times in the Woodwork Room, as Trevor opened his mouth and taught 2F, saying:

'Now you're all too young to remember woodwork lessons when we had a reasonable supply of wood. So there's a big treat in store. You're going to make two bookends, instead of one. A pair. Not one, but two.'

Trevor always laid special emphasis on sophisticated concepts like the number two, as opposed to the number one.

'You can tell your parents you'll be bringing home two bookends at the end of term and they won't need a wall at the other end. They can have their walls back.'

'Sir, please sir, my Dad says will they have to buy a book, sir?'

'Tell him you can borrow books from the library. And you can keep other things between your bookends. Compact discs. Empty beer bottles. Elderly relatives.'

Books were top of the agenda in Jill's classroom.

'Now . . . hands up everybody with a copy of *Tess of the D'Urbervilles*.'

All the hands went up.

'We've done well, haven't we, miss?' said Sharon.

'You've done very well. This is almost like education used to be in the olden days. I wonder if I can still remember how to do it?'

'Morning, sir.'

'Morning, sir.'

'Morning, men.'

Inspector Hobson was alarmed. Joe and Ben stood smartly to attention in front of his desk. They looked eager and professional. It was ominous.

'A brief word, if we may, sir,' said Joe.

'Keep it brief. I have an appointment with Commander Blake in ten minutes' time.'

'Commander Blake. Quite so. Message understood,' said Ben.

The message was not understood. The detectives had never heard of Commander Blake and had no idea why the name was supposed to impress them. Instinctively they filed the name away for future use: they could discuss Commander Blake for at least an hour, as a creative alternative to investigation.

Ben took the initiative.

'Item first. Another video has come into our possession. We would like to entrust it to your scrutiny.'

'Leave it on my desk.'

Ben placed the video-cassette on the desk. It was still in the wrapper, exactly as they had found it at the cricket match. They had decided not to tamper with it for fear of annoying the lads from Forensic and breaking their policy of non-involvement in enigmas not of their own making.

'I generally keep videos . . . here,' said Hobson, moving the package six inches to the left and re-aligning it to true north.

'Item second and last,' said Joe, picking up on the semantic style he and his partner had first heard and admired during the halcyon days of *Hill Street Blues*, 'we need your guidance, sir.

More specifically, we need to know your policy guidelines in the matter of dawn swoops.'

'Dawn swoops?'

'It obviously wouldn't be a dawn swoop in the true sense, since dawn has already, so to speak . . .'

'Dawned,' said Ben.

'That being so, we are probably talking in terms of a mid-morning swoop.'

'I have no idea what you are talking about.'

'Dawn, as in day-break, the moment when the leading edge of the sun peeps over the horizon. Swoop, as in . . .'

'I know the meaning of the phrase!' said Hobson, sharply. 'I simply have no idea on what or whom you intend to swoop. Upon. Or why.'

He had lost control of the situation. He had lost control of his grammar too.

'San Quentin High School, sir,' said Ben.

'Hockey sticks, sir,' said Joe.

'We figure there could be a connection.'

'Sort of a *prima facie* hunch based on information received.'

'Hockey sticks?' said Hobson.

'Affirmative, sir,' said Joe.

Hobson looked at his watch. He checked it against his wall clock and the digital read-out on his word processor. They were exactly in synch. Commander Blake was due at 10.30 and it was already 10.28.37.8.9 . . .

'Very well. I leave it entirely to your discretion. But if things go wrong, I shall not be available for help. I have a top level meeting in this office with Commander Blake and . . .'

'Commander Blake. Understood, sir,' said Joe.

'Be careful in here,' said Ben, as they left the office.

They inquired of the duty sergeant about Commander Blake. Apparently, the Commander was from a branch of the police force so special even Special Branch was unaware of its existence. The detectives, with their highly-tuned speed of response, left the building and the area as quickly as possible. They were allergic to senior officers; extreme seniority brought them out in a rash. Distance was the solution.

Mr Carter stood by the staffroom window. It was the morning break. The room was foggy with Woodbine smoke and resentment.

'I spy strangers,' he said.

His colleagues ignored him. It was the usual reaction and he enjoyed it. Soliloquies were his main comfort in an imperfect world. In the words of the old cigarette commercial: you were never alone with a soliloquy. Except you were. That was the point.

'What have we here? The bailiffs? The official receivers? The broker's men? Two gentlemen from Whitehall here to tell us we are henceforth forbidden to use pencils because of their phallic significance.'

Jill paused by the window, on her way to the sink with her coffee jug, a cheerful item bought by mail order to help the peasants of Central South America.

'They're policemen,' she said, recognising Joe and Ben.

'Nonsense, Mrs Swinburne. If they're policemen, where are their whistles and truncheons and handcuffs? They look more like double-glazing salesmen.'

'Plain clothes policemen.'

'Even so, they should be wearing big boots.'

Trevor joined them at the window.

'No point in double-glazing salesmen coming here. Most of the school hasn't even got single glazing.'

As his original theories tottered, Mr Carter glimpsed a more tantalising possibility.

'If these chaps really are bobbies, as you say, I am forced to the conclusion that the headmaster's perversions have caught up with him at last.'

'Which ones?' said Trevor.

'Who knows? The silk underwear. The graven images. The guinea pigs.'

'Do you have evidence?' said Jill.

'I never let evidence get in the way of my prejudice, Mrs Swinburne. Otherwise it wouldn't be proper prejudice.'

Trevor shrugged.

'They'll probably just do him for receiving stolen property.'

'The headmaster? Receiving stolen property?'

Mr Carter's eyes sparkled.

'That's even better than perversions.'

Mr Wheeler sat behind his desk, swivelling uneasily in his chair as Joe looked at the receipt signed outside St Amber's Church the previous day.

'And this document purports to be . . . what?' said the detective.

'A receipt. And it does not purport, officer. It *is* a receipt.'

Joe handed the document to Ben, who read aloud:

'Books, footballs, netballs, hockey sticks, a vaulting horse . . . these items are here now, in the school?'

'Obviously. Why else would I sign a receipt?'

'And where did they come from?'

'An anonymous benefactor. A former student of the school who has become a successful businessman and wishes to show his gratitude to his Alma Mater.'

'Alma Mater, was that?' said Joe, making notes.

'Yes. Alma Mater.'

'And the name of this anonymous benefactor?'

'How can I possibly give you the name of an anonymous benefactor?'

'Point taken.'

Ben decided to be Columbo for a while, and shambled across to the window in the manner of Peter Falk. Joe realised what he was up to and left him to it; it was impolite to trample on a partner's dreams.

'Mr Wheeler,' muttered Columbo, 'I need to get a handle on how these items found their way into the building. These are artefacts of size and substance. Did they appear on your doorstep, in dead of night, like a foundling child?'

'A man brought them on a lorry.'

'Ah! We have a man. We have a lorry. We are getting, in the

jargon of the policeman's trade, somewhere. May I ask who, in your estimation, was driving this . . . er . . . lorry?'

'He claimed to be a gravedigger, doing a favour for a friend.'

'Sounds like Charlie,' said Joe, as himself.

Trevor was explaining the principles and practice of a saw to a First Form class.

'A saw, as you can see, has a handle at one end. Always hold it by the handle. That is why the thoughtful manufacturers put it there.'

The door of the Woodwork Room opened and Sharon peered in.

'Please sir, Mr Chaplin sir, Mr Wheeler says will you come and help the police with their inquiries?'

'Now?'

'Yes sir.'

'Right.'

Trevor turned to the class.

'Don't do any sawing while I'm out of the room. Find a nice piece of wood and look at it till I get back. Study the grain.'

Jill was outside the corridor.

'You as well?' said Trevor.

Jill nodded.

'Yes. We both have to do our duty to God and the Queen.'

'Is Mr Wheeler going to prison?' said Sharon.

'No,' said Jill, 'nobody is going to prison.'

'But if it has to be anybody . . .' said Trevor.

'Well, I suppose, given the choice . . .'

'Just as long as you don't say anything about Yvonne. You won't, will you, sir, you won't, will you, miss?'

They were startled by the urgency in Sharon's voice, especially as they had no idea what it was they were not supposed to talk about.

'No, we won't say anything about Yvonne,' said Trevor.

'Thank you, sir, thank you, miss.'

Sharon walked off along the corridor, trying to remember where she had left her class.

'What's all that stuff about Yvonne?' said Jill.

'No idea.'

'If I'm not supposed to talk about things, I like to know what it is I'm not supposed to talk about.'

'Funny. With me it's the other way round.'

They met Joe and Ben on the stairs.

'Good morning,' said Jill, brightly, keen to grab the initiative. 'I understand you have some inquiries that require our assistance.'

'Correct,' said Joe. 'Inquiry number one. Where are we?'

'San Quentin High School.'

'That much we understand. Beyond that, we are baffled. It seems to be impossible to proceed from A to B in this building, without the use of a staircase, even if A and B are on the same level.'

'That's true. We think of it as an amusing architectural quirk, inspired by the Ministry of Education.'

'Where would you like to be?' said Trevor.

'Perhaps a dark secluded place where we can talk in confidence over a cup of coffee?' Jill suggested.

The detectives agreed this was an excellent idea. They made their way, via two staircases, to the staffroom. While Trevor made coffee, Jill studied the receipt bearing Mr Wheeler's signature.

'Are you trying to tell us that this is stolen property? Is that the burden of your case?'

'That is our current understanding, ma'am,' said Ben, slipping back into Columbo mode.

'Bollocks.'

Ben reverted to his regular identity, and quickly.

'Is that your considered opinion?'

'I'm sure you don't expect me to say: it's a fair cop, put the cuffs on, I'll come quietly.'

'People very rarely say that to us, as a matter of fact,' said Joe. 'Makes our job very much harder.'

'Here's your dark secluded coffee,' said Trevor.

'All part of San Quentin High's policy of friendly cooperation with the police,' smiled Jill. 'Now, about your inquiries. If I read you correctly, you don't really *want* to check every item on this list, do you? Hundreds of books?'

'Hundreds of bits of wood?' said Trevor.

'Not to mention the footballs and netballs.'

Joe and Ben considered the prospect: hours of tedious checking and cross-checking. Swoops were not supposed to be boring. Swoops were supposed to be swift and dramatic, with flashing blue lights and raids on a number of houses across North London. Maybe they were wrong. Maybe swoops only worked properly at dawn.

'We are open to offers,' said Joe.

'How about a random sample?' said Jill.

'That's fine by me. Didn't we do a short course on random sampling techniques?'

Ben nodded.

'I remember it well. It was a Thursday afternoon, at the Poly.'

'Wait there,' said Jill.

She and Trevor left the staffroom.

'An impressive woman,' said Joe.

'An unimpressive man,' said Ben.

'He seems to have impressed her.'

'But that's real life. There's no accounting for real life.'

Trevor was the first to return, carrying an assortment of pieces of wood which he dumped on the floor between the detectives.

'A random sample. Oak, ash, pine, mahogany, walnut and good old-fashioned deal. Help yourselves.'

Joe and Ben each picked up a piece of wood. Each of them scrutinised his sample with cool analytical zeal concealing total ignorance.

'All this arrived at the school on a lorry, driven by Charlie the moonlighting gravedigger?' said Joe, playing for time.

'Yes. I helped unload it. Charlie sang a couple of songs. He's got a nice voice. Knows all the old favourites.'

Joe persisted with his impersonation of an investigating officer.

'In your professional experience, Mr Chaplin, does wood carry any means of identification?'

'You can tell what sort of tree it came from. Mind you, I already told you that. Oak, ash, pine, mahogany, walnut and good old-fashioned deal.'

Ben looked along his sample, like a snooker player checking his cue for signs of warping: a pointless exercise but it gave off a faint odour of authority.

'And having established what manner of tree this sample comes from, what do I do next?'

'Not my problem. I suppose your best bet's to check on the police computer about stolen trees. Compare them with my bits.'

The detectives swopped samples, a symbolic gesture indicating defeat: it was game, set and match to Trevor Chaplin, unimpressive man. They were relieved to see Jill return to the staffroom with a pile of books.

'Books,' she said.

'Another random sample?' said Joe.

'I made it as random as possible.'

'*Tess of the D'Urbervilles*,' said Ben, taking the top book from the pile.

'It's a set book for O Level.'

'It's about this woman who's oppressed and eventually destroyed by men,' said Trevor.

'We'll have to take all this stuff away and have it checked,' said Joe.

'That's fine,' said Jill, 'providing you give us a receipt.'

'Of course.'

It was tangible success of a kind: a load of stuff to take back to the station. They could bung it off to Forensic and forget about it.

'Anything else?' said Jill.

There was one more item and they had almost forgotten.

'Hockey sticks,' said Ben.

'Would that be a gymnasium job?' said Joe.

Trevor nodded.

'A treat in store.'

'Maybe we can take a look at the vaulting horse,' said Joe.

'Ask it a few routine questions?' said Trevor.

They walked along a corridor, up some stairs, along a corridor, down some stairs, out of a door, across the playground, through a door, along a corridor, arriving at a large pair of double doors, chained and padlocked. The chains and padlocks were rusty and ineffective. Jill pushed one of the doors. It fell over.

'Welcome to San Quentin's Temple of Physical Culture.'

It was not so much a gymnasium as a disturbing dream, a bleak parody, a joyless pastiche of the real thing. Ropes and wall-bars hung in clusters from a shattered roof. Brown water dripped onto crusted tarpaulin sheets covering unidentified motionless objects. It had been declared unsafe and unhygienic five years earlier, and had since achieved mythic status, with rumours of mushrooms and scaly creatures cheerfully breeding in the welcoming dankness. Slitherings had been heard after dark. One of the better-read neighbourhood vandals had written on the far wall: SAN QUENTIN WELCOMES CAREFUL TRIFFIDS.

The vaulting horse stood close to the double doors, garlanded with the hockey sticks from the gravedigger's lorry.

'Is that the horse?' said Joe.

'That's the horse,' said Trevor.

'I'll skip the questions.'

Ben took a careful pace forward. The floor creaked, triggering sympathetic vibrations under the tarpaulin. The vibrations hinted at legs and paws.

'I take it this place is not in use?' he said.

'Not by human beings,' said Jill.

'So how do the young people maintain the high levels of physical fitness required in a competitive society?'

'If it's fine they go on the field, being careful to avoid the subsidence.'

'And if it's wet?'

'Silent reading. If we can find any books.'

'Or they go home, or have a smoke round the back of the cycle sheds, or they hang around the shopping precinct,' said Trevor, keen that the detectives should have a comprehensive overview of the socio-econo consequences of dereliction.

'It's really up to Mr Bickerstaffe,' he added.

'Bickerstaffe?' said Joe.

'Teaches PE.'

'Where is he?'

'Hasn't been seen for months.'

'But we think he went out of his mind,' said Jill, keen they should have a psycho-emotional overview of Mr Bickerstaffe.

'Two rashers short of a bacon butty?' said Ben, the jokiness concealing an urgent need to get the hell out of this place. It gave him the creeps. He hated the creeps.

Jill sensed his nervousness.

'Oh look,' she said.

'What is it?' said Ben.

'Sorry. Don't worry. Trick of the light. I thought I saw a tentacle.'

'Do you want to take the horse away for forensic examination?' said Trevor.

'No,' said Joe, firmly.

He reached out, very carefully, and selected the shiniest hockey stick from the stack leaning against the vaulting horse.

'One random sample hockey stick.'

'Don't forget the receipt,' said Jill. 'And if there are any further problems, questions or matters arising, have a word with Big Al.'

'Big Al?'

'Big Al?'

Driving back to Sherlock Road, the detectives formulated their conclusions.

'The trail begins with Big Al,' said Joe.

'Travels in a great big circle.'

'And ends up back at Big Al.'

'In which case?'

'We might as well give our midfield Napoleon this hockey stick and forget the whole business.'

'And no way do we go back into that gymnasium.'

Jill and Trevor sat in the dining hall, contemplating Today's Special and their encounter with the police.

'Those books you gave them. Are they incriminating?'

'Of course not. I said to Sharon: I need six copies of *Tess* to give to the police. She selected them very carefully. She said: don't worry miss, they're kosher. What about your wood? Is that incriminating?'

'No. Mostly bits of old desks and chairs we chopped up last term.'

Today's Special was sausage-and-mash. Trevor poked the sausage. A shadow fell across it.

'May I join you?' said Mr Carter.

'Certainly,' said Jill. 'What are you planning to kindle today?'

'You might be surprised if I confessed to you about the current state of my kindling.'

'Feel free. We're all mature adult citizens.'

'No we're not,' said Trevor, as Mr Carter sat down, squeezing himself between them.

'My confession is professional.'

'You've given up erotic fantasies?' said Jill. 'Is it Lent?'

Mr Carter was unusually serious. He was always gloomy, but it was a gloom reflecting the outside world, like a black mirror. Today's gloom was internal, drawn from a deep and long-neglected well.

'I hold you responsible, Mr Chaplin.'

'Me? I've never been responsible for anything.'

'That speech you made. I will fight, nay if necessary I will steal, in order to give my child a decent education. I was powerfully impressed. It was like being back at Agincourt. It took me back to when I was a young teacher. I arrived here, running over with evangelical zeal. I had wisdom to share. A blazing torch to pass on.'

'So?'

'So, Mr Chaplin, when you made your speech the other day, you reminded me. I had forgotten that I once carried a blazing torch. And you reminded me. I will try to find it in my heart to forgive you.'

It was Mr Carter's turn to prod a sausage. It whimpered. Jill and Trevor pushed their trays aside and stood up.

'Where are you going? Have I upset you?'

'We have an urgent appointment,' said Jill.

'What can it be this time? The bowling green? The police station?'

'Home,' said Trevor.

'Home? Why are you going home? You can get all that at home.'

'Top-level talks with our child-minder.'

'A nappy crisis?'

'Criminology.'

'Of course. Silly of me to ask.'

Trevor and Jill never went home during the lunch-hour but Yvonne was not surprised to see them, if only because she was never surprised by anything; but she noticed an unfamiliar urgency in Jill's questioning.

'Before we talked to the police, Sharon said to us: don't say anything about Yvonne. She said it to both of us. Why did she say that?'

'She wouldn't want you to tell the police about the shoplifting and such.'

'Does that mean you have been shoplifting . . . and such?'

'Just a bit. Not ever such a lot. Mostly I was coordinating things.'

'Coordinating what things?'

Trevor and Jill, realising their planned casual conversation was turning into a detailed cross-examination, sat down to listen.

'Well, you needed stuff at school. I organised a few of the kids to, like, get things. Just a few things. Things Big Al couldn't get hold of. Mind you, he got a bit stroppy when he found out we'd been nicking them. He doesn't like people nicking things. He says it's against the law and you can get into trouble.'

'You *can* get into trouble,' said Jill.

'You can go to prison. Places like that,' said Trevor.

'Not bothered. First offence, I'd get probation.'

'That's bad enough,' said Jill.

'It doesn't matter. What have I got to lose?'

'A great deal, I should think.'

'Sod all.'

'What about your parents? Do they want you to go to prison?' said Trevor.

'My Dad works Monday to Friday doing a crappy job down South on account of you can't even get crappy jobs up here. The money stinks so he stays in a doss-house. My Mam's zonked out of her brains on Valium. The only decent thing I've got is my job. Working here. Looking after First-Born. I love doing that. I don't love anything else.'

'Thank you,' said Jill.

'And if I got into trouble, you wouldn't sack me, would you? You like people to be villains and ex-cons and refugees, don't you, miss? You're into all that.'

'We also like jazz musicians and footballers,' said Trevor.

'Hush Trevor.'

'I think I'll hush.'

Jill Swinburne had been soundly beaten over the head with her own morality. There was guilt among the bruises, too. Until this moment, she had known nothing of Yvonne's parents and what passed for their life-style.

She settled for short-term pragmatism. She would work out the morality later.

'Let's try this, Yvonne. Will you promise me, in future, that you only steal, or coordinate other people's stealing, if and when we ask you to? Will you promise me that?'

'No problem, miss. Fair enough. I promise.'

12

Can You Hear the Music?

Commander Blake arrived at Sherlock Road Police Station at four o'clock in the afternoon. He was preceded by a series of messages, via telephone, telex, Fax and osmosis, saying he would be late. There were no explanations and no apologies. When he turned up, the local force understood why. The aura of authority entered the building ten minutes before the man. He wore a uniform that obviously went to the dry-cleaners every hour, on the hour. But the power was in the shoes. The toe-caps shone with a transcendent radiance, like a trailer for the Second Coming.

The shoes said it all. They had shone upon better people in better places than Sherlock Road. They carried within them residual reflections of cabinet ministers, miscellaneous crowned heads and nameless officials who worked in tall buildings for the FBI, the CIA, the MCC and, more recently, the KGB.

'That guy is a heavy hitter,' said the desk sergeant, watching the Commander as he made his way to Hobson's office. There was nobody to hear him. The rest of the force had gone into hiding.

'Hope you haven't been hanging around wasting your time,' said Blake.

'Absolutely not, sir,' said Hobson.

In reality, Hobson had been at his desk, sitting to attention, since ten-thirty in the morning. He had taken incoming telephone calls. He had read the messages from the telex and

Fax machines. He had been static and passive. Now the Commander had arrived, he remained so.

'My late arrival doesn't indicate any lack of urgency. One or two things cropped up in Whitehall. Heads rolling in Washington and Brussels. Usual nonsense.'

'Of course,' said Hobson, gently implying that he had to deal with similar nonsense in Ilkley and Horsforth.

Blake opened his brief-case. To Hobson's surprise, it had no security locking mechanism. Perhaps it was programmed to self-destruct if touched by the wrong hands. He might ask the Commander about this later. Or, more likely, he would not ask about it later.

'You need to find this man.'

Commander Blake handed Hobson some photographs.

The Inspector looked at them, half-expecting an instruction to learn them by heart and then eat them. On top of the pile was a standard prison photograph, showing a man in full face and profile. His name and number had been blanked out. The other pictures showed the same man in the outside world, carrying out routine civilian activities: standing at a bus stop, going into a launderette, buying a newspaper. They illustrated a truth well-known to security services the world over: human behaviour, however innocuous, becomes highly sinister when photographed from a distance, with a long lens, and subjected to grainy enlargement in the dark rooms of the powerful.

'Who is he?' said Hobson.

'He works under several different names. I am not in a position to reveal any of them.'

'I see.'

'What has he done?'

'He tilts the world on its axis.'

'Really?'

Hobson shook his head, frowned and tutted quietly. He tried to signal profound concern about axis-tilters.

'We know this man has been in your area during the past few days.'

'Is he violent?'

It felt like a safe question.

'Heavens no! Quiet as a lamb. Model prisoner. Bit of a charmer from all accounts.'

'But dangerous?'

'Lethal.'

'I see.'

'Our American cousins, in their somewhat melodramatic way, have identified him as Global Enemy Number One.'

Commander Blake handed Hobson a sheet of paper.

'Perhaps you'd like to read his CV.'

Hobson scanned the document. He had done a speed-reading course in his spare time; but even so, what he read slowed him down to a browse.

'He caused the Stock Market crash of '87?'

'With a little help from his friends.'

'Gosh.'

Hobson remembered the crash. His mother's share portfolio had dropped in value by fifty per cent in the course of an afternoon. She had come out in a rash and was unable to show her face at bridge for three months.

'The central problem is that he seems to regard the whole thing as a game.'

'Computer fraud?'

'Precisely. Straightforward bank robbers are no problem, as we know. We can also handle the Robin Hood syndrome. Arrest the middleman before the money gets to the poor.'

'Quite so.'

'But this man is different, Inspector. His aim, apparently, is to dismantle the financial institutions of the world. I need hardly remind you, if we do not take those institutions seriously, we perish. The precise balance of currencies . . . the pound, the dollar, the mark, the yen . . . the symbiosis of the stock markets of London, New York, Tokyo and Hong Kong . . . on these sacred temples we all depend. Whether we like it or not, they are our bread and butter. Our life and death.'

Hobson caught a sliver of irony in the Commander's words:

the characteristic English upper-class music that told you, I only do this sort of thing out of respect for my ancestors – given the choice, I could just as easily be knocking up a double century at Lord's.

Hobson, who had been to a very minor public school, felt empowered to seek clarification.

'Our bread and butter? Our life and death?'

'We are all paid to believe that. Ergo, we believe that.'

Hobson acknowledged the importance of the situation. The fiscal universe must be protected at all costs. It was bad enough last time. His mother had been on the phone three times a day, with updates about the state of her rash.

To hell with it, he thought: I'm going to impress this man.

'I once wrote,' he said, 'the man who controls the computer, controls the world.'

'You wrote that?'

'Yes.'

'That's rather impressive.'

A fanfare rang out in Hobson's head. He had impressed the Commander! It was a giant step nearer shiny shoes of his very own. And oh, how they would glisten!

'We shall find this man, Commander.'

'Please do. If he tilts the world too far on its axis, we all fall off the edge. Imagine it. Think of all the paperwork.'

'Global implications,' said Hobson, examining the photographs carefully, almost as a silent reprimand for Blake's flippancy.

'As you say. Global implications.'

There was a knock at the door.

'May I?' said Hobson.

'I don't wish to be an impediment to the smooth running of your unit. Please feel free.'

'Come in!' said Hobson, with cavalier confidence. He had proved he could handle the shiniest Commanders in the business. He could handle anything that walked through his door.

Joe walked through his door, brandishing a hockey stick.

'Is this yours?'

'Certainly not!'

'That's how it goes,' said Joe to Commander Blake. 'You win some, you lose some.'

Ben was waiting for his partner outside in the corridor.

'What's he like then? Blake?'

'Shiny shoes. Looks tall even when he's sitting down.'

'Wonder if he's related to Sexton.'

'Sexton who?'

'Sexton Blake. He wrote *Jerusalem*.'

A limousine took Commander Blake to the airport. An executive jet was waiting on the runway. The Commander went on board quietly and without fuss.

'Snotty-nosed bugger,' said a baggage-handler.

Hobson sat in his office, still frozen at attention. He stared at the photographs. They showed Ivan the refugee, bank robber, computer genius, tilter of axes, lover of cool music, admirer of Bix Beiderbecke, the cornet player who made a sound like bullets shot from a bell.

Hobson knew none of this. In addition, he was perplexed. Why would such a man, intending to overthrow the universe, start here, in the moonstruck outer limits of Leeds?

It was a good question and his computer could give him no satisfactory answers. He decided to phone his mother.

'Home sweet home,' said Jill.

'There's no place like it,' said Trevor.

Equilibrium had been restored at 17, Hotspur Street. The refugees had fled. The house had resumed normal transmission.

It was a standard issue early summer night. First-Born was asleep in his room, dreaming of sand and seagulls. Jill was reading Maya Angelou. Trevor was watching world championship snooker with the sound turned down. He loved the game but hated the cliché-ridden commentaries. He sometimes gave three-hour lectures on the subject.

Jill sighed.

'It's a mess, isn't it?'

'I wouldn't say that. He can hit the red if he plays off the side cushion with a bit of left-hand side.'

'I don't mean the snooker. I mean the world.'

'Oh yes. That's a mess.'

'Our educational system can only operate on a basis of organised crime.'

'Most other things work that way so what's the odds? Read your book.'

She retreated into her book. Trevor concentrated on the match. It was between a dour Canadian and a dour Australian. It had all the sparkle of a breeze-block. Trevor relished every brooding minute. It was a rude and defiant gesture at the hustlers and hucksters who wanted to turn snooker into show business. He was a Northerner, born and bred, and knew in his bones that sport was much too serious to be treated as entertainment. Obviously this belief still survived in parts of Australia and Canada.

The match crept unwillingly towards a gruelling climax. Trevor touched Jill on the arm. She glanced at the screen.

'What has he lost?' said Trevor.

'Position?'

'What has he not got?'

'He has not got the right angle on the blue.'

'In order to what?'

'In order to screw into the pack.'

'Terrific. I'm proud of you.'

She had paid attention to the three-hour lectures. He still found it surprising.

'It's like I said to your ex-husband, when we were paddling. Go with the tide.'

'What's the tide got to do with snooker?'

'I'm not talking about snooker. I'm talking about education. If the tide says you've got to organise a bit of shop-lifting on the side to survive, well, go with it . . .'

'Where does it end?'

'It doesn't.'

'Yes it does. It ends in D Wing. Three to a cell. Slopping out every morning.'

'The tide doesn't end. It just goes in and out. For ever.'

Again her attention switched to the television screen. It showed the dour Australian sitting in his chair. The people in charge had a programme policy. To hell with the game – let's see personalities in close-up: human interest in bite-size lumps.

'My turn,' said Jill. 'That man in the chair. What is he doing with disaster?'

'He is staring it in the face.'

'You are a remarkable human being, Mr Chaplin.'

'Everybody's remarkable. You told me that years ago.'

'If you're going to insist on remembering what I say, I shall stop talking altogether.'

'Promise?'

'Knock it off. Now be quiet. I'm trying to read.'

The dour Canadian missed a shot. The dour Australian got up from his chair. There was a tide in the affairs of snooker players as there was in education. The Canadian sat down, assembling his features ready to stare disaster in the face. He lit a cigarette. He knew that would make the cameras go away. It was all in the programme policy.

Trevor made a short announcement.

'There are three of us living in this cell. We slop out every morning. And I am very happy. Is that ridiculous?'

'Sorry. Wasn't paying attention.'

But she was.

Ten days later the monsoon season arrived in the outer limits. There was no cricket at Headingley. Old men gazed from the pavilion windows at the black sky and agreed it might fair up a bit later on. Then they read their morning papers. The Ouse had burst its banks in York, flooding many houses. It lightened the gloom in the pavilion. It served people right. If they insisted on living in a nice place like York, they deserved to be flooded.

The rain beat down on the windows of San Quentin High School and, where there was no glass in the windows, on the staff and students. Serious attempts at scholarship had to take place in corridors or under the stairs. The playing field became a primeval swamp though the difference was only apparent to the sensitive eye. The holes caused by subsidence doubled their diameter overnight. Sharon claimed to have seen turtles hatching their eggs in one of them.

The lorry battled its way through the storm with a formidable display of smoke, steam and occasional defiant sparks. It stopped outside the school but continued to shudder, even when the engine was switched off. Above the noise of the wind, sometimes at gale force, a familiar voice rang out:

'I'm singing in the rain
Just singing in the rain
What a glorious feeling . . .'

Charlie paused in his celebration of the weather as Mr Wheeler, sheltering under a large black umbrella, carefully edged his way from the main door of the school to the lee of the lorry, his body at forty-five degrees to the horizontal.

'Another delivery for you, sunbeam.'

'I am not a sunbeam and I am not expecting any further deliveries, from you or anybody else.'

The headmaster peered warily under the tarpaulin covering the lorry's cargo.

'Don't waste your time nosing under there, flower. Them's not for you. Them's coffins. You wouldn't want a load of coffins, would you?'

'No. We do not require coffins.'

'*That's* for you.'

Charlie handed Mr Wheeler a large parcel, wrapped in brown paper and tied up with string, like a Christmas present from a bygone age.

'What is it?'

'Me, I'm no expert, but it looks to me like a brown paper parcel with your name and address on it. In my book, that makes it none of my business, petal. Happen your best plan's to unwrap it and have a look inside.'

'But . . '

'Sorry. Can't hang about. Got to get my skates on. That film's on telly tonight and I've got a load of coffins to get rid of.'

Mr Carter watched from the staffroom window as Charlie reversed the lorry out of the school grounds, embellishing the manoeuvre with a pleasing version of 'You Are My Lucky Star'.

'I have been observing the great cycle of nature since its first revolution. What we have just witnessed outside the school will be followed, as night follows day, by a summons to Mrs Swinburne and Mr Chaplin. The headmaster would like to see you in his study. Immediately!'

It was a soliloquy. Mr Carter was alone in the staffroom. His own room, officially called a History Laboratory in accordance with some long-discredited Whitehall whim, was flooded to a depth of two feet. He had left a notice on the door reading: HISTORY – CLOSED FOR RE-WRITING and retired to the staffroom, saying, 'I shall devote myself full-time to being a chorus, in the Greek tradition, on the warp and weft of human frailty.'

There were no witnesses to his acute prediction, but Mr Carter was right. Jill and Trevor had been summoned to Mr Wheeler's study. They met outside in the lobby.

'What's going on?' said Trevor.

'No idea. Probably a plague of frogs or locusts.'

'Howay then. Let's count the frogs.'

Trevor knocked at the door.

'Come in!' barked the headmaster, in his familiar tones of stifled hysteria.

'Oh look,' Trevor murmured to Jill as they entered the study. 'No frogs.'

'I beg your pardon, Mr Chaplin'

'A trivial and meaningless aside, Mr Wheeler.'

'Well, if you are able to divert your mind from trivialities, perhaps you can explain this.'

He drew their attention to the brown paper parcel on his desk.

'It's a parcel.'

'I am well aware it's a parcel, Mr Chaplin.'

Trevor increased his offer.

'An old-fashioned brown paper parcel, just like my mother used to make?'

Mr Wheeler had already removed the string, winding it into a neat ball ready for a rainy day. Now he pulled aside the brown paper to reveal the contents.

'Oh look,' said Jill, 'it's a parcel full of money.'

Trevor inspected the contents more closely.

'Yes. Mrs Swinburne's right. That's certainly money. In used notes. Fivers and tenners. You can use them to buy things.'

'This parcel contains fifty thousand pounds.'

'Fifty thousand pounds?' said Jill.

Trevor seemed puzzled.

'You'd expect it to be a bigger parcel.'

'There was a message inside. Pay attention while I read it to you.'

Jill and Trevor paid attention: fifty thousand pounds focusses the mind something remarkable.

'Perhaps this will help in some small way to repair your gymnasium roof. I wish it could be more. Perhaps one day it will be more. Please give my kind regards to Mrs Swinburne, Mr Chaplin and their First-Born. Tell them I still envy their simplicity. All of this is, as they will realise, a joke.'

Mr Wheeler passed the note to Jill for her inspection.

'There is no signature.'

'Probably anonymous,' said Trevor.

'But what am I supposed to do with all this money?' cried the headmaster.

'Repair the gymnasium roof?' Jill suggested.

'Certainly not! It's out of the question!'

'You can get a couple of estimates,' said Trevor, quietly.

* * *

'Fifty grand?' said Big Al.

'To fix a roof?' said Little Norm.

'For fifty grand in cash, we can put a roof over the whole of the West Riding.'

'I'm not putting a roof on Bradford.'

'Excluding Bradford, obviously, Norm.'

They were sitting with Jill and Trevor in the bowls hut. Rain had stopped play three days earlier. The bowlers had taken the opportunity to hold their first Annual General Meeting since 1978. Big Al had been elected President. Little Norm had been elected as the committee.

'Does that mean the answer's yes?' said Trevor. He and Jill had arrived with an unwritten and unspoken mandate from their timorous headmaster. It amounted to: get the roof fixed if you can, no questions asked but don't drag my name into it.

'We will restore the gymnasium roof with pleasure and in the best traditions of British craftsmanship.'

'Terrific,' said Trevor.

'Don't forget, Trev. I was made redundant from the building trade during the last recession but two. Or was it three? It's difficult to tell. These recessions all look alike to me. But your gymnasium will be my renaissance.'

'We haven't had a nice renaissance for ages, have we?' said Norm.

Al chuckled. It was a dark brown, peasant gurgle.

'Tell you what. He's a lad, that Ivan, isn't he?'

'We were very impressed,' said Jill.

'The police have been round, asking about him. They seemed a bit het up. Have they been to see you?'

'Not recently,' said Trevor. 'And we haven't been under surveillance for well over a week.'

'What did you tell them?' said Jill.

'Very little. Gave them a six-to-one winner at Redcar and a couple of hockey sticks. Sent them away happy.'

'If the police come to us, what do we tell them?'

'Tell them the truth, Mrs Swinburne.'

'The truth?'

'Within reason.'

The truth, within reason. It was a fair summary of Big Al's world-view where high authority was concerned. He had now moved to the next item on the agenda.

'Norm. We need a weather forecast for the benefit of our membership.'

Norm looked through the single small window of the hut.

'There's a sunny period approaching from the South.'

'The first for a thousand years,' said Big Al.

The detectives had asked for another identity parade in Inspector Hobson's office. They stood side by side, each bearing a hockey stick in the Present Arms position favoured by the armed forces.

'That isn't mine. Nor is that one.'

'But full marks for trying, sir?' said Ben.

'Full marks for trying, but will you now please stop.'

It sounded like an order.

'Stop?' said Joe.

'Yes. Stop. Let me remind you where your priorities now lie.'

He pointed to his notice-board. It carried a dozen assorted photographs of Ivan.

'Finding that man is all that matters.'

'We have been pursuing him with unceasing vigilance, sir,' said Ben.

It was true. They had consulted Big Al. His advice had been straightforward and very helpful: don't waste your time, lads, he's right out of your league and mine. The last bit had really hit home. Al was deeply and passionately aware of his own worth. He would sit down in his hut with the mightiest in the land, with Kings and Queens, Popes and Cardinals, and look them in the eye on strictly level terms. Therefore, the fugitive was a bit tasty.

Joe and Ben had taken his advice. They were going through the motions but no more than that. If Al respected the man's fancy footwork, there was no point in their working themselves into a frenzy over a fruitless quest.

'Indeed, sir,' said Joe, 'it was during that very pursuit that we picked up the hockey sticks, *en passant*, so to speak.'

'Well, as I say, relax on the hockey sticks. That will be all.'

The detectives hesitated.

'May we burden you with one more item,' said Ben, 'accepting as we do the already intolerable work-load under which you are labouring . . .'

'Whatever it is, will you please say it!'

Hobson had grown a little snappy since Commander Blake's visit. His toe-caps were shinier too.

'The video, sir.'

'What video?'

'The suspect video we passed on to you following our surveillance at Headingley cricket ground, reference suspected stolen sports equipment. We wondered whether you'd had time to look at it yet, in view of your other priority concerns, ie, that is, *per se*, Global Enemy Number One.'

News had leaked out about the FBI's description of the wanted man. It had made a big impression in the canteen. The general view was they should have at least ten Global Enemies on a permanent basis. Joe and Ben suggested that five of the Enemies should be easy marks. That way the force was guaranteed a fifty per cent clear-up rate with high public credibility and little danger to life and limb.

'No, I haven't had time to look at it yet.'

The cassette remained in its allotted space on Hobson's desk.

'Perhaps we could assist you. A burden shared is a burden halved,' said Joe.

'Or, in this case, shelved,' said Ben.

'You are volunteering?'

'Sir!'

Their four heels clicked in unison.

Hobson was suspicious. They were manipulating him again and he wanted them to stop. Then, in a moment of what he later decided was pure inspiration, he remembered something his mother had mentioned on the telephone the previous evening.

'This sudden zeal . . . is it connected with the fact that the film *Singin' In The Rain* is on network television this evening? Is it your intention to re-cycle this tape for domestic use?'

'Sir. Do you really imagine that we . . .?' said Joe.

'Yes, you damn well would!'

'I cannot tell a lie,' said Ben. 'It did drift fleetingly across our occasionally unworthy minds.'

'The video stays on my desk and you will leave my office, taking the hockey sticks with you.'

After they had gone, Hobson preened. It was, he felt, a well-merited preen. He had won a small battle. The hours spent buffing his toe-caps had not been in vain.

Keen to savour the taste of victory, he loaded the video into his machine and pressed the PLAY button. On the screen, he saw a well-defined image of a familiar yellow van outside an equally familiar terrace house.

After running the tape a couple of times, he concluded that he was watching pictures of a group of people setting off for a day at the seaside. After another viewing, he identified three of the people as Trevor Chaplin, Jill Swinburne and, he deduced, their baby. After re-running the tape slowly, a frame at a time, he realised the child was in the arms of Global Enemy Number One.

Trevor handed Jill a kleenex.

'They don't make films like that any more,' she said, dabbing her eyes.

'What are you crying for? It was mostly about people singing and dancing and kissing each other.'

'You can cry for happiness.'

'I've been sitting here waiting for that bit when he walks into the sea.'

'That was James Mason in *A Star Is Born*.'

'No wonder it was a long time coming.'

The doorbell rang.

'If that's Ivan, we are not at home.'

'If it's anybody, we are not at home.'

Trevor answered the door. He returned to the living room with Inspector Hobson.

'It's all right,' said Trevor. 'He doesn't want to stay the night.'

'Do forgive the late hour, but I took the liberty of waiting until the film was over. Were you watching it?'

'We watch it every time it's on,' said Trevor, 'waiting for the bit when he walks into the sea.'

'Isn't that *A Star Is Born*?'

Jill stepped in firmly before the conversation turned into Mastermind with the specialist subject: common misunderstandings about Hollywood movies.

'Is this a search, a surveillance, a swoop or a social visit?'

'It is, I have to confess, a business call. Have you seen this man?'

He handed each of them a photograph of Ivan. He had decided on upfront shock tactics, following his triumph over the detectives. From now on he would be decisive, within limits.

Trevor and Jill glanced at the photographs.

'Oh look. It's Ivan,' said Jill.

'Before you answer,' said Hobson, 'I should warn you that we have powerful circumstantial evidence that you know this man.'

'Of course we do. He stayed at the house,' said Trevor.

'And any denials on your part,' Hobson continued, 'could result in quite serious consequences.'

'We're not denying it,' said Jill.

'We have witnesses. We have photographs. We have video pictures. We . . .'

He stared at them.

'He stayed here?'

'We've been trying to confess but you wouldn't listen,' said Jill.

'How long did he stay here?'

'About a week, on and off. He left us a week past Sunday. Trevor drove to the coast. And this man sailed away in a boat with my ex-husband. What else would you like to know?'

'Could you describe the boat?'

'Kind of a pea-green. It's possible he's gone to the land where the Bong-tree grows,' said Trevor.

'Mr Chaplin . . .'

'OK. We have no idea where he is. But I hope he's found a place where he can hear some good cool music.'

Trevor returned the photograph to Inspector Hobson, then crossed to the shelves that housed his record and tape collection. He had designed and built the shelves himself. They were full.

'He really liked Bix.'

Beiderbecke's elegant grace notes strung themselves around the room like tinsel at Christmas.

Jill picked up a plastic, pushalong Volvo from its garage beneath the settee.

'You should make a note of this, Inspector.'

'What is it?'

'A toy car. We bought it for First-Born, with the money you gave me.'

She whizzed it across the floor to him. He picked it up carefully, as if it were a clue bearing fingerprints. Then, with a whisper of a smile, he whizzed it back across the floor to Jill.

'We were going to get him a police car, but they were a pound extra,' said Trevor.

'Very nice,' said Hobson.

'The car or the music?' said Trevor.

'Both. That's a very pretty tune.'

Explaining the difference between jazz and pretty tunes was, as Jill knew well, a three-hour lecture. Trevor gave him the short version.

'Inspector. There are only two kinds of people in the world. Those who hear the music and those who don't.'

'The cool and the uncool,' said Jill.

Hobson nodded appreciatively, almost in tempo. He left while Bix was still playing. He had a report to write.

* * *

It was Sunday. At the crack of noon, the telephone rang.

'Don't answer it,' said Trevor. 'It might be a refugee or a relation. Today we are running away into the hills.'

'You're amazing when you're masculine and powerful.'

'Like macho?'

'Like silly.'

'That's fair.'

Now they stood on the brow of a hill in Swaledale: mother, father and child. Yorkshire lay before them in its Sunday best.

'I needed this,' said Trevor.

'Me too,' said Jill.

'Thanks for dealing me in,' said First-Born.

'I look at all this,' said Jill, 'and I can't work out how we turned it into what we've left back there. Where did we go wrong?'

'The precincts and the takeaways?'

'And kids trying to sell cavity wall insulation by telephone.'

'And me saying: I will steal for my child's education.'

'And everybody cheering.'

'Thanks anyway, Dad. It was a nice thought,' said First-Born.

'Trouble is,' said Trevor, 'people don't hear the music.'

'Back to music?' said Jill.

'Certainly. What else is there?'

'Bix?'

'And Duke and Bird and Prez.'

'The Beiderbecke Connection.'

'That's the sanity clause. You only have to listen.'

'You know how to listen, don't you? You just put your ears together and . . .'

'Hush,' said Trevor.

'Listen,' said First-Born.

They listened. They heard the music. Then, after they had eaten their sandwiches, they climbed into the little yellow van and drove into the sunset.